Queen

By Cynthia White

Compilation and Introduction copyright © 2007 by
Triple Crown Publications
PO Box 6888
Columbus, Ohio 43205
www.TripleCrownPublications.com

Library of Congress Control Number: 2007933036
ISBN: 0-9778804-0-0
ISBN 13: 978-0-9778804-0-9
Author: Cynthia White
Cover Design/Graphics: www.MarionDesigns.com,
Aaron Blackman Davis – www.elevado.us.com
Typesetting: Holscher Type and Design
Associate Editor: Kiristin Reid
Editorial Assistant: Elizabeth Zaleski
Editor-in-Chief: Mia McPherson
Consulting: Vickie M. Stringer

First Trade Paperback Edition Printing August 2007

10 9 8 7 6 5 4 3 2 1

Printed in the United States of America

This book is dedicated to everyone who told me I couldn't do it. I want to thank you all for adding fuel to my already burning fire. You made me fight harder and stay focused on my goals. For that I will forever be grateful.

Triple Crown Publications presents . . .

iv

Cynthia White

chapter

One

I SAT DOWN IN THE UNCOMFORTABLE, worn out chair and picked up the phone. I put it up to my ear and opened my mouth to speak. Nothing came out. I looked up at him. He smiled at me. He was as handsome as ever. His skin was still smooth and unblemished. His teeth were still perfect and white as snow. His hair was longer and was starting to turn gray around the edges. I didn't like him with braids. They made him look too thuggish. Even though he was sitting across from me, locked in prison, he was no thug.

"Hi, baby." His deep voice penetrated my soul.

"Hi, daddy." I forced myself to smile.

"How are you?" he asked, concerned.

"I'm the one who should be asking you that."

"Baby, I'm fine. Your old man's tough." He stuck out his chest proudly.

"I know but—"

"But nothing," he interrupted me. He knew what I was

about to say. It was my fault he was in this situation. I should've been the one behind bars, not him.

"I miss you, daddy," the little girl in me whined as my eyes began to fill with tears.

"I miss you, too, baby girl." He closed his eyes in an attempt to hold back his own tears.

"I'm goin' to go talk to your lawyer tomorrow."

"You will do no such thing," he scolded me.

"But you don't deserve this. You don't deserve to die." I put my hand up to the glass.

"Baby, I'm at peace with God." He put his hand up to the glass as well. His was twice as big as mine. He smiled at me. I wanted to hug him so badly.

"I just don't know what to do," I confessed.

"You live your life. I know it hurts, baby. It's okay to be sad sometimes. You don't always have to be so strong."

"Yes, I do." I looked back up at him.

"That's why you have a husband."

"Barely." I laughed out loud as I thought about the problems my husband and I had been having lately.

"What's wrong, baby?"

"We're just driftin' apart."

"I'm sorry to hear that. You'll work it out," he said.

"I doubt it."

"Are you saying that he's done something to you? If he has, I'll—"

"Daddy, no. I can handle my own problems. It's not that serious. You said you're at peace with God so don't do anything to mess that up."

For a while we just stared at each other. It was almost time. We knew that this was the last chance we would ever have to speak to one another.

Cynthia White

"I don't want you to come tomorrow." Now he was the one who couldn't look me in the eye.

"But daddy—"

"No!" he shouted.

"Fine. If you don't want me to come, I won't come." A single tear fell from my face onto the JLO jeans I was wearing.

"It's not that I don't want you to come. I just don't want that to be the last image you have of me stuck in your head."

"Okay." I lowered my head as I began to cry uncontrollably.

"Queen, baby, please don't cry," he begged.

"I'm sorry, daddy." I tried to control my emotions, but I just couldn't get ahold of myself.

"I love you, baby." His words were simple, yet they meant so much to me.

"I love you, too, daddy." I wiped away the tears.

We got up at the same time and walked away from each other. The next day, my father was to be put to death for murdering my mother. The fucked up thing about it was that he was innocent. He didn't do it, and I knew who did.

It was me.

*****

I walked out of the prison in a daze. I got into the limousine and Jeffrey our driver shut the door behind me. I could feel my husband looking at me, but I paid him no mind. I had bigger things to worry about. How could I live with myself knowing that my father died for something I did? It was eating me alive. I couldn't sleep. I couldn't eat and I could barely think straight. It never should have gone that far. We used to be so happy. We were the family that everyone envied. We had it all.

My father was a self-made millionaire. He clawed his way out of the projects by committing petty crimes for small time crooks. He did whatever he had to do. He started when he was only twelve years old so he mostly delivered packages for my Uncle Moe. Moe wasn't really my uncle but he was as close to a brother as daddy ever had. Uncle Moe was an intimidating man at six-foot-nine and three hundred pounds. He had skin as dark as the hair on my head and eyes as yellow as buttered popcorn. I was terrified of him when I was a little girl until he started giving me hundred dollar bills every time I saw him. I used to think I was rich. From as far back as I could remember, Uncle Moe was always there. He was even there the night I killed my mother.

*****

It was three years ago on my sixteenth birthday. Daddy had thrown me a huge party at our house on the lake. Everyone I had ever met in my entire life was there. My first crush, Carmen, was even there. It was the first time I had seen him in four years. He had gone off to college and come back with a pregnant girlfriend. He was looking fine, but I couldn't be too disappointed, because I was with Gauge.

Gauge was my boyfriend at the time. He was five years older than me, and at first my father did not approve. A twenty-one-year-old man dating his sixteen-year-old daughter was out of the question. I begged daddy for months to just give him a chance. I told him how good he was to me and how he never tried to push me to do anything I wasn't ready to do. Just hearing that I was still a virgin was music to daddy's ears.

Gauge told me how daddy had taken him into his office to discuss our relationship. "Sit down, son. I want to talk to you," daddy said. He locked the door then went and sat

Cynthia White

behind his huge antique cherry desk.

"Sir, I just want you to know that Queen is a very special girl." Gauge tried to break the ice with daddy.

"You don't have to tell me that. I know how special my daughter is."

"Of course you do, sir." Gauge looked around at all the pictures of me that daddy had on his desk.

"Cut it out with this 'sir' bullshit. My name is Hershey Aaron. You can call me Mr. Aaron."

"Okay, Mr. Aaron. I just want you to know that I love your daughter."

"You love my daughter?" daddy questioned suspiciously.

"Yes, Mr. Aaron, sir."

"Have you touched my daughter?"

"Touched?" Gauge asked.

"Yeah, boy, are you stupid or something? Have you had sex with my daughter?"

"Oh, no. We have not had sex yet."

"Yet? So you plan on having sex with my daughter?" daddy asked.

"I don't really feel comfortable talking about this." Gauge looked around nervously because he knew this was something he could never comfortably discuss with my dad.

"Good! You shouldn't feel comfortable. It's not a comfortable subject. How do you think I feel? Do you have any kids, boy?"

"No, sir, Mr. Aaron," Gauge said.

"Well, one day when you do you'll understand, especially if you have a daughter. Queen is a very beautiful girl and every time I turn around some grown-ass man is looking at her like she's a piece of meat. I won't have any man disrespecting my daughter."

"No, sir, Mr. Aaron. Neither will I," Gauge assured him.

"You realize that being with her is not like being with any other young lady. She has to be protected." Daddy's whole demeanor changed. He didn't really want to drill Gauge. He just wanted to make sure I was safe.

"I do realize that, sir."

"Listen closely, 'cause I'm only going to tell you this once. If you hurt my daughter in any way, they'll never find your body. I won't hurt you. I won't send you away. I will fuckin' kill you with my bare hands."

"I understand, Mr. Aaron." Gauge didn't back down.

And that was that. My father was the type of man who only warned you once. Gauge knew that he couldn't fuck up or his life was over. It was just that simple. You didn't fuck with Hershey Aaron. He was known for not taking any shit from anyone, including his family. I was a good girl so daddy didn't have to worry much about me. My mother was another story.

Hilary Aaron was an ex-model who was known for dating high-profile men. She met my father while doing a photo shoot for a famous men's magazine in Mexico. My father and a few of his friends were there on business. He had a connect there who was about to supply him with the most potent dope the U.S. had ever seen. Everybody who was there said it was love at first sight. I think my mother smelled money. Uncle Moe said that it was like watching a romantic movie. He said that he didn't know shit like that happened in real life.

My father was twenty-two then and already on his way to being the top nigga in his crew. My father and Uncle Moe founded The Black Mafia and to this day it is the deadliest gang in the entire city of St. Louis. To make a long story

Cynthia White

short, my mother flew home with my father and moved into his apartment when they got back to town.

My mother was a gorgeous woman, and sometimes the more beautiful a woman is, the more scandalous she is. She was no fool. She knew that she could get anything from a man because of the way she looked. She was five-foot-eleven with long legs, big breasts and a round ass. She had light skin, long hair and turquoise eyes. She was what you would call an exotic beauty. My father pampered her, giving her any and everything her heart desired. She had luxury cars, expensive jewelry, designer clothes and even a custom-built home in an affluent neighborhood. She was pregnant within a month and they were married within two. She moved fast. I'll give her that.

*****

I was born into a life of privilege. I was the princess of The Black Mafia. I had twenty-seven uncles. None were related by blood, but they all would have given their lives for mine. Anything I wanted I could have. I had the world at my feet. I was too young to realize it then, but my father was a leader. He was their king. Hundreds of people worshipped Hershey Aaron like a god. No one ever disrespected him.

Everyone loved my father, everyone except my mother. I was six the first time I saw her with another man. My father was out of the country on business, and I came home from school and found her in bed with our pool boy. Even though I was just a little girl, I knew it was wrong.

"Queen, this is our little secret. You don't want your daddy to be mad at you, do you?" she whispered into my ear. She always was a good manipulator.

"No," I whispered back in my little six-year-old voice.

"That's mommy's girl." She smiled and then kissed me

on the cheek. The only time she showed me any affection was when I was doing something for her.

"But mommy, why was Hector in daddy's bed?"

"Hector was just helping mommy with something." She smiled mischievously.

"What?" I wanted to know.

"That's none of your business. You just make sure not to tell your daddy. Do you understand?" She grabbed me by the shoulders and shook me wildly.

"Yes, mommy," I cried.

"Good girl." She patted me on the head then sent me on my way.

It happened again the following summer when I turned seven. It was three times with three different men when I was eight, and by the time I turned nine there were so many I had lost count. My mother was a notorious whore. Everyone was too afraid to tell my father; everyone except for good ole Uncle Moe. I was twelve by the time the shit hit the fan. Daddy had just gotten home from yet another business trip when Uncle Moe sat him down and had a long talk with him.

"I didn't want to have to be the one to tell you this, Hershey, but everybody else was too scared." Uncle Moe couldn't even look him in the eyes, but somehow he managed to break the news.

"It's okay, Moe. I'm glad you told me." Daddy sat down on the couch in his office with a distant look on his face.

"I'm sorry. I know how you feel about her." Uncle Moe put his huge hand on daddy's shoulder as a small gesture of support.

"She's the mother of my child. I can't kill Queen's mother."

Cynthia White

"Would you like me to handle it for you?" Uncle Moe offered.

"No, I don't want my daughter to have to grow up without a mother."

Little did my father and Uncle Moe know, I was listening at the door. I was glad that he finally knew. I was so tired of carrying that burden all by myself.

My father grew up without a mother and he didn't want me to suffer the same fate. I couldn't have cared less. My mother was a snake and I wanted her gone. She didn't love my father and she didn't love me. She only had me to secure her place in my father's life. I didn't know what he saw in her. If a woman could manipulate a man as smart and powerful as my father, Lord help the rest of them. They didn't have a chance.

For years he acted as if nothing happened. We would be sitting at the dinner table and I would be looking over at him just waiting for him to snatch her up and whoop her ass. What I didn't understand was that my father's love for me was stronger than his hatred for her. He suffered with a lying whore of a wife for years just so I could go on believing that I had the perfect family. He didn't know that I knew everything and I didn't have the heart to tell him. I loved him too much.

For my sixteenth birthday, daddy bought me not one car but two. I hadn't been able to decide whether I liked the Mercedes-Benz CLK320 two-door coupe or the SL500 convertible better, so he got me both. They were both red, my favorite color. I was so happy I stuck by my father's side the entire night. I just had this feeling that he needed me. Of course he would never admit it, but I knew just the same.

My father and I were kindred spirits. I was so much like

him that Uncle Moe used to call me a chip off the old block. He used to swear that when I grew up, I would be the first female leader of The Black Mafia. Daddy wouldn't hear of it. He wanted me to live a normal life. The main reason he did the things he did was to guarantee me a better life than he had.

"Daddy, thank you so much for the cars." I stood on my tippy toes and hugged him tightly.

"You're welcome, baby." He smiled but there was something desolate in his voice.

"Daddy, what's wrong?"

"Nothing, baby. Everything's fine." He didn't even realize that he wasn't smiling anymore.

"Daddy, I'm not a little girl anymore. You don't have to lie to me."

"This is your special night," he said as he turned and looked away.

"And it's only special because of you."

"You should go back out and enjoy it with your friends."

"I'm not leavin' you like this. Please tell me what's wrong," I begged.

"Your mother and I ..."

"You have to leave her, daddy. You deserve so much better." I exhaled. It felt good to finally get that off my chest.

"What are you saying?"

"I know everything," I confessed.

"How long have you known?" he asked.

"Since I was six."

"What?"

"I came home from school one day and found her in bed with Hector," I said softly. As much as I hated my mother, I knew this was hard for daddy to hear.

Cynthia White

"The pool boy?"

"Daddy, there were so many others. I wanted to tell you so bad, but she said that you would be mad at me if I told."

"She said what?" He started to yell but regained his composure.

"Then when I was old enough to know better I just couldn't tell you. I didn't want to hurt you, daddy." I began to cry.

"Come here, baby." He opened his arms and invited me in.

"I'm so sorry, daddy."

"Shhhhh. You have nothing to be sorry about. This has nothing to do with you. Your mother was wrong for involving you. This is between me and her," he said.

I felt so safe with his massive arms around me. There was something else I wanted to tell him, something that I hadn't told anyone.

"Daddy?" I looked up at him.

"Yes, baby?"

"Can I tell you anything?" I asked, searching for his acceptance.

"Anything," he assured me.

"When I was thirteen …"

"You can tell me," he urged.

"Daddy, Hector raped me." As soon as the words left my mouth, I regretted saying them. It had happened over three years ago, but it was still fresh in my mind.

One hot summer afternoon, I was out by the pool reading a book when my mother called Hector inside. He was in there for a while so I decided to go for a swim. I took off the long T-shirt I had over my black Juicy Couture one-piece swimsuit and dived in. I was only in for about ten minutes

when Hector came back outside. I couldn't see what mama saw in him. How could she cheat on a man like daddy with this piece of scum? He had that kind of skin that always looked dirty. His hair was long and oily and there was something dark in his eyes. I didn't trust him. I tried my best to stay away from him, but I was just a little girl. I had been sheltered my entire life, and I had no idea that there were adults in this world who preyed on children.

"Hey, how you doing, Queen?" he asked slickly.

"I'm fine." I jumped out of the pool and put my T-shirt back on.

"How old are you now, fifteen or sixteen?"

"I'm thirteen." I started to walk toward the house.

"I wouldn't go in there if I was you."

"Why not?" I wanted to know.

"Your mama is busy, if you know what I mean." He put his finger up to his nose and made a sniffing sound. I knew my mother had a heavy cocaine habit, and I also knew that I didn't like being anywhere near her when she was high.

"Did you give it to her?" I may have only been thirteen but was bright enough to recognize that whenever he came around, she was high.

"Who, me? Nah, I'm a good guy."

"Yeah right." I rolled my eyes and snaked my neck.

"You know, for only being thirteen you sure have a nice body on you. I bet you'll be as tall as your mother and probably as freaky, too."

"If my daddy heard you talk like that he'd kill you," I warned him.

"He would? Well I guess it's lucky for me he's not here."

Without warning he put his hand over my mouth, picked me up and carried me into the pool house. He locked the

Cynthia White

door behind him then pulled a knife out of his back pocket. I was terrified. He threw me down on the hard marble floor and raped me, holding the knife to my throat the whole time.

Nothing was the same after that day. *I* was never the same. I started spending a lot of time over my friend Jennifer's house. Jennifer was Puerto Rican and her father did business with my father. They lived in the house next to ours, but it was still far enough that I had to be driven over. Even though I told her everything, I couldn't tell her this. I was afraid that if I told anyone Hector would came back and kill me. The only person I knew would protect me was my daddy, but I was too ashamed to tell him. I didn't want him to know what Hector had done to me. So I did what I thought was the next best thing and I told my mother.

"Queen, I'm disappointed in you. How could you make up such a horrible lie about a man as nice as Hector?"

"But mommy, I'm not lyin'," I cried.

"You keep this up and your father and I will send you away to boarding school."

"But—"

"But nothing! You go upstairs to your room and don't come out until it's time to go to school in the morning." She yelled at me like I was the one who had done something wrong. I was crushed that my mother didn't believe me. In the time that followed, she even continued to have an affair with the monster who had violated her own daughter. I went up to my room and collapsed onto my bed. I cried and cried until finally I fell asleep. I had a nightmare that Hector climbed into my bedroom window and raped me again. When I woke up, it was two a.m. I plugged in the nightlight that I hadn't used since I was seven years old and sat in my

bed until the sun came up. I was safe then.

As I began to get ready for school, I looked into my vanity mirror and saw my mother looking back at me. I was becoming her. I looked exactly like her. I stared at myself with a strong hatred. If I looked this much like her, did that mean that I would also start to act like her? I opened my top drawer and pulled out my scissors. I proceeded to cut inches and inches off of my long hair. I didn't want to look like that woman who called herself my mother. When I was finished, the hair that was once halfway down my back was now right below my ear. Now I looked like my own person.

"Queen, what in the world did you do to your hair?" my mother asked as I joined her and my father at the table for breakfast.

"I cut it." I looked over at her and rolled my eyes.

"What in the world did you do that for?" she asked like it was her hair I cut.

"Because I wanted to."

"I like it, baby." Daddy smiled at me.

"Thank you, daddy." I smiled back at him.

She didn't say another word after that. If Hershey Aaron said it was okay then it was okay and that was all there was to it. She could never understand the bond between my father and me. We loved each other and that was a foreign concept to her. The only love she knew was the love of money. The gold diggin' bitch was so used to sucking and fucking to get the new Dolce & Gabbana that she completely lost sight of the things that were really important in life. Our relationship used to bother me. I prayed that one day we would become closer like a normal mother and daughter. Then I realized that being close to the devil was the last thing I wanted. If you played with fire long enough,

Cynthia White

you were bound to get burned.

*****

"So you told your mother what Hector did to you and she didn't believe you?" daddy asked me like he was recording our conversation. Never in my life had I seen my father shed a tear, but they were welling up in his eyes.

"She didn't even ask him about it," I cried with my face buried in my father's chest.

"I wish you would have told me." He just hugged me tighter like he never wanted to let me go.

"So do I, daddy. I'm sorry."

"You have nothing to be sorry for." He gently stroked the back of my head. I knew what he was thinking. If only I would have told him a few months ago, he could have done something about it. Now it was too late. Hector had died four months previously from a drug overdose. The day I found out was one of the happiest days of my life. I watched my mother cry for that bastard. She had the audacity to mourn the man who took away my innocence and peace of mind. I didn't think it was possible, but I hated her even more at that moment.

Daddy and I stayed in his office for a while longer. We didn't talk anymore. There was nothing left to be said. He just held me in his arms like I needed him to. I would forever be his little girl. I knew that there was nothing in this world my father wouldn't do for me. For that brief time when I was in his arms, I was safe. I knew that no one could get to me. Not even my mother. I knew that sharing my truth with him would change everything forever.

Daddy called one of the guards in. He ordered him to find my mother and bring her to him. That was easy. I knew that she was wherever the men were. The guard called

daddy on his walkie-talkie and told him that she refused to leave some Dominican business men she was entertaining. Daddy called Uncle Moe and told him to bring her by any means necessary. He had to pick her up and throw her over his shoulder, but just like always, he came through.

"Hershey, I don't appreciate being summoned like a child," my mother bitched.

"Shut up." My father's tone was stern and intense.

"Excuse me?" She had the nerve to try to get an attitude.

"I said shut the fuck up!" Daddy yelled so loudly and with so much power that even I jumped.

"What's going on here?" She looked from my father to me.

"How long have I put up with your bullshit?" daddy asked her in a very direct manner.

"Come again?" she asked like she had absolutely no idea what was going on.

"Bitch, you heard me. I've known for years," he spat at her.

"Known what?" She still tried to play it off.

"Don't patronize me. Did you really think that you were that slick? Did you really think that no one would tell me?"

"Hershey, I don't know what you're talking about."

"I'm talking about you spreading that lame-ass pussy all around town." He looked at her like the trash she was.

"Don't talk like that in front of our daughter."

"My daughter," he corrected her.

"I gave birth to her," she retorted.

"And I've raised her for the last sixteen years."

"So I'm not the best parent in the world," she remarked nonchalantly.

"No, you're not the best parent in the world. You're not

Cynthia White

the best wife in the world, either."

"I've always been there for you," she lied through her teeth.

"Me and every other man with five dollars in his wallet."

"How dare you?" She tried to act all high and mighty.

"How dare I? Bitch, how dare you? How can you even sit up here and try to act like you're a lady? You were a whore when I met you and you're an even bigger whore now."

"Hershey, please don't talk like that in front of my daughter."

"Don't call me that." I had to speak up.

"You are my daughter, Queen."

"You're nothin' to me," I spoke honestly.

"Are you happy? You've turned our daughter against me!"

"Bitch, you did that all on your own."

"And how exactly did I do that?" she asked like she did-n't already know.

"When you forced me to cover up your affairs and lie for you. You told me that if I told daddy he would be mad at me. I was just a little girl."

"Queen, that was a long time ago." She brushed me off.

"What about Hector? What about what he did to me?" I asked her, begging to be validated.

"Don't start with that shit again." She continued to brush it off like it was nothing, like I was nothing.

"He raped me!" I yelled. This time I wanted her to hear me.

"He did not. You just wanted some attention."

Daddy smacked her so hard she fell to the floor.

"You stupid bitch! My daughter was raped because of you!" He began beating her viciously. She screamed for

help, but no one came. They all knew better. He punched her and kicked her like she was a man. I knew it was sick of me, but I enjoyed it. It made me feel better about all the pain I had endured because of her. She deserved everything she got.

"Hershey, please stop! Please! Please!" She yelled and screamed but there was no stopping him. She had messed with the one thing he loved more than anything else in the world – me.

"I'm gonna kill you, you stupid bitch!" he yelled like a madman as he pulled his 9mm from the waistband of his pants. He pointed it at her and she froze.

"Daddy, no." I walked over and took the gun out of his hands.

"That's right, baby. Don't let him kill your mother." She smiled as she looked up at me. Her eyes pleaded for sympathy. I had none.

"Let me." I aimed the gun at her and emptied the entire clip. Something overtook me. I felt free.

I knew instantly that she was dead. I felt no pity or remorse, just satisfaction. I looked around. There was blood everywhere. My daddy had to pry the gun out of my hands. Within minutes we heard the police sirens. They were coming for me. I knew I was going to jail for the rest of my life, but I didn't care.

Daddy had other ideas. He called Gauge in and told him to get me out of there. I didn't want to leave. I knew what he was about to do and I didn't want that.

"Take her away, now," daddy ordered Gauge.

"No, daddy, I wanna stay with you," I whined.

"Baby, listen to me. You have to get out of here."

"But—"

Cynthia White

"But nothing. Now you do as I say," he ordered.

"Yes, sir." I fell in line like a good little soldier.

"Stay with her," he instructed Gauge.

"I will, Mr. Aaron." He took me by the hand and led me to his car. I said nothing the entire ride.

*****

When Gauge finally brought me back home, the place was crawling with guards. There had to be twenty more than usual. We went inside and I turned on the TV. My father's face was on every channel. They finally had something to convict him of, and it was all my fault. It wasn't supposed to be this way. I didn't want him to pay for my crime. He was the last person in the world I wanted to hurt.

"You have to take me to the police station," I begged Gauge.

"Yo' father told me to stay with you," he reminded me.

"But I have to confess."

"Confess to what?" he asked.

"Gauge, I did it. I killed my mother," I blurted out.

"What?" He looked at me like I was crazy. I proceeded to tell him everything.

After the long story, he was speechless. He didn't know what to say. My life wasn't as perfect as everybody thought it was. Then he did something that changed everything. He put his arms around me and held me just like my father would. I felt safe. Someone besides my father finally understood me. Things went further that night. It wasn't just him holding me anymore or us kissing and freaking. We were going to make love that night for the first time.

"I'll always be here for you, Queen. I'll protect you now," he reassured me.

"You promise?" I asked as I looked up into his big brown

eyes. I was searching for something. For what, I did not know.

"I promise. I love you."

I didn't care if he meant it or not. I needed so desperately to hear it. I put my hand on his hand and I felt a spark. I kissed him. We both knew where it was going. The kiss grew more and more intense every time I heard my father's name mentioned on the TV. Finally, Gauge picked me up and carried me upstairs to my bedroom. He laid me down gently on top of my white satin comforter. I looked up at him with innocent eyes. I wanted him to make me forget. He took off his shirt. His body was amazing. Both of his arms were covered in tattoos. His stomach was ripped like he did a thousand sit-ups a night. I looked up at his face. He was so fine. His dark eyes told on him. He had been wanting to do this for a long time. I motioned with my finger for him to come to me. He obeyed.

His lips were like candy, sweet and juicy. His kiss made me want to do more. I unbuttoned my white blouse exposing my white lace bra and my full breasts. He kissed them then sucked them. It was the first time I had ever wanted a man. No one had touched me since Hector, nor had I wanted them to.

Gauge did things to me that night that I had only read about. By the time he took my panties off, I was so wet and ready that he could have had me any way he wanted me. He pushed himself inside me and it hurt so damn good. I didn't know whether I should just lay there and take it or get up and run for my life. When it was over, I just lay in his arms until I eventually fell asleep. I was a woman.

*****

"I love you, Queen," he whispered into my ear as I woke

Cynthia White

up the next morning still in his arms.

"I love you, too." I smiled innocently at him.

"Marry me?" he asked out of the blue.

"What? I can't marry you. I'm only sixteen," I tried to rationalize.

"Yo' mother's gone and who knows what's gonna happen to yo' father. Let me take care of you."

"But do we have to get married?" I asked.

"You said you loved me," he reminded me.

"I do, but I don't know anything about being a wife."

"And I don't know anything about being a husband, but we can learn together." He looked at me like he wanted this, really wanted this. My heart said go for it, but my head told me to slow down.

"Please, Queen?" he begged.

"Okay." I gave in.

The previous night was our first time together and now suddenly we were engaged. It was all so overwhelming. In twenty-four hours my life had completely changed. My father was arrested for my mother's murder. My prints were on the gun. I was missing from my own party, yet they didn't even attempt to question me. They got what they wanted. They didn't care if he killed her or not, just as long as they got their names in the paper for busting Hershey Aaron. They thought that with the big dog behind bars, The Black Mafia would perish.

They were wrong. My father still ran shit. Uncle Moe let muthafuckas know that this was still their town. If anything, they got stronger. Being locked up gave my father more time to plot and strategize. He was worse than ever. Within a few months, only a few other gangs remained. You either got down with us or you got laid the fuck out.

chapter *Two*

I WENT TO VISIT MY FATHER all the time. We spoke mostly in codes that nobody besides the two of us understood. He seemed to be doing well. That was more than I could say for myself. I missed my daddy so much. I wanted him back home with me. He wanted the same, but deep down he knew that there was only one way he was leaving that prison.

The judicial system was a joke. They had an innocent man locked up while a cold- blooded killer went free. I wrestled with my conscience constantly. Daddy and Uncle Moe both drilled it into my head that no matter what I said or did, they would never release my father. They said that they would just think that I was covering for him, lying to get him off the hook. I would have lied to God himself to save my father's life.

"Hi, daddy." I put on my biggest, brightest smile.

"Hi, baby. You look nice. Is there something different

Cynthia White

about you?"

"I'm engaged." I held up my hand to show him the flawless 3 carat round diamond on my finger.

"Engaged? Queen, you're only sixteen years old." His smile disappeared and was replaced with a look of concern.

"I know, daddy, but I'm all alone now," I whined.

"You still have your Uncle Moe," he reminded me.

"I know, and I love Uncle Moe just like he was my real uncle, but Gauge loves me. Please just say it's okay?" I begged.

"It's okay, baby." He smiled at me.

"Thank you, daddy." I smiled back at him.

"You're welcome, baby. I want you to be happy."

"I know you do. That's why you koot eht emalb rof em." That was part of our code. It was "took the blame for me" backwards.

"That's exactly why." He confirmed what I already knew.

After my visit with daddy, I needed some time alone. I had my driver take me to the park. It was so peaceful out there. It was just me and the ducks. They didn't bother me so I didn't bother them. The bench right next to the lake was my favorite spot. The cool breeze relaxed me and all the trees shaded me from the rest of the world. I thought about the young lady I was and the woman I wanted to become. I had no idea what I wanted to do career-wise, but I did know that I wanted to go to college. Daddy had taught me a long time ago that a degree was a very powerful asset for a black person in America. Without an education, you were pretty much doomed to work a dead-end job until you were too old to work any longer. I didn't want that. I was a boss bitch and whatever I ended up doing, it had to be on that level.

After two hours alone at the park, I decided to pay my

girl a visit. "Hey, girl." I greeted my best friend Jennifer at her front door.

"Hey. Come on in."

I followed her into her house. "Where yo' folks at?" I asked as I looked around the empty house.

"My mom is at a doctor's appointment and my dad is out of the country."

"Is yo' mother okay?" I asked, concerned.

"Girl, she's fine, just gettin' a little Botox."

"Botox? See, that's why I'm glad I'm black. We don't do crazy shit like that." We both laughed.

"Did you go see yo' father today?" she asked.

"Yeah, that's where I'm comin' from now."

"How is he?"

"He seems fine, but it's not like he would tell me if he wasn't," I said sadly.

"Well at least you have a father that cares. All my father does is throw money at me and wave goodbye," Jennifer said bitterly.

"Girl, yo' father loves you. Some people just have a hard time showin' emotion." I understood because I had that same problem myself. The only person I truly trusted with my heart was my daddy.

"I guess. Anyway, did you tell your father about you and Gauge gettin' married?"

"Yeah. At first he wasn't with it, but eventually he came around."

"That's because he loves you and he wants you to be happy." She smiled at me as she tried to straighten up her messy room.

Jennifer and I had known each other ever since we were a few months old. Our birthdays were a day apart and we celebrated together every year. Our nannies used to meet up at the park each and every morning so that we could spend the majority of our days playing together. It was always just me and Jennifer. We never played with any other kids. She was also an only child so we pretended that we were sisters. Since I was a day older, I was the big sister. I bossed her around and made her sit in the corner.

*****

"Girl, why the hell do you have a convertible if you're not gonna drop the top?" Jen asked on our way to the mall.

"Are you happy now?" I asked her as I dropped the top.

"Oooooh, girl turn that up. That's my song!" she screamed as some new song by Ciara came on the radio. I had never heard it before. I just turned it up and pretended like it was my song, too. Because of my father's case, I didn't listen to the radio anymore. I was tired of hearing them talk about what a bad guy he was. They didn't know him. They never talked about what a good father he was, and I never heard them mention all the money he donated to various charities. Or what about all the turkeys he gave away to poor families at Thanksgiving? They had to tear him down in order to build themselves up. My father's fall was the best thing that ever happened to the media.

The mall was crowded as usual. It was more like a club than any actual club I had ever been to. Girls came to meet dudes and dudes came to meet girls. No one actually shopped. Jennifer and I were the exception to the rule. We loved to get our shop on. I'd still prefer a nice pair of Carlos Santana stilettos over a nigga any day.

"Damn! How you doin', sexy?" some fine young tender asked me as we walked past Foot Locker.

Jennifer and I just laughed. Even though we lived hectic

lives, we were still only sixteen years old. The mall was always where we had the most fun.

"What's ya name, ma?" he asked with a little bit of East Coast flava.

"Queen," I stated proudly.

"Queen, huh? I like that. Who gave you that name?" he asked with the sexiest smile I had ever seen in my life.

"My daddy."

"He a king?" he joked.

"King of this city," I stated boldly.

"What, is he the mayor or somethin'?"

"No, he runs The Black Mafia," I informed him. I didn't know the name of our mayor, but every person living in this city knew who my father was.

"Yo' father's Hershey Aaron?"

"Yes." I smiled proudly.

"Then you know my father?" he asked.

"Who's yo' father?"

"Maurice Darrin."

"Never heard of him." I rolled my eyes.

"Everybody calls him Moe."

I couldn't believe my ears. "Uncle Moe is yo' father?" I asked excitedly.

"Uncle Moe?" he asked, confused.

"Yeah, that's what everybody in the family calls him."

"Well at least y'all get to see him," he said and looked away.

I saw the sadness in his eyes. We were all missing our fathers in different ways. "You never told me your name," I reminded the young tender.

"Isiah."

"Well, Isiah, it was nice meetin' you. I'll tell Uncle Moe

Cynthia White

you said hi."

"So you gonna just brush me off like that? We're practically family. Let me buy you lunch?"

"I can buy my own lunch, thank you."

"I know you can. I'm just tryin' to be a gentleman. My homeboy likes the way yo' girl looks. Let's make it a group thang." He smiled. He had the cutest dimples. He was fine as hell and very charismatic. How could a girl say no?

We headed down to the food court. He paid for everybody's food then we sat down to eat. I kept noticing him looking at me. It made me blush. I felt like a normal teenager. We didn't talk about anything too heavy. He didn't ask me a million questions about my father and I really appreciated that. I couldn't get over how fine he was. He was just as black as Uncle Moe with long, neat braids and two big diamond studs in his ears. He was tall, around six-foot-three, and cocky like he worked out a lot. He probably played football. I could picture him out on the field dominating. He was dressed nicely, wearing all the new fly shit. He had a brand new pair of wheat Timberlands on his feet. I didn't know what it was, but I just loved a nigga in some Timberlands. He had on a red G-Unit cap, jacket, T-shirt and jeans. Red was a good color on him.

"What school you go to?" he asked, knocking me out of my fantasy.

"St. Mary's."

"Private school, huh? Y'all wear those little plaid skirts?"

"Yes, we do." I laughed.

"You have a pretty-ass smile," he complimented me.

"Thank you." I blushed.

"What you so shy for?"

"I'm not," I lied.

I wasn't usually shy, but there was just something about him. The chemistry was automatic. I had never had that kind of instant connection before. It was as if we had already met.

"But for real though, I know what's goin' on with yo' pops. I'm real sorry about that," he told me sincerely.

"Thank you." I appreciated that so much.

Jennifer and his boy Nate talked amongst themselves as Isiah and I talked and even flirted a little. I really liked him, but I knew that nothing could come of it. I was engaged and I had to honor that. I loved Gauge. I wasn't really sure about marriage, but I did love him. I was honest and upfront with Isiah. I told him about my situation, but he didn't seem to care. I liked his carefree attitude. He didn't seem to let anything bother him, and I wished I could be like that. Just as I had predicted, he was a quarterback on the football team. He invited us to a game that night. Luckily, we were at the mall because I needed something new to wear.

Isiah and Nate had to go, but Jennifer and I had four hours before the game to shop. I wanted to look good but not out of place. I knew that Prada was too lavish for a high school game and Dolce & Gabbana was out of the question. I decided on a pair of skin-tight Baby Phat hip-hugger jeans with a white and gold Baby Phat halter top. Next I needed shoes. I got a pair of metallic gold Baby Phat sandals with a three-inch wedge heel and a gold Baby Phat handbag to match. Jennifer got the same outfit in black instead of white. We still had a little time to kill, so we stopped at the nail salon and had our French manicures touched up. When we were done, we jumped in my Benz and headed back to Jennifer's house to get ready.

"So what did you think about Nate?" I asked Jennifer as

Cynthia White

I looked in the mirror and put on my big gold hoop earrings.

"He's cute," she confessed.

"What about Rico?" I asked cautiously. Rico was somewhat of a touchy subject with Jen. He had been her boyfriend for the last two years.

"What about him? He's in New York livin' it up and probably ain't even thinkin' about me."

Rico had moved to New York the previous fall to go to college and ever since then, Jennifer had been a little down. She knew in her heart that he was probably with another girl, but he never had the balls to come out and tell her.

"Do you still love him?" I asked sincerely.

"Of course I still love him. He was my first boyfriend, but I'm not gonna sit around waitin' for him to come back to me. I like Nate, so I'm goin' to have some fun with him tonight."

That meant she was going to fuck him. Jennifer and I were a lot different when it came to sexual experience. She had been with ten guys to my one. Most of the men she dealt with were a lot older. I think she was searching for a father figure or just looking for a way to get her father's attention.

We arrived at the game twenty minutes after it started. We were known for being late. All eyes were on us as we squeezed past rows of people to get to a seat. We both went to private school, so this was a very different scene than we were used to. It was exciting. Everywhere I looked there was some fine young man admiring me. I didn't know much about football, and the game wasn't really that interesting to me, so Jennifer and I sat and gossiped most of the time. I kept hearing people yelling out Isiah's name, so I knew he was doing something good.

After the game we walked around trying to get a feel for

our surroundings. People were staring at us like we were celebrities or something. I thought that at any minute someone was going to come up and ask me for my autograph. At least nobody knew that I was Hershey Aaron's daughter. My father had always protected my identity. I wasn't ashamed of him or anything like that, I just didn't feel like answering any questions about his case. Tonight I was just a normal sixteen-year-old girl.

"Queen!" I turned around as I heard Isiah call my name. He came running up to me just as Jennifer and I were about to bounce.

"Hey." I reached up and put my arms around him, hugging him tightly.

"You not leavin' already, are you?" he asked, sounding a little bit disappointed.

"Well, the game is over," I said.

"I'm still here. Why don't you and yo' girl shoot back to my crib with me and Nate? I'm havin' a few of my folks over and I'd like it if you'd come."

"What you think?" I turned and asked Jennifer.

"I'm down." She shrugged. "I ain't got shit else to do."

"I guess we'll be there." I turned back to Isiah.

"Good." He smiled. "Give me ten minutes to hit the showers and I'll meet you in the parkin' lot. I drive a black Navigator."

"On some 26-inch dubs?"

"How'd you know?" he asked.

"I'm parked right next to you."

"See, it was meant to be." He kissed me on the cheek.

As he ran off to go take a shower, I couldn't help but smile. There was something about him. I was attracted to him and there was no denying that, but there was something

Cynthia White

more. I was instantly comfortable with him. It felt like I had known him all my life. He let me be me and that was enough for him. With Gauge I always felt like it was more about my father than me.

"If his boy plays his cards right, he just might get fucked tonight," Jennifer whispered in my ear as we walked back to my car.

"He might not be the only one," I confessed.

"You really feelin' him, huh?"

"Like crazy." I couldn't help but smile.

"Just make sure Gauge don't find out," she warned.

"This is just a one night thing."

"You hope."

"I know. In some ways Gauge is nothin' like my father, but when he gets angry, I can't tell them apart. My father was never like that with me, but in the end he despised my mother. I never want Gauge to feel that way about me," I confided in my best friend.

"Then maybe we should just go home. I don't want you to get in any trouble." Jennifer might have been wild, but she always looked out for my best interests.

"I'm cool. Gauge ain't getting back from Chicago 'til tomorrow. Anyway, I deserve to have some fun." I laughed.

"Yes, you do." She threw her arm around me.

We got back to my car and got in. I dropped the top and turned up the stereo. Christina Milian's new song was on the radio. Now that was my shit. I turned my stereo up even louder. Girls mean-mugged as their boyfriends admired us. It was nothing new. I had been dealing with haters my entire life. I just did my own thang and tried not to worry about anybody else. I was a good person. I got good grades, went to church and respected my elders. I couldn't help that I was a kingpin's daughter nor did I want to change it.

Sure, my car was worth over a hundred thousand dollars, but my father worked hard so that he could give me nice things. I never took anything he gave me for granted. I treasured each gift whether it was a car or a new pair of shoes. My father grew up dirt poor and I knew how good it made him feel to provide for me and my mother. We would never have to be on welfare and food stamps the way his mother was before she died. He didn't talk about it much, but I knew how hard that was on him.

"Y'all ready to roll?" Isiah popped out from nowhere.

"Lead the way."

He jumped in his truck along with Nate and we followed them back to his place. He had a very nice townhouse on the south side. I was surprised to learn that he lived there by himself. How could a seventeen-year-old high school student afford a place like that? The downstairs was beautiful. The living room had a black leather sectional sofa, a huge 70-inch TV, an Xbox 360 and a monster stereo system. It was a teenage boy's paradise. The kitchen had all stainless steel appliances, cherry wood cabinets, a center island and marble counter tops. It also looked like it had never been used before. The only things in the refrigerator were beer and cold pizza. The dining room had a beautiful table and chair set that also looked like it had never been used. The last room downstairs was the bathroom. It was just a half bath with a toilet and a sink, but the black marble floors and the beautiful artwork on the wall made it extraordinary.

Upstairs there were two bedrooms and two more bathrooms. The master bedroom was huge. It was furnished with a beautiful modern mahogany bedroom set. There was a sliding glass door that led out to a balcony with a magnifi-

Cynthia White

cent view. The master bath was three times as big as the one downstairs. It had a separate tub and shower, two huge walk-in closets, a double sink, a vanity and of course marble floors. I was impressed. He definitely had style. The town-house, the truck, the rims and the expensive designer clothes were all enough to keep me interested. It wasn't that I was attracted to him just because of what he had. He was myste-rious. I wanted to discover all there was to know about him.

"Are you havin' a good time?" Isiah asked me as we danced together.

"Yeah, it's cool."

It was more than cool, but I didn't want to sound overly excited.

"What time do you have to be home?" he wanted to know as he grinded on my booty.

"Whenever I get there." I smiled. We both had the same thing in mind.

"You want to stay here with me tonight?"

"We'll see how the night goes," I teased. I already knew I wanted to stay. I just didn't want him to know that. Jennifer and Nate were already upstairs doing the damn thang. Sometimes I wished I could be bold like that. To be able to just go after any guy you wanted had to be liberating. I would never know. I just wasn't that type of girl.

It was a little after four a.m. when the party finally start-ed to wind down. I was starting to get nervous. I knew it was now or never. This could be my only chance to be with Isiah. I loved Gauge, but I was just a kid. I needed to explore more before I committed the rest of my life to one man.

He took me by the hand and led me up the stairs. My heart was pounding. I could hear Jennifer screaming from the hallway. Nate must have been laying it down. I followed Isiah into his bedroom. He closed the door then locked it. I looked up at him. I wanted him and he wanted me. I took a step closer then he kissed me. I liked it. I put my hand up under his shirt and explored his chest. His muscles were like mountains, up and down, up and down. He reached down and grabbed a handful of my ass. He was aggressive like I needed him to be.

I didn't know how we got on the bed, but that's where we ended up. He looked me directly in the eyes as he unbuttoned my jeans. He kissed my bellybutton and I giggled. I was so scared and so eager all at the same time. He pulled my pants off then put his hand down my panties.

"Uhm …" I moaned as he began to play with my kitty.

His hands were good, but his tongue was even better. I lost control. Within minutes he had me purring his name. My heart and my mind were getting all jumbled up. Usually I could keep the two separate, but this time was different. I tried desperately to get a grip. I had just met dude. I didn't want to fall too fast for someone who might not feel the same way.

"You sure you want to do this?" he asked me like he was scared he was going to catch a case.

This was my last chance to back out. All I had to do was say that I had changed my mind. I could get in my Benz and drive home where I needed to be anyway.

"I want to do this with you, Isiah," I assured him then kissed him passionately.

He pushed himself inside me and I damn near passed out. He was so big. I thought Gauge was big, but he was much, much bigger. I'm talking about thirteen inches. It was thick, too. I was too young for this.

Cynthia White

"Am I hurtin' you?" he asked as he lay on top of me in complete control of my body.

"I'm fine," I lied.

"You sure?"

"Yeah, I'm okay." It didn't take much to get him back in the swing of things. He went right back to thrusting and grinding inside of me. After a while I started to get into it. It took me a while to get used to his size, but once I did, it was on. I was up on top riding that dick like his name was Mister Ed. I rode that big muthafucka so good he couldn't close his mouth. Now he saw how I felt.

"Damn, Queen ... shit ... uhm, girl ..." He moaned and made faces.

"This pussy good to you, daddy?" I asked in my most seductive voice.

"Hell yeah!"

"Who dick is this?" I asked boldly.

"It's yours, ma!" he cried.

"Whose is it?" I asked again just to feed my ego.

"It's yours."

"That's right."

I leaned forward and grabbed the headboard as I swirled my pussy like a tornado for his ass.

"Damn, girl, you gonna make me cum."

"Come on, daddy." I started to bounce up and down.

"Damn!"

"Come on, daddy. Cum in yo' pussy."

He looked up at me and our eyes locked. I was almost there.

"Oh shit!"

"Uhm ..." I moaned as we came together. It was like the Fourth of July. So much yelling and sweating and grinding

to bring us to that one perfect moment. It was beautiful. That was my first orgasm.

As I lay in his king-sized bed with his arms wrapped around me, I knew I had just made a big mistake, but I didn't care. I was so relaxed. He reached into his top nightstand drawer and pulled out a big box of blunts. He opened up the box and it was filled with everything we needed to make the night perfect. Besides blunts there were bags and bags of weed, razor blades and lighters. I could smell the weed and he hadn't even opened up the bags yet. I knew it was some fire. He rolled two so we could each have our own. I was on cloud nine. I felt every care and concern I had vanish into thin air.

"I really like you, Queen," he confessed.

"I like you, too."

"I hope I can see you again," he said.

"I don't know about all that."

"Come on now. You can't just put it down on a nigga like that and just expect me to let you go."

"I told you I'm engaged," I reminded him.

"Yeah, that's what you told me, but you showed me something different."

"I think I should go." I got up out of the bed and started putting my clothes on.

"So it's like that?" he asked in a hurt voice.

"It ain't like shit. I gotta go."

"Why you tryin' to play me like that?"

"I'm not tryin' to play you. I like you but …" I stopped myself from saying too much.

"But what?"

"But I have to go."

"No, you don't," he pleaded.

Cynthia White

"Yes, I do. I'll talk to you later."

I had his number but no plans to use it. I liked him so much it scared me. I didn't want to turn into my mother. I felt guilty for cheating on Gauge, but with time I could get over that. I couldn't get over the things I felt in that bed with Isiah. For the first time in my life, I felt sexy. I was nastier than I ever thought possible, but somehow he made that okay.

"So, how was it?" Jennifer asked me in the car on the way home.

"It was cool."

"Cool? Queen, I'm yo' best friend. Don't lie to me."

"What?"

"Don't *what* me. Bitch, I heard you yellin' all the way down the hall." She laughed.

"No, you didn't." I tried to defend myself but it was useless.

"Really? Well does this sound familiar? Oooooh ... right there, daddy ... right there ... this yo' pussy!" She laughed.

"I know you ain't talkin', the way Nate had you yellin' like ya ass was on fire," I shot back.

"It was. Girl, that nigga ain't no joke."

"It was good, huh?"

"It was fabulous. Him and Isiah are comin' over to my house after school," she added.

"What? Girl, I don't want that nigga knowin' where I live!" I yelled.

"Why not?"

"Because I don't wanna get my ass kicked."

"Girl, please, Gauge knows if he ever lays a hand on you, he's dead. Fuck The Black Mafia, yo' Uncle Moe would kill his ass."

"And that's another thing. Uncle Moe doesn't know I'm kickin' it with his son," I revealed.

"So instead of Uncle Moe he'll be your father-in-law," she joked.

"Bitch, I'm glad you think this shit is funny."

"Girl, mellow the fuck out. You like the nigga and you got fucked. That's a win-win situation if you ask me."

We went home, took quick showers then changed into our uniforms. We were late for school, but we didn't care. They were teaching us the same ole shit anyway. Each day it was the same thing. I was so tired of school. I couldn't wait until I graduated and went to college. More and more, moving out of town seemed like a good idea. There was nothing here for me anymore. If Gauge really loved me, he would come with me. If he didn't then that was cool, too. Life never turned out the way you planned it anyway. I learned that from my father.

After school we went back to Jennifer's house. Her father was still out of town and her mother was at a five-star hotel recovering from her breast augmentation surgery. That woman had more fake shit than the flea market. She was a beautiful woman, but the more surgery she had, the less beautiful she got. She thought that bigger breasts would keep her husband at home, but she was sadly mistaken. He was in the game. I knew his life all too well. Nothing could keep him at home because he loved the lifestyle too much. These women would never learn. You can't change a man, at least any man worth having. I liked strong men. Go out of town for two weeks and come back with two-hundred grand. Make me miss you. Have me lying up in my bed at night thinking about you and playing with myself. That's gangsta.

"What's up, ma?" Isiah greeted me as he got out of his

Navigator.

"I'm good. How you doin'?" I tried to play it off like I wasn't open.

"I'm good now." He licked his lips. I knew what he had in mind. I was thinking the same thing.

"Come here," I commanded.

"My pleasure." He got as close to me as possible.

"I missed you," I confessed as I put my arms around him and hugged him tightly.

"You smell so damn good," he whispered into my ear.

"Thank you." I smiled. It was nice to get compliments without having to fish for them.

My entire attitude had changed when Gauge called me and told me that he wouldn't be getting back from Chicago until next week. I took advantage of the situation and decided to have some fun with Isiah. The four of us hung out at Jennifer's place for a while. We rolled up a few blunts, ordered pizza and then hit the pool. I was looking too good in my red Donna Karan string bikini. I was lounging on one of the patio chairs with absolutely no plans to get in the water. My hair was looking fly and I didn't want to get it wet. I was high as a kite and all seemed right with the world. Then Isiah picked me up and threw me into the pool.

"You look good wet." He laughed as he put his hands under the water and on my legs.

"Did I say you could touch me?" I asked playfully.

"Did I ask?"

"I don't belong to you," I asserted.

"Not yet."

"Not ever."

"That nigga you engaged to will fuck up and when he does, I'll be right here to swoop in and pick up where he left

off," he said in a serious voice.

"So you just know he's gonna fuck up, huh?"

"Most niggas do," he admitted.

"And what about you?"

"I'm not most niggas."

"Come with me," I instructed him. I got out of the pool and wrapped a towel around myself. We got into my Benz and I drove down to my house.

"Damn! You live here?"

"Yep."

I got out and walked up to the front door.

"Hey, Queen," Jimmy C, one of the day guards, greeted me.

"What's up, Jimmy? How you been?"

"I'm good."

"Have you seen my Uncle Moe today?" I asked.

"Yeah, he's inside. I think he's in Mr. Aaron's office."

"Something goin' on?"

"Just between me and you?" He looked around before he went any further.

"Always."

"The Black Mafia is plannin' somethin' big. I don't know exactly what, but I do know that it has something to do with Jin Yang and his crew."

"Yang? I go to school with his daughter, Hung."

"Well, whatever's goin' down, I just want you to know that I'd lay down my own life before I let harm come to you," he said as he looked in my eyes.

"That's sweet, Jimmy. Thank you."

Jimmy C had had a thing for me ever since he started working for my father two years ago. He was cute, but I wasn't into Puerto Ricans. I loved my black brothas.

Cynthia White

"I'm serious. If you need anything, you know where to come," he offered.

"Yeah, she knows where to come." Isiah stepped to him.

"Who is this *puta*?" Jimmy asked as he looked Isiah up and down.

Now I wasn't exactly fluent in Spanish, but I did speak enough to know that Jimmy had just called Isiah a bitch.

"What the fuck did you just call me?" Isiah asked as he stepped to Jimmy C.

"Guys, come on. We all on the same side here." I got in between the two of them.

"Who the hell is this clown, Queen?" Jimmy C asked, heated.

"This is Uncle Moe's son, Isiah."

"Moe has a son?" he asked.

"Yep, so I suggest you keep the bitch comments to yo'-self unless you want Uncle Moe to deal with you," I warned.

"It's nice to meet you, sir." He extended his hand to Isiah.

"So you called me a bitch, huh?" Isiah squeezed his hand so hard that Jimmy's entire face started to turn red.

"Stop it!" I yelled at both of them. Suddenly I felt like I had two little brothers.

Isiah followed me into the house. He looked around like he was in a museum or something. I guess if I didn't live there I would've been impressed, too. We had twelve bedrooms, fourteen bathrooms, a game room and a theatre. We also had an indoor pool, an outdoor pool and a pool house that was as big as most people's primary residence.

"Damn, this is nice," he said in awe.

"Thank you." I stopped at the door to my father's office and knocked.

"Who's there?" Uncle Moe yelled from the other side of the door.

"It's me, Uncle Moe!" I yelled back.

"Queen? Girl, come on in here. You know you don't have to knock."

"Come on." I grabbed Isiah's hand.

"I'm not goin' in there." He pulled away from me.

"Why not?"

"I don't want to see him," he said angrily.

"Why? He's yo' father."

The concept that somebody may not be happy to see their father was completely lost on me. I would have given anything to be able to hug my daddy.

"Look, I'm not goin' in there."

"You said you liked me."

"I do," he said.

"And you want to keep kickin' it with me."

"True."

"Then do as I say." I grabbed his hand again and this time he didn't pull away. We walked in that office hand and hand like we were Bonnie and Clyde.

"Hey, baby." Uncle Moe turned around to greet me and got the shock of his life. Even though he hadn't seen him in years, he recognized Isiah immediately.

"I believe you know my friend?"

"Yeah, I know him," he said in a still voice.

"What the fuck is wrong with you, Uncle Moe? Why didn't you tell me you had a son?" I asked, completely pissed off.

"I ... I just ..."

"You just what?!" Isiah interrupted him. He was mad as hell and there was no way to hide that.

Cynthia White

"I wanted you safe, you and your mother," he tried to explain.

"My mother's dead."

"I know, son," Uncle Moe said in the saddest voice I had ever heard.

"Don't call me that. I'm not yo' fuckin' son!" Isiah yelled.

"Did you get the package I sent you?"

"Yeah, I got yo' money!" he yelled like he was offended. That explained the truck and the fly-ass crib.

"I just wanted you to have a normal life."

"I'm seventeen years old. I have no family and I live on my own. That's real fuckin' normal."

"Isiah, what are you even doin' here?" Uncle Moe asked.

"He's my guest," I explained.

"Queen, I know you meant well, but this is no place for him."

"Well, get used to it 'cause I ain't leavin'. Come on." He grabbed my hand and practically dragged me out of the office.

We went upstairs to my room. I locked the door then showed him where I kept my stash. He wasn't the only one with some fire-ass weed. I knew what he needed. I was still high from the four blunts we smoked over at Jennifer's house, but I knew he needed a booster. As he lay on my bed smoking his blunt, I began to undress him. I started with his shoes and then his socks. He had nice feet for a man. I loved my daddy, but his feet looked like they had been through some terrible things. I sat down on the bed and proceeded to give him a foot rub.

"That feels good," he moaned.

"Does it?"

"Uh huh."

"I know what will feel even better."

"What?" he asked.

I could show him better than I could tell him. I climbed up his body and straddled his waist. I raised his T-shirt and started kissing all over his chest. He liked it, but that wasn't what I had in mind. I licked a warm trail from his chest all the way down to his boxer shorts. He was curious. He wanted to know if I was a head tease or if I would go all the way. I was my father's daughter and Hershey Aaron didn't make no punks. I unzipped his khaki Phat Farm shorts. I looked up at him to see where his mind was at. He looked me in my eyes and we communicated without words. Silently he was begging me to suck him off and although I would never admit it to him, I wanted to badly.

First I tasted it. I stuck my tongue out and licked the head like it was a lollipop. I was not about to have no nasty dick in my mouth. But it was different than I thought it would be. It wasn't nasty and I didn't feel dirty.

Ten minutes later, he was sitting on the edge of my bed and I had my knees on the floor sucking his dick like it was laced with crack. I was a quick learner. This was my first time giving head and already I was a natural. I had him cursing and moaning like crazy. He especially liked it when I hit his dick up against my tongue like it was a drum. Now I wanted to watch the movie "*Drumline.*" I was high and trippin'. Isiah grabbed a handful of my hair and pulled my head back. He leaned down and kissed me passionately. Now my pussy was aching for him.

"You are so fuckin' sexy," he told me as he licked and kissed on my neck, driving me crazy.

"Fuck me, Isiah."

"Come here," he commanded.

Cynthia White

He pulled me up from the floor. He lay back and I climbed on top of him. His dick was brick. He practically ripped my bikini bottom as he tried to get to my pussy.

"Uhm …" I moaned as I slid down on his dick.

It felt so damn good. I twirked my pussy like a pro. I had him calling out my name and professing his love for me. I was no fool. I knew this nigga didn't love me just like I didn't love him. But whatever it was that I was feeling, it was profound. The deeper I got, the deeper I wanted to go.

"Oh shit!" I hollered as he entered me from behind.

This was yet another first for me. His dick felt ten inches bigger. It hurt like hell at first, but I took it like a soldier. The harder he fucked me the better it felt. A few minutes in and I was throwing it at him like Beyoncé. Nobody could tell me shit after that. I was grown, and fuck anybody who tried to tell me any different.

Three and a half hours later we lay in my bed trying to recover. That was as close to death as I had ever come. It was such a rush. I wanted to do it again, but I didn't think my body was ready. I just inhaled the chronic through my mouth then slowly released it from my nose.

"Come on now." Isiah laughed.

"What?"

"You know you look sexy as hell when you do that."

"Do I?" I toyed with him.

"Yes, you do." He kissed me softly.

"What was that for?"

"For bein' you," he said sweetly.

"Just for bein' me?"

"That's right. I have to keep on remindin' myself that you got a man. I kept catchin' myself thinkin' about you all day at school."

"Really?" I blushed.

"I care about you, Queen," he confessed.

"I care about you, too."

"Do you, or are you just sayin' it because I said it first?"

"I wouldn't say something just because you said it or just because I thought you wanted to hear it. My father raised me to be a leader, not a follower. I said I care about you because I do."

"Good, 'cause I'm sprung like a muthafucka and I ain't lettin' you go," he asserted. I liked him like that.

I spent the next few days with Isiah having fun and getting dicked down. We went shopping together, to the movies, out to eat and to a party at one of his boys' houses. Jennifer and Nate were kickin' it, too, but on a whole other level. For the two of them it was just sex and they seemed to like it that way. Whatever made my girl happy, I supported. Not everyone clicked instantly like Isiah and I did. I wished that I had met him before I met Gauge.

Those days, nothing about my life was easy. I had some guilt about shooting my mother. I often wished that I could go back and find a better way, but I knew that what was done was done. There was no bringing her back. I didn't miss her. I had no love left for her. I just realized that I had no right to take another person's life. God would deal with me in due time.

I felt most guilty about my father. He would be free if it hadn't been for me. That hurt the most. Isiah helped me to forget about all the bad stuff. He made me smile when I thought I had forgotten how. He was there for me when Gauge wasn't. It was his arms that held me when I woke up in the middle of the night from a nightmare. He whispered in my ear and told me that everything was going to be okay.

Cynthia White

He stayed up with me until I fell back asleep. I was starting to think that maybe I was about to marry the wrong man.

chapter

Three

GAUGE GOT BACK FROM CHICAGO the following week. I was glad to see him, but on some level I wished he would have stayed longer. It was so much easier to have feelings for another man when he wasn't there. It wasn't that having him home made my feelings for Isiah go away, they were just hidden in the back, away from the light. Things were so complicated. With us being engaged it was all set for Gauge to become a member of The Black Mafia. He wouldn't have as much power as my father or Uncle Moe, but he would still be more powerful than most.

"This is for you." Gauge placed a small, black velvet box in my hand.

"What is it?"

"Open it." He was so excited.

I opened the box and damn near melted. Inside was a 7.5 carat canary yellow diamond mounted on a platinum setting. It was gorgeous. Gauge took off the 3 carat round diamond,

Cynthia White

which now looked like a trinket.

"I couldn't resist. I saw this and I knew this was the ring you needed on your finger." He took it out of the box and slid it onto my finger. "You can still keep the other one, of course."

"Gauge, it's beautiful."

"I'm glad you like it." He kissed me softly on the lips. I felt dirty and not in a good way.

"Thank you," I whispered.

"No, thank you for makin' me the happiest man on the face of this earth."

I had the perfect chance to tell him and still I said nothing. I should have never let him put that ring on my finger. I knew I wasn't ready to be his wife. I was barely ready to be his girlfriend. With him back home, I didn't get to spend any time with Isiah. I told Jennifer to tell him that I would call him as soon as I could.

A week turned into two and soon a month had gone by. I thought that surely Isiah had forgotten about me. He was young, fine and rich. I was convinced that he had moved on. Still, five and a half weeks after our last encounter, I sneaked into the backyard with my cell phone and dialed his number.

"Hello," he answered. His voice was like the antidote to my sickness.

"Hey, it's me," I spoke sweetly.

"Me, who?" he questioned. That hurt.

"Oh, it's like that?" I asked with a bit of an attitude.

"I was just playin'." He laughed.

"You betta be."

"I missed you," he confessed.

"Did you?" I smiled even though no one else was there to see it.

"I wanna see you."

"I wanna see you, too," I admitted. "I have an idea. I'll be there in half an hour."

I hung up with him and called Jennifer on her cell phone. It rang fives times and the freak didn't answer so I hung up. Maybe it just wasn't meant to be. Just as I turned and started to walk toward the house, my phone rang. I looked at the screen. It was my girl calling me back.

"Hello," I answered.

"What's up, freak? You called me?"

"Yeah, where you at?"

"At some sleazy-ass motel with Nate."

"Did you take yo' car or did he pick you up?"

"He picked me up. Why?"

"I'm tryin' to sneak over to Isiah's place, but I need your help."

"Name it."

"I'm goin' to tell Gauge that I'm goin' over yo' house. Just in case he decides to investigate I'll park my car out front ..."

"... and drive my car." She finished my sentence.

"That's right."

"You a sneaky little freak. I'm gonna have to get you to scheme up some shit for me."

"It would be my pleasure."

"My car keys are in my room on my dresser. Call me and let me know how it turns out."

"I will."

Everything was set and ready to go. I went into the house to find Gauge. As I was searching for him I realized just how damn big our house really was. I searched the entire downstairs and still couldn't find him. I climbed the stairs and started on the second floor. I searched everywhere except for the maid's room. He had no reason to be in there. Maybe he had left to run an errand when I was out back on the phone with Isiah. Just as I turned to go back downstairs, I heard his voice. He was talking really low and the door was shut so I couldn't hear him that well. What I did hear didn't sit right with me.

"I need more time. It just can't be done by then. All I need is another month." He was bargaining with someone.

What the hell was going on? Who the hell was on the other end of that phone? I was already a very suspicious person but hearing that put me over the top. I didn't run and hide. I stayed right there. He stopped dead in his tracks when he saw me, looking like a deer caught in the headlights.

"I'm goin' to Jennifer's house," I informed him.

"Alright. I'm about to leave myself. Do you want me to drop you off?"

"I'd rather drive my own car."

"Well, I'll see you later." He kissed me on the cheek.

"Bye." I turned and walked away.

I didn't know what he was up to, but I would find out soon enough. I didn't ask him any questions about being in the maid's room because I was in no mood to hear his lies. He knew he was busted.

I got in my Benz and drove down the street to Jennifer's house. I parked my car out front then went around back where the door was always unlocked. We could never do that at my house. Her father had just enough power so that they could live comfortably, but not enough that people would try to murder him to get his position. My father, on the other hand, was a Don. Every little wannabe thug in

town wanted his position. There was a thin line between power and all-powerful. Daddy never wanted to be this large, he just was.

Jennifer's car keys were right on her dresser where she said they would be. I smiled at the picture on her mirror of the two of us together in the eighth grade at our school's Valentine's Day dance. Neither one of our fathers would let us date yet, so we went together. We joked that she was my bitch and I was hers. We had so much fun that night. We had our dresses custom made. They were five thousand dollars apiece but they were worth it. Hers was pink and mine was red. The ringing of the phone snapped me out of my daydream. It rang twice before the answering machine picked up.

"Jennifer, this is Oliver. I been thinkin' about you. I had fun last night. I was wonderin' if we could kick it sometime without Nate, just me and you. Call me when you get this message. You know the number." *Click*. He hung up. Who the hell was Oliver? What the hell was going on today? Was everyone living a double life?

I got into Jennifer's white Lexus ES 350 and took off. I had a strange feeling. It seemed as if everything in my life was changing and not in a good way. I turned off the AC and let down the windows so I could get some air. I felt sick to my stomach. The thing with Gauge was really bothering me. I had to find out what was going on with him. It was then that I realized just how little I really knew about him. He always told me just enough to satisfy my curiosity. He never talked about his family. He didn't have any friends. Then it hit me that I didn't even know when his birthday was.

"Hey, baby," Isiah greeted me at his front door.

"Hey." I wrapped my arms around him and rested my head on his chest.

"What's wrong?"

"There's something goin' on with Gauge," I confessed.

"Something like what?"

"I don't know yet. I was lookin' all over the house for him and guess where I found him?"

"Where?" he asked.

"In the maid's room."

"What was he doin' in there?"

"I don't know." I didn't want to believe the worst.

"You think he's fuckin' the maid?"

"I hope not. She's sixty-five years old." I laughed to cover my pain.

"Then what?"

"I don't know. He was on his cell phone talkin' to some-body. The conversation was real sketchy. He was sayin' just enough to answer them without incriminating himself."

"Did you tell my father about this?" he asked.

"No. You think I should?"

"Hell yeah. It ain't no tellin' what that nigga's up to."

I dug in my Coach handbag and felt around until I found my cell phone. I took it out and dialed Uncle Moe's number. It rang six times and just as I was about to hang up, he answered.

"Hey, baby." He sounded so upbeat that I hated to ruin his mood.

"Hey, Uncle Moe."

"What's up?"

"Can you talk right now?" I asked.

"Yeah, shoot."

"I think there's something goin' on with Gauge."

"I already have that under control," he informed me.

I was shocked. Why didn't anybody ever tell me what was going on? "What do you know that I don't?" I asked, quickly becoming disgusted with the entire situation.

"You know I can't talk about that over the phone."

"Just tell me this. Is he dangerous?"

"Not to you."

"But to the family?"

"Where are you?" He attempted to change the subject.

"I'm at Isiah's place." He was silent for a moment.

"You're safe there. Don't tell him this, but I have guards sittin' on his place twenty-four seven."

"That's good to know."

"I'll keep you informed."

"Same here."

I hung up the phone feeling much better than I did before. Uncle Moe always had my back. I was so grateful to have him in my life.

"What did he say?" Isiah wanted to know.

"He said he already knew."

"And he didn't tell you?"

"He thought it was betta that he didn't."

"Cocky muthafucka."

"Don't talk about my uncle like that."

"He's my father."

"Then act like it," I snapped.

"Look, I don't want to fight with you about this."

"Then don't."

"Do you always have to win every argument?" he asked.

"Every single one."

"You really do think you're a Queen, don't you?"

"I don't *think* anything," I asserted.

Cynthia White

"You just know, huh?"

"You said it."

I walked right past him and headed upstairs to his bedroom. He followed me just as I knew he would. I sat down on his bed. He sat down beside me. I turned and looked at him, wondering what he was thinking. I had something on my mind. Something I wanted to do. He leaned in to kiss me. I turned my head.

"It's like that?" he asked with wounded pride.

"If we get rid of Gauge, are you ready to take his place?"

"Are you askin' if I'm ready to be yo' man?"

"That's exactly what I'm askin'."

"I'd do anything to be with you." He said it with such honesty it caught me off-guard.

"Anything?"

"I love you, Queen." His words were so sincere and authentic.

"I love you, too." I leaned over and kissed him softly on the lips.

"I have to tell you something." His whole expression changed.

"Go ahead." I braced myself.

"After I graduate, I'm goin' to the Army."

"The Army?!" I asked, full of shock and bewilderment.

"I've thought long and hard about this."

"Well then you need to think again."

"Queen, I'm not like you," he argued.

"And what the hell is that supposed to mean?"

"I barely made it through high school. I have no desire to go to college, nevermind the fact that no college would accept me."

"College is not the only option," I said.

"I don't have it like you. You're set for life. You never have to work a day in yo' life if you don't want to."

"So I'm supposed to feel bad because my family has money?"

"That's not what I'm sayin'," he tried to reason.

"Then what the hell are you sayin'? It seems to me like you're tryin' to run away from your problems instead of facin' them like a man."

"I am a man."

"No, you're not, not yet. If you were, you would go talk to your father and squash this bullshit once and for all."

"Why does it always have to come back to my father?"

"That's who you're runnin' from, ain't it?" I asked. I was heated and tired of his hatred for Uncle Moe.

"I'm not runnin' from anybody."

"Prove it. You want to join an army, then join your father's army."

"The Black Mafia?" he asked like he had never even considered it.

"Why not?"

"For one, I'd have to see his face every day."

"Are you really gonna let yo' pride fuck you out of an opportunity like this?"

He was silent for a while. He was more like his father than he realized. I had done exactly what I had set out to do. I planted a seed of doubt in his head. I wasn't about to let him walk away from his destiny.

I stayed with him that night. We didn't discuss joining The Black Mafia any further. Just my being there with him was enough to make him think twice. I knew that he wanted me, but was that enough? It would have to be. After we fucked for two and a half hours, we smoked two blunts and

Cynthia White

I fell asleep in his arms.

*****

The next morning, Isiah accompanied me back to my house. Uncle Moe was in my father's office as usual. I took it upon myself to arrange an unscheduled meeting between the two of them.

"I don't know if I want to go in there," Isiah confessed to me as we stood outside the door.

"Look, do you want to spend the rest of your life wonderin' what could have been or do you want to get in the game and make some shit happen?" I proceeded to open the door and walk in the office.

"I don't know about this," he whispered in my ear.

"Hi, Uncle Moe." I ignored Isiah's concerns.

"Hey, baby. Hello, Isiah," he said, addressing his son.

"What's up?" Isiah greeted his father coldly.

"Uncle Moe, we have somethin' we need to discuss with you."

"Sit down." He graciously offered us his valuable time.

"I want to join The Black Mafia," Isiah blurted out.

"What?" The look on Uncle Moe's face said it all.

"It's either that or he's joinin' the Army," I informed him.

"The Army? Where is all this comin' from? Now I know that you and Queen have been spendin' a lot of time together ..."

"No offense, Uncle Moe, but this ain't got shit to do with me. Isiah came to this decision all on his own. Now if he wants to be a soldier then why not let him be a soldier in yo' army? You are a founding member. Isn't that his birthright?" I added fuel to the fire. Daddy used to tell me that I should be a lawyer because I never lost an argument.

"I guess it is." Uncle Moe took a deep breath.

"I'd rather stay here, but if you decide not to let me join, I'm enlisting. It's yo' decision." Isiah put it all out there. I couldn't have said it better myself.

"Alright, you can join, but it won't be easy. You want to be a boss, you have to work hard."

"I understand."

"Do you?" Uncle Moe challenged.

"Yes, I do."

"I hope so."

Uncle Moe wasn't exactly glad that his son was joining up, but what could he do? It was time for people to stop telling us that we were too young and just let us live our lives. I was a mafia princess, soon to be a mafia queen. I needed a king on my arm. That's where Isiah came in. It was perfect. I wasn't lying when I told him that I loved him. Everything I was doing, I was doing for us. Our future would be secure if it was the last thing I did.

My mother was a fool. She could have had the world at her feet if she would have just played her cards right. You have to let your man know that you believe in him. Tell him he's fine even if he's ugly as hell. Make him feel strong even if he's a hundred pounds soaking wet. Tell him he's the only man for you even if you're fucking the entire hood.

"I feel like I can do anything with you by my side," Isiah confessed as we sat on my bed smoking a blunt.

"You can do anything. You're a king." I continued to feed his ego.

I told him he was the best kisser, the best lover and the best pussy eater. I wasn't lying. He was the best I had ever known.

"What did I do to deserve you?" he asked as he looked at me like I was his ticket to utopia.

Cynthia White

"I keep askin' myself the same thing about you."

"I love you so much," he said.

"I love you, too. I wish there was something I could do to prove that to you."

"You don't have to prove anything to me."

As we kissed, my head began to spin. He made me feel like I was high even when I wasn't. Kissing him was almost enough. Fucking him was too much. I felt like if he asked me to jump off a building, I would. That was chilling. To know that another person had so much control over me shook me to my core. We fucked for a few hours before he had to get ready for his game. Jennifer and I would be there cheering for our football stars.

After Isiah left, I grabbed my bags and headed over to my girl's house. As usual, she was the only one home. We put on the new Trina CD as we got dressed. I looked in the mirror and I could have sworn I saw my mother standing over me. I freaked out.

"Did you see that?" I asked in a panic.

"What?" Jennifer looked at me like I was crazy.

"My mother."

"Okay, no more weed for you," she joked.

"I'm serious." I tried to keep my composure but I could feel my hands trembling. I started messing with my hair to hide that I was shook.

"Do we need to contact Sylvia?"

"Who is Sylvia?" I asked.

"This psychic that's always on Montel. She can talk to the dead."

"I don't wanna talk to that bitch. I just want her to leave me alone." I laughed. I brushed it off, but it really did shake me up a little.

*****

That night we went in Jennifer's Lexus. It wouldn't have mattered if we were riding the bus. Hoes would still hate. I was fine as hell and that was being modest. Jennifer had that whole Jenny from the block thang going on. Like Jennifer Lopez, she had a pretty face and a ghetto booty. I had on a fitted pair of ultra low-rise jeans and a red lace shirt with a red bra underneath. My red leather Dior handbag matched perfectly, as did my red leather Dior sandals and my red Dior shades with pink tinted lenses. Jennifer was wearing a white button-down shirt that she tied above her navel to reveal her new butterfly tattoo. Her khaki Bermuda shorts were skin tight and looked good with her mother's dark brown leather Jimmy Choo sandals and Carlos Falchi handbag. We were dimes in a sea of pennies.

Just like last time, Isiah and his team were victorious. I couldn't understand why some college wasn't scouting him. He was a god out on that football field. There were twenty girls just praying that they would be the one that night. They would have to be disappointed. I would be the one that night and every other night that followed.

"Hey, baby." Isiah wrapped his arms around me and kissed me passionately. Everybody was looking at us, but I was used to it.

"Good game," I complimented him.

"You weren't even watchin'."

"Yes, I was. I didn't know what the hell was goin' on, but I was watchin'."

"You proud of yo' man?"

"I'm always proud of you, baby." I kissed him, throwing in a little tongue for all the haters.

"Get a room," Jennifer joked.

"Oh, we will," I assured her.

We all went back to Isiah's townhouse for a private after-party. As soon as we hit the front door, they went their way and we went ours. I walked right past his bedroom and went into the master bathroom. Isiah followed me. I grabbed ahold of his shirt and pulled him close to me. The heat was undeniable.

"I just want you to know that there is nothin' in this world I wouldn't do for you," I told my man as I looked up into his eyes.

"Same here."

"Tell me what to do."

"Take yo' clothes off." His voice was deep and penetrating.

As my shirt and bra hit the floor, he took my naked breasts in his hands. He touched them the way I always dreamed my man would. He squeezed them firmly then sucked them. His tongue was warm. My nipples were as hard as diamonds. I stepped out of my jeans. Standing there in nothing but my red lace thong and my four inch heels, I felt powerful. His eyes scanned my entire body. He licked his lips. He wanted me so badly. I walked slowly over to the shower and turned on the water. Within seconds the room was filled with steam. I took off my shoes and got into the shower. The hot water felt so good on my naked flesh. Isiah followed my lead. He took off his clothes and got in. My long hair curled up as I stood underneath the water. I reached down and firmly gripped his rock hard dick. It was calling my name. I kissed the spot on his chest I had picked out for him to get a tattoo of my name.

"Tell me what to do."

"Suck my dick," he ordered me, and I obeyed.

I wanted him to feel like he was in control. Whatever my man wanted, I would provide. I went down and sucked his dick like I knew no other broad could. Even if she was a better dick sucker than me, she could never make him feel as good as I did. I had his mind and that was more powerful than any physical action. I wasn't stupid. I knew that if another chick gave him head he would enjoy it. He was only a man made of flesh and blood like the rest of us. However, I also knew that before I came along, he had nobody. I loved him when he so desperately needed to be loved. I let him lead when I thought it was necessary, then took over when he was in over his head.

I moaned as I sucked him off like his dick was the most mouthwatering thing I had ever tasted. He looked down at me and admired my work. Every time I did it, I just got better and better. I was thinking of putting it down on my college applications as my special talent. Seriously though, it turned me on. I loved the way he moaned and panted when he was in my mouth. I was used to his taste. Now, no other man would do.

*****

I got home at around five o'clock the following morning. I was feeling so good that I greeted all twenty guards one by one. The sun was shining and the birds were singing. It seemed that all was right with the world. This was the effect Isiah had on me. He made me happy in ways that I had never imagined before. I used to think that love was bullshit until I fell for him. I thought to myself that this is what life is all about. I was finally living instead of sitting on the sidelines waiting for other people to tell me what to do.

"Queen, we need to talk." Uncle Moe stopped me as soon as I walked through the front door.

Cynthia White

"What's up?" I asked, trying to hide the fact that I was exhausted and had no plans on going to school today.

"I need you to stop seeing Isiah."

"Here we go." I rolled my eyes and threw my hands up in the air.

"Just until we get this situation with Gauge under control."

"And what situation is that? You want me to help you, but you won't tell me what the hell is goin' on. I'm a part of this family, too."

"Come with me."

He grabbed me by the arm and took me into daddy's office with him. We sat down on the couch as he struggled with whatever it was he was trying to tell me.

"What is it, Uncle Moe? I can handle it," I reassured him.

"Queen, Gauge is working undercover."

"Undercover? Are you tryin' to tell me that I'm engaged to a pig?"

"Yes," he hesitantly admitted.

"Oh my God." I felt sick. "What have I done?"

"Queen, it's not your fault."

"The hell it isn't!" I yelled, taking my frustrations out on him instead of the person I was really mad at.

"Baby, try and calm down."

"I brought him in. I introduced him to daddy."

"You didn't know," Uncle Moe tried to reassure me.

"I should have. I wasn't thinkin'."

"It took us this long to figure it out, and we've been in the game for over fifteen years."

"Daddy knows?" I asked.

"He knows."

"Is he mad at me?" I worried.

"No."

"I slept with him, Uncle Moe. He was my first," I confessed.

"I'm sorry, baby."

"Are they allowed to do that? Can they just sleep with the people they're investigating?" I began to cry.

I could no longer hear Uncle Moe. I saw his lips moving, but all I could hear was my own guilty conscience. I had failed my father once again. Not only had I let him down, I had let the entire family down as well. I felt like I was about three inches tall. Gauge had made a fool out of me, but he would never get a chance to do it again.

I sat on that information all day and night. I waited for the right time to make my move. I thought about all the times I had let that pig touch me. I took three scalding hot showers, but I couldn't wash away my shame. Never in my life had I ever felt so low, so used. He had to pay for this.

*****

"Hello," Gauge answered his phone half asleep.

"Did I wake you?" I asked like I really gave a fuck.

"Queen, what's wrong? You sound strange."

"I need you."

"You want me to come over?" he asked excitedly.

"No. I'll come to you. Is that okay?"

"That's fine," he said.

"I'll be there in twenty minutes."

Downtown was deserted this time in the morning. Nobody was out and that's exactly what I had banked on. I was dressed in all black like I was on my way to a funeral. My scarf hid my hair and a pair of dark shades hid my eyes. I didn't have to knock. He was waiting for me at the door. I

Cynthia White

walked right past him and into his tiny one bedroom apartment. I didn't want anyone to be able to distinguish my voice.

Once inside, I opened up my coat, but didn't take it off. All I was wearing was a black lace bra and a black lace thong. His eyes were happy. He didn't say a word. He walked over to me and put his hands on my body. I felt dirty. I kissed him even though it turned my stomach. I felt his dick grow hard. I wondered if that was a part of his job description. I pushed him down on his bed. He smiled. If he liked it when I was aggressive, he was about to love my ass. I climbed on top of him and continued kissing him. Isiah's face popped into my head. As Gauge grabbed my breasts, I reached my right hand behind me and pulled the 9mm from the inside pocket of my chinchilla coat. I pointed it at his face.

"I am in no mood to play with you," I warned him sternly.

"Queen …"

"Shut the fuck up. Just tell me the truth. Are you a pig?" I tried to remain as calm as possible.

"Yes," he answered in an almost inaudible voice.

"Are you undercover right now?"

"Yes."

"Are you tryin' to take down the family?"

"Yes."

"You used me."

"No," he lied. I smacked him in the face with the gun.

"I told you, I'm in no mood to play right now. You knew I was Hershey Aaron's daughter and you used me."

"I'm sorry." He tried to apologize, but I wasn't hearing it.

"Did you really love me or was that just an act, too?"

"I did love you. I still do."

"I love you, too." I kissed him softly on the lips, then put a pillow over his face and shot him.

I looked around his apartment. Even though I had just committed my second murder, I was thinking very clearly. I scanned every single inch of that place looking for evidence that I had been there. I'd been wearing gloves the entire time so they would not find my fingerprints. Of course they would suspect The Black Mafia, but they had no proof. Then I remembered something I heard my father once tell Uncle Moe. If they can't find a body, they can't prove a crime has been committed. I called the one person I knew would understand.

Isiah was there in ten minutes. I helped him cut Gauge's body up into small pieces and didn't so much as flinch. We put the pieces into these huge storage containers and then, one by one, took them out and put them into his truck. I picked up the plastic tarp we had laid down on the floor before we cut up the body and took it with us. I scanned the apartment one last time. There was nothing there that could incriminate either one of us. We left the place clean enough to cover up the crime, but not too clean to look suspicious.

We drove for an hour until we came to my father's old warehouse. The Black Mafia had used the place to dispose of bodies back in the day. It was completely desolate. Isiah poured the gasoline and I lit the match. We watched from a distance as the entire place burned to the ground. Gauge was no longer a problem and I could close that chapter of my life.

Cynthia White

chapter *Four*

Three days after I murdered my fiancé, I went down to the police station and filed a missing persons report. I cried and acted all distraught. The officers tried to comfort me as I told them how much I loved Gauge and didn't know how I could go on without him. You would have thought I was Halle Berry or somebody the way I was acting. I deserved an Oscar for that performance. They asked me a few questions that I gave my perfectly rehearsed answers to. I told them about our plans to get married. They didn't know that I knew he was working with them to tear my family and my entire world apart. I could never let that happen. I would destroy anyone who stood in my way.

*****

"Hey, girl," I greeted Jennifer at her front door.

Her house was the first stop I made after I returned from the police station. I wanted to run straight to Isiah, but I knew that wasn't a good idea. For this to work, we had to be smart. I knew the police would be watching me so I had to play my part.

"How you doin'?" she asked as she hugged me.

"I'm okay." I tried to sound as sad as possible.

I wanted to tell her what I had done, but I couldn't. The fewer people who knew, the better. Besides, I didn't want her to be an accessory. If they ever questioned her, all she could say was that I was upset and as far as she knew, I had nothing to do with my fiancé's disappearance.

"Do the police know anything?" she asked as she sat down on the lounge chair next to the pool.

"Nothing. It's like he just vanished."

"Maybe it was The Yang Family?" she wondered aloud.

"I doubt it. They're at peace with The Black Mafia."

"Are you sure?"

"Positive. They're desperate for product and we have it. It's a lot more expensive than they're used to payin', but it's also a higher quality," I explained.

"Girl, listen to you. You sound like a commercial for the mafia," she laughed.

I didn't think it was funny. I took my family's business very seriously. "I am what I am."

"It wasn't an insult. It was just a joke," she said lightly.

"Well, it wasn't funny."

"Queen, calm the fuck down. What's wrong with you? You actin' like we ain't girls or somethin'. We joke about everything." She tried to rationalize but it was no use, I wasn't having it.

"Not this." I got up and left.

I knew Jennifer didn't mean to offend me, but she did. Her father was in the game. She knew better. Some things are sacred and just shouldn't be joked about. I loved her to death, but sometimes she got on my last nerve.

Since I couldn't go see Isiah, I went back to my house. Jimmy C was at the front door when I walked up.

"Hey, Queen. How you been?" he asked as I walked up to the front entrance of my home.

"I'm okay, Jimmy. Thanks for askin'."

"I was sorry to hear about Gauge," he said sincerely.

"Yeah, me too."

"You think they'll ever find him?"

"I don't know. Maybe he doesn't want to be found," I suggested.

"What do you mean?" he asked with a confused look on his face.

"When we got married, he would be next in line to be a boss. Maybe that was too much for him."

"That makes sense. Everybody ain't cut out for this life."

"No, they're not."

"How are you holdin' up? Do you need anything?"

"I'm fine. I just want to be alone right now."

"I understand. If you need anything ..."

"I know. Thank you, Jimmy."

"No problem." He smiled empathetically.

I felt his eyes on my ass as I walked away. Somehow I knew he was going to turn out to be trouble. I ignored my intuition and went upstairs to my bedroom. I ran myself a warm bubble bath and let my body relax for a while.

I gave you all the love I got
I gave you more than I could give
I gave you love
I gave you all that I have inside
And you took my love

You took my love ...

As Sade's *"No Ordinary Love"* played on my stereo system, I lay back in my whirlpool tub and thought about the last year of my life. So much had changed. I would've given anything to have my life back the way it was, but I knew that was never going to happen. All I could do now was move forward.

The next day was my birthday. I would turn seventeen years old and I prayed to God that nobody would remember.

*****

I woke up the next morning and went to school as usual. I sneaked out before Uncle Moe got up just in case he remembered. This day carried a lot of baggage for me. Besides being my birthday, it was also the anniversary of the day I murdered my mother. Most importantly, it was the day my father got arrested. As far as memories went, that one was the worst.

"Happy birthday." Jennifer stopped me in the hall and gave me a present.

"Thank you."

"About yesterday—"

"Don't worry about it," I cut her off.

"No. I was wrong. I'm sorry. Can you ever forgive me?" she asked as she made her sad puppy dog face.

"That depends on what you got me," I joked.

I opened the box and immediately started to cry. Inside was a musical carousel with pretty white horses. She was the only other person who knew about that.

On my seventh birthday, my father had rented me a huge carousel for the entire day. It was so beautiful. Jennifer and I rode that thing all day and half the night. Daddy even rode

Cynthia White

it a couple of times with us. We had so much fun. There wasn't a cloud in the sky that day. Not like today. Today it looked like it might start pouring down at any moment. That was how I felt. I hoped that somewhere there was a rainbow at the end of all this rain.

"Come here." I opened my arms to my best friend and hugged her like I never wanted to let her go.

"Happy birthday, Queen. I love you."

"I love you, too."

"Let's never fight again, okay?"

"Okay," I agreed.

People looked at us like we were crazy as we walked down the hall together, crying and laughing at the same time. We didn't care. I loved that girl and I needed her to know that. I knew that she felt the same way about me. She was the only female I shared my life with. She was the only female I trusted. Even my mother was a traitor. When I was hurt in the worst way possible, she didn't care enough to listen. Believing her child meant that she would have to give up her good times and face reality. She was a drug addict and a whore and needed some professional help. She chose not to listen to me then, so I chose not to listen to her when she begged for her life. Ain't payback a bitch?

*****

After school, Jennifer rode with me to the prison to visit my daddy. This was the best part of my entire birthday. As soon as I saw his face, I felt better. He smiled at me and suddenly I was seven years old again.

"Happy birthday, baby," he greeted me through glass.

"Thank you, daddy." I smiled.

"I can't believe my baby girl is seventeen years old. I'm getting old."

"You're not gettin' old, daddy. You're gettin' betta."

"You know how to make a man feel good about himself."

"You should feel good about yo'self. You're the best father a girl could have." I tried to hold back my tears. Once his fell there was no stopping mine.

"Queen, I hope you marry a man who's smart enough to realize what a special girl you are."

"I will."

"Don't settle for anything less," he cautioned.

"I won't. I'll hold out for a man as wonderful as my daddy."

"I love you, baby."

"I love you, too, daddy."

After my visit with daddy, Jennifer and I headed back to my house to change. We had been in our uniforms all day and were desperate to get into some normal clothes. Our plans crumbled as soon as we pulled into the driveway and saw the police cars. There had to be fifteen of them. It was ridiculous. They were everywhere like they owned the place. I got out of my car and stormed up to the front door.

"Can I help you, young lady?" some ugly-ass, red-haired, freckle-faced pig asked me as I breezed right past him.

"No, you cannot."

"Hey, did I say you could go in there?"

As soon as he grabbed my arm, Jimmy hit him in his face hard enough to send him crashing to the ground. I smiled. He had my back just as he always told me he would. Of course he got arrested for assaulting a police officer, but I would remember to reward his loyalty.

"Tell me where he is, Moe." Some cracker-ass, wannabe Steven Seagal had my Uncle Moe up against the wall holding him by the collar of his shirt.

Cynthia White

"Take yo' hands off of him," I ordered.

"Go to your room, little girl." The cop smugly tried to order me around.

"Little girl? My name is Queen, and that is how you'll address me."

"Queen, aren't you the one who's engaged to Gauge Derek?"

"Yes I am, and instead of you harassing my uncle, shouldn't you be out lookin' for him?"

"We've looked everywhere. There's no sign of him. Your uncle—"

"Officer, I would advise you to be careful what you say about my uncle while there are witnesses around. He just might decide to sue you for slander."

"I just might." Uncle Moe smiled an almost devious smile.

"We have reason to believe that someone in The Black Mafia crime family may have harmed your fiancé."

"And why would you think something like that? I love Gauge. My family loves Gauge. I assure you that no one here did anything to harm him. In fact, I find it extremely offensive that you would come here throwin' around these ridiculous accusations while I'm still in pain. You act as if you know my fiancé is dead. Do you?"

"No, I do not."

"Then why exactly are you here, officer?" I asked as I looked him directly in those beady-ass eyes of his.

He wanted to challenge me, but he didn't. He was pissed off. It must have been humiliating for him that a young girl knew more about the law than he did.

"What, are you in law school or something?"

"I could never be a lawyer." I laughed.

"Why not?"

"It doesn't pay enough. How much do you make a year, officer? What, thirty thousand? I make that much on a bad day." That did it. I had him good and pissed now. I wanted him to make a move. He didn't.

"I'll be seeing you," he sneered as he walked past me. I read the name off his badge. Officer Jenkins. I wondered what a redneck cop like him was doing with a black name like Jenkins.

"I'm sure you will, but a word to the wise, the next time you come into my home, make sure you have a warrant," I warned him. He scampered away like the coward he was.

"I'm impressed." Uncle Moe hugged me.

"Thank you. That means a lot to me."

"I have to ask you something, and I need you to be perfectly honest with me."

"Yes."

"Yes, what?"

"I did it," I confessed.

"I thought you might have."

"Don't worry. They can't prove anything."

"You're that good, huh?" he asked.

"I like to think so."

"Was Isiah involved?"

"Uncle Moe, don't ask questions you really don't wanna know the answers to."

"Enough said. I just don't want the two of you to get in any trouble," he said like a worried parent.

"I understand that, but I assure you we were very careful."

"You're more competent than half the niggas I got workin' for me."

Cynthia White

"Speaking of which, somebody needs to go bail Jimmy out," I remembered.

"What the fuck did he do?"

"One of the pigs grabbed me by the arm and he punched him."

"In that case, I'll go bail him out personally."

*****

The following month, Isiah graduated from high school. That was the first time I had seen him in thirty-seven days. Yes, I counted. I was overjoyed to be present at one of the most important days of his life. His father was also there. They still had a long way to go, but at least they were making some progress.

"Yeah, Isiah!!!" I screamed at the top of my lungs as he went up on stage and got his diploma. I was so proud of him. All the white people in the audience looked at me like I was crazy, but I didn't care. I was there to support my baby.

"He looks just like his mother," Uncle Moe spoke out loud even though I didn't think he meant to.

I could tell by the look on his face that he had loved her. "How did she die?"

"She committed suicide." His eyes dropped to the ground.

I knew there was nothing I could say to make it better so I just laid my head down on his shoulder and sat quietly as he reminisced.

*****

As a graduation present, I rented Isiah and myself a house for two weeks in Hawaii. We left the day after his graduation. We flew first class and were greeted at the airport by some beautiful Hawaiian ladies. Isiah just watched as I joined them in a sensual native dance. I knew what he was thinking. I was thinking the same thing.

"I got you later," I whispered into his ear as we sat in the backseat of a white stretch limo.

"What?"

"You know." I smiled.

"Queen, I have no idea what you're talkin' about."

"Well then, I guess you'll just have to wait and find out," I teased.

The island was beautiful. Never in my life had I seen the sky look so blue. The air was intoxicating. It was as if pollution didn't exist there. The weather was warm, but not too hot. Everything was just right. I could see myself making a life there. I thought how maybe in a few years, Isiah and I would start a family. It would be the ideal place to raise our children. The people spoke, acted and even dressed differently. I didn't notice a single person wearing any major designers except for the tourists. It must have been so liberating to just throw on a pair of shorts and a top and not have to worry about everyone judging you.

The house was magnificent. It was located right along the famous Kehena Beach. Inside there was over ten thousand square feet of living space. The four bedrooms and six bathrooms were more than enough for the two of us. Out back there was an infinity edge pool, an outdoor shower and several Koi ponds. The landscaping was meticulous. Everything was in its perfect little place.

"Look at that pool." Isiah's eyes lit up. He was the only thug I knew who loved the water.

"Get in."

"What about you?"

"I'm comin'. I'm just waitin' on a delivery," I said nonchalantly.

Cynthia White

"What kind of delivery?"

"It's a surprise. Now will you just go?" I pushed him toward the sliding glass door.

He took off every single stitch of clothing he had on and got in the pool. I just stood there watching him. I wanted him, but I was trying to be patient. Someone knocked on the door. That had to be my surprise.

I opened the door, and it was her. Launi worked for my father and Uncle Moe. She was just as cool as one person could get.

"Hello, Queen." She smiled then hugged me.

She smelled like lavender. Launi was a beautiful girl. She was about five-foot-seven with golden skin and long, wavy black hair. She wore a white bikini with a red and white floral sarong tied around her waist and white flip-flops. She followed me out to the pool.

"Isiah, this is Launi."

"Nice to meet you, Launi." He looked a little embarrassed.

I had caught him off-guard. He didn't know anyone else would be there.

"Launi's gonna join us for a swim."

"Queen, I don't have any clothes on," he whispered even though Launi was standing right next to me and could hear everything.

"That's the point." I smiled mischievously.

I put my hands on Launi's body then I kissed her. I began to take off her clothes as she began to take off mine. Our kiss grew more and more passionate. I pulled her head back by her hair and began to suck on her breasts. I looked over at Isiah. He was enjoying the show.

We joined him in the pool and it became a full-fledged

freak show. We both attacked Isiah, kissing him and sucking him with such intensity. The water was cool and felt good on my warm pussy. I kissed Isiah as Launi sucked my breasts. Talk about doubling your pleasure. I had the best of both worlds. They were both sexy as hell, but in different ways. Isiah had a hard body with striking, dark skin and a handsome face. Launi was soft and delicate. Her breasts felt so good up against mine. She ate my pussy underwater while Isiah watched.

"Uhm ... sssssss ... oooooh ..." I moaned in pleasure.

The girl had skills. She moved her fingers in and out of my pussy slowly as she licked my clit. I tried to keep my eyes open, but it was a struggle. I wanted to watch Isiah. I wanted to enjoy his reactions.

When Launi surfaced, I told her to sit on the side of the pool. She obeyed. I spread her legs and tasted her pussy. She lay back with her back on the concrete. Isiah came up behind me. I could feel his hardness. I wanted them both so much. He reached around and grabbed my breasts as he kissed and licked on the back of my neck. I was so turned on that I felt like I was about to explode. He lifted my leg and forced his dick in my pussy from the back. I gripped Launi's hips tightly and licked her inside out. I just wanted it to be special for Isiah. I wanted to show him that his wish was my command. I didn't trip when he fucked Launi. I didn't trip when she sucked his dick. The truth was, I enjoyed watching the two of them together. They were sexy and sexy was always good.

*****

"Where did you come up with that idea?" Isiah asked as he and I sat in the hot tub together drinking champagne. After four hot hours together, Launi had to go to work.

"It just came to me," I lied. I had been planning it for a

Cynthia White

while.

"Why?"

"Don't act like you didn't like it."

"I'm not. I just don't want you to think you're not enough for me."

"I don't think that. I just wanted this trip to be special."

"Just havin' you here makes it special."

"You don't have to kick game. I know you enjoyed being with both of us. I enjoyed it, too." I laughed.

Just how much I enjoyed it he would never know. Though Gauge was my first male lover, Launi was my first female. The first time it happened, I was fourteen. I came to the island with my mother and father for summer break. Launi was a couple of years older than me but she treated me like I was her age. We kicked it. She showed me all the hot spots and even where to get some fire-ass weed. We smoked on the beach. She told me I was beautiful. Nobody besides my father had ever said that to me. She wanted me. I was curious. Our first kiss was tender. The second was intense. Before I knew it, she had her head between my legs turning me the fuck out.

*****

The next morning, Isiah and I headed out to go sightseeing. Everybody was so kind to us. It felt good to be in a place where I didn't have to be surrounded with bodyguards to feel safe. The beach was my favorite place. I carried my sandals in my hand the entire day. I loved feeling the sand between my toes, and the warm sun on my skin. We sat down and enjoyed the peace and tranquility. Isiah sat between my legs. I rubbed his strong shoulders as he looked out at the ocean. I laughed when he tickled my feet and bit down on my bottom lip when he kissed the inside of my

thighs.

"Thank you for bringin' me here."

"My pleasure." I kissed him softly on the lips.

"What have you done to me?"

"What?"

"I have never felt this way about a broad. I think you put some of that voodoo shit on me," he joked.

"You crazy." I laughed, too.

"You know I love you, right?"

"I know," I said.

"Let's get married."

"Just tell me when and I'll be there," I said seriously.

"Just like that?"

"Just like that," I assured him.

He smiled then shook his head like he couldn't believe I was real. I was. I was real as they got.

We lounged on the beach for a while then went and had lunch. The lobster stuffed with shrimp was delicious. Isiah had some pasta dish he kept on trying to get me to taste, but I wasn't having it. I didn't like white sauce. I'm ghetto. If it wasn't marinara sauce, then I couldn't fuck with it.

I had so many tropical drinks that I thought I was going to pass out before we got back to the house, and I almost did. Isiah had to give me a piggyback ride. He had his braids freshly done before we left, and his hair smelled good. I had to find out what that girl put in it when we got back home. Isiah always took really good care of himself. Some niggas get braids and don't take proper care of them. They go too long without getting them redone and their hair starts to smell like shit. Not Isiah. He got his done every two weeks. He smelled as good as he tasted.

The next few days were more of the same. We enjoyed

Cynthia White

the island so much that we barely slept. Each day just seemed to blend in with the next. Who needs rest when you're in paradise? We partied at some local nightclubs, made love on the beach, ate some delicious meals and had way too much to drink. It was hard, but soon it was time to go back home.

I looked out on the island as our plane flew over it. I was missing it already. Isiah promised me that we would be back soon, but I knew better. He was about to join an organization that was going to take up most of his time. I wasn't complaining. I knew what I was getting into when I asked him to join. I just wished we could have taken a piece of that island home with us.

*****

"Welcome home," Uncle Moe greeted us as we got inside the limo that was parked right in front of the airport.

"Thank you." I smiled.

"How was the trip?"

"It was wonderful."

"Are you ready to get to work?" he addressed Isiah.

"I'm ready," Isiah assured him.

As they spoke about the business, I tried my best to block out their conversation. I didn't want to know any more than I already knew. Two weeks away wasn't enough. I was back to riding around in a black limo with bulletproof glass. There was a guard sitting on my right and one sitting on my left. It was time to let go of the fantasy in my head. I had to come to grips with reality. My father was never getting out of prison. Isiah and I were soon to reign. He would need me to meet his highest potential. Uncle Moe wouldn't be around forever.

*****

"Hey, freak!" Jennifer screamed as she hugged me.

"Hey, hoe!" I screamed back.

"Tell me everything."

"I don't think you want to know everything," I teased as we sat down on her couch.

"What happened?"

"Remember Launi?"

"Yeah."

"We had a threesome with her," I blurted out.

"What? I'm offended."

"Why?"

"I'm yo' best friend and you didn't ask me."

"That's because I didn't want things to get weird between us."

"You know I ain't even like that. What, you think Launi's finer than me?" she asked with attitude.

"Girl, would you quit trippin'? Launi was there and you weren't. That's the only reason I asked her instead of you."

"It better be. I would have asked you first."

"That's because I'm the only female you know," I shot back.

"So what. The point is, I'm thoughtful and you're not," she pouted.

Jennifer was very jealous when it came to our friendship. She didn't like me kicking it with any other chicks in any way, shape or form. Don't get me wrong, it wasn't a sexual thing. We were strictly friends. I didn't look at her like that and she didn't look at me like that. She just wanted to be the only bitch in my life. I wasn't really into the whole girl-on-girl thing. I thought Launi was sexy as hell, but I wouldn't want to make it a regular thing. I mostly did that for my man. Fantasy was a big part of reality. I knew once he got

Cynthia White

involved with The Black Mafia, his stock would go up. Hoes that never even looked twice at him would be standing in line to suck his dick. Too bad for them I would already be down on my knees handling my business. If they wanted to take my man, I wouldn't make it easy for them.

Uncle Moe insisted that Isiah move into the house while he completed his training. He gave him a bedroom all the way downstairs, as far away from mine as possible. It didn't matter much. If I wasn't in his room, he was in mine. We fucked every day, sometimes three or four times a day. It was never enough. He would come home and tell me these stories about how he whooped some bitch-ass nigga's ass or how he killed some snitch. It was like Spanish Fly to me. It turned me on to the highest level. I was a freak that way.

"Queen, baby, you 'sleep?" Isiah asked as he sneaked into my room at four-thirty in the morning.

"Huh?" I answered back, still half asleep.

"I got something for you."

He went underneath the covers and pulled up my gown. I wasn't wearing any panties. As soon as his warm tongue touched my pussy I was wide awake. He licked and sucked me so good I came without any dick needed. I felt like I had just been healed. I no longer cared that it was the crack of dawn.

"Uhm …" I moaned loudly as he pushed his dick inside of me. I tried my best to be quiet. Uncle Moe's room wasn't too far down from mine. I didn't want him to hear me fucking his son.

We were deep in the throes of passion when we heard it. It sounded like something exploding. I remembered that sound. My mind flashed back to the day I shot and killed my mother. Then it hit me. Somebody was shooting inside my

home.

Isiah jumped up and put his pants on. I had never seen somebody move so quickly in my life. He put his finger up to his lips silently telling me not to talk. I was perfectly quiet. I opened my top nightstand drawer and pulled out my 9mm. Daddy taught me to always be prepared. Whoever raised Isiah must have taught him the same. He pulled his 9 from underneath my mattress where he always put it when he was in my room. He said something to me. It was too fast. I couldn't read his lips. I threw up my hands.

"Get in the closet," he whispered.

"No. I'm comin' with you," I whispered back.

He tried several times to convince me to hide. Fuck that! It was my house and I was not about to hide in the closet like a child. He opened the door slowly to make sure that it wouldn't creak and tip off whoever was in the house. I followed behind him like his shadow. The door to Uncle Moe's room was open, and I got a bad feeling.

The first thing I saw when I entered the room was a man standing over Uncle Moe's bed. He was big. At least six-foot-four and maybe two hundred and eighty pounds. He was dressed from head to toe in all black, and a ski mask covered his face. As he attempted to turn and escape out the window, Isiah fired one shot, hitting him in the back of the head. He hit the floor like a ton of bricks. I knew instantly that he was dead. It was then that I turned and saw my Uncle Moe lying in his bed covered in blood. I couldn't breathe.

"Is he ..." My mouth wouldn't even say the word.

He was the last real family I had left. No, he wasn't blood, but he was my heart. I loved that man to death. I couldn't take losing him. Not now. Isiah went over to him. He put his fingers on his neck, checking to see if he had a

Cynthia White

pulse. I felt completely useless. Instead of reading all those damn law books, I wished I had read some medical books.

"He has a pulse. Call 911," he ordered.

I ran over to the phone and picked it up. The line was dead. They had cut the phone wires. This was a professional hit.

"It's dead."

"Where's his cell?" He asked the next logical question.

I searched the room with my eyes. I saw the picture of the two of us together at Christmas last year and almost started to cry. Then I saw the cell phone. I ran and picked it up. Thankfully, unlike me, Uncle Moe always remembered to charge his cell. I made a mental note to be more responsible. I called 911. As they asked me all the stupid-ass, unnecessary questions they do, I looked over at Isiah with his father. He was sitting down on the bed beside him holding his hand. I shed a tear. I prayed to God, *Please don't let this be the end.*

I was so distracted that I almost didn't see the second intruder enter the room. He raised his gun and pointed it at Isiah. Isiah's back was to him. He couldn't see the coward, but I could. Without saying a word, I raised my 9 quicker than my lazy ass had ever done anything in my life and I shot him. With two bullets in his head, he fell lifeless to the floor. Isiah turned around just in time to see me fall to my knees.

"Queen, are you okay?" he asked over and over again.

I didn't answer him. I couldn't. I wouldn't know if I was alright until I knew if my uncle was going to make it.

"Where the fuck is the ambulance?" I cried.

"I don't know." He stared at me blankly.

As we sat there, we heard the sirens in the distance.

"Here they come. He's goin' to be okay, isn't he?" I asked

Isiah like he had all the answers.

"I don't know," he answered me honestly.

"What the fuck do you know?!" I yelled at him in frustration.

"I know you saved my life."

He tried so hard to hold that one tear back. It was too powerful. I watched it roll down his face then fall onto the floor. I grabbed him and held him firmly in my arms. I was never letting go.

Cynthia White

chapter *Five*

THE HOSPITAL WAITING ROOM WAS FILLED with members of The Black Mafia. I looked around at each one of them. These men had lived incredible lives. Young and old, they all stood together. My Uncle Carmine was there when daddy and Uncle Moe were first starting out. He was older than both of them, but still served under them. He looked different. There was a peace that surrounded him. I guess retiring and moving to Italy agreed with him. At almost sixty years old, he was still a very attractive man. His hair was still dark and his olive skin bore no wrinkles. As usual, he was dressed in an Armani suit with pair of custom-made crocodile loafers on his feet.

He sat down next to me and reached for my hand. I tried to smile. I couldn't. My face wouldn't let me fake what I wasn't feeling. We still didn't know if Uncle Moe was going to make it or not. The surgery that they told us would take two hours was now closer to five.

"How are you doing, sweetheart?" Uncle Carmine asked me as he put his arm around me. He still had that thick Italian accent I remembered.

"I don't know yet. I haven't had time to think." I rubbed my weary eyes.

"I know things are tough with your father behind bars and Moe's future still uncertain. I just want you to know that if you need me, I'll come back."

"Uncle Carmine, I can't ask you to do that," I said hesitantly.

"You don't have to. I offered."

"You were in the game for so long."

"Ever since I was thirteen years old. I'm fifty-eight now."

"That's forty-five years. How did you survive so long?"

"It was different back then. There was a sense of honor. Now it's just about the money." He seemed to grow upset.

"Isn't that what it always comes back to, money?" I asked myself out loud. I looked over at Isiah staring out the window.

"Is that Moe's son?"

"Yeah, that's Isiah." I smiled.

"He's gotten so big."

"You remember him?" I was surprised.

"Of course. Your Uncle Moe was crazy about that boy. I'm surprised you don't remember."

"I don't."

"It was like the two of you were destined to be together. You were like a tiny little couple. You couldn't have been more than four and five years old, but you were so good for each other. You played together all the time and even then you took care of him. You were the bossy one."

"I still am." I laughed.

Cynthia White

"You love him, don't you?"

"Yeah, I do," I admitted.

"I can tell by the way you look at him."

"He asked me to marry him," I confessed.

"What did you say?"

"I said yes. How could I not?"

"Because you're scared. He's one of us now. There is no turning back," he said.

"I know."

"You want to know what I think?"

"What?" I gave him my undivided attention.

"I think that if any woman can handle the life, it's you. You've grown up in the middle of all this chaos and still managed to be quite an amazing young lady."

"Thank you. You don't know how much I needed to hear that." It was true. I needed to hear that desperately.

"Just remember one thing: Moe might survive today, but one day when he's gone, Isiah will reign. He will be tested and re-tested day after day. It'll be hard on him. Try to be understanding. Don't make the same mistakes your mother did with your father."

"I'm nothin' like her."

"You never were. I look at you and even though you look exactly like Hilary, all I see is your father."

"*De tal palo tal astilla.*" I repeated the phrase I had heard my entire life. It was Spanish for "a chip off the old block."

"Indeed." He smiled at me like he used to when I was a little girl.

The time seemed to pass slower than usual. I figured that every minute that passed without the doctor coming out to speak to us was another minute my uncle was still alive, but I couldn't take this waiting bullshit. I felt so damn helpless.

There was nothing I could do. I looked up and noticed Jimmy C staring at me. He quickly looked away. I knew what he was thinking. He was feeling sorry for me. First my mother was murdered, then I was separated from my father, next my fiancé comes up missing and now this. He didn't know as much as he thought he did. I killed my mother. Fuck that bitch. I would've spit on her grave if I hadn't insisted on having her cremated. The hardest part of all of it was having people think that my father killed her. I seriously doubted that he would have ever pulled the trigger. I believe the only reason he pointed that gun at her was to frighten her. He wanted her to feel like she had made him feel all of those years. Deep down I knew he loved her. He also knew that she didn't love him back.

"What the fuck is takin' so long?" I yelled out in frustration.

"Maybe it's bad and they don't wanna come out and tell us," Vince, who referred to himself as Lil Vinni, responded.

"Are you really that muthafuckin' ignorant or do you just lack consideration?" I asked him, my blood boiling.

"Why is everything about you?"

"Excuse me?" I asked with attitude.

"You heard me." He had the nerve to try to get loud.

I jumped out of my seat and got all up in his face. "Why don't you try sayin' that shit to my face?" I challenged him.

"Queen, I ain't scared of you." He laughed.

"I don't give a fuck about yo' little bitch ass. If you think you put fear in me, you're sadly mistaken. Every man in this room would stand behind me. Can you say the same thing?" I looked him dead in the eye.

"Fuck y—"

Before the words left his mouth, Isiah hit him in the face

Cynthia White

with a hard right. "Watch yo' muthafuckin' mouth," Isiah warned him.

"Get him the fuck out of here," I told anyone who was listening. Gino and Raymond each grabbed an arm and escorted him out.

"You're out," Isiah informed him.

"You can't be serious?"

"You're no longer a member of The Black Mafia."

"Isiah ..."

"Leave," was the only response Isiah gave him.

"It was just a little misunderstanding," he reasoned.

"You disrespected Queen. Hershey wouldn't have it, my father wouldn't have it, and I damn sho won't have it."

"Yo' father ain't even dead yet, and you already tryin' to run shit," he bucked.

"If I see you again, you're dead," Isiah warned him.

Lil Vinni knew Isiah was serious. We didn't have a three strikes policy. You fucked up and you were out on your ass. He violated that, so now he was on his own. My father only let him in as a favor to his father, anyway. Nick was a good man. He was killed when Vinni was eleven. Soon after that, his mother kicked him out of the house. He was smoking and drinking and had completely stopped going to school altogether. She didn't know what to do, so she turned to daddy for help. He tried to help the young man, but some people don't want to be saved.

When he turned eighteen, he asked for a job and daddy reluctantly gave him one. That was five years ago and he was still just as big a fuckup as he was then. Twenty-three years old and still acted like he was eleven.

"You okay?" I asked Isiah as I wrapped my arms around his waist.

"I'm fine."

"Isiah, don't lie to me."

"If you knew I wasn't okay then why'd you ask?" He seemed annoyed.

"To see if you were goin' to lie to me."

"Why do females have to be so fuckin' difficult all the time?"

"Well, I'm sorry for carin'." I walked away from him and walked right into the doctor who was performing Uncle Moe's surgery.

"Ms. Aaron."

"Yes?"

"The surgery ran a little longer than we had anticipated. We were met with a few complications. There was a lot of internal bleeding. Also some damage was done to his—"

"Is he goin' to live?" I asked the only question that mattered to me.

"Yes, he is going to live."

"Thank you so much." I threw my arms around him and squeezed tightly.

He kept right on talking, but I stopped listening. All I cared about was that my uncle was alive. They wouldn't let us see him so soon after his surgery, but I didn't care. Isiah and I stayed in that waiting room all day and night. It was after midnight when we finally decided to go home for the night.

I didn't want to go back to my house just yet, so we went to Isiah's townhouse. He had guards posted at the front and back and two cars doing laps around the neighborhood. I was exhausted. Now that I knew Uncle Moe was going to be okay, I could finally close my eyes and get some rest.

Isiah was another story. I woke up at three a.m. to find

Cynthia White

him staring out his bedroom window. I couldn't help but wonder what he was thinking about. I wanted him to know that I was there for him and that he could always count on me.

"Hey," I whispered into his ear as I came up behind him and put my arms around him.

"Hey."

I never knew one little word could sound so sad.

"What's wrong?"

"I was just thinkin' about my father," he confessed.

"He's gonna be fine."

"This time."

"I don't know what to say. Nothin' I say will make you feel betta. I love you and I want to be with you, but if you want to leave the family, I'll understand."

"Would you come with me?" He turned around and asked me face to face.

"You know I can't do that. This is my life. It's who I am."

"But does it have to be all you are?"

"It's not all I am."

"Queen, I'm afraid for you," he confessed.

"Meaning?"

"Meaning, I don't know how all this is gonna play out, but I think me and you should chill until then."

"Chill, huh? So basically what you're tellin' me is that you don't wanna fuck with me no more?"

"It's not even like that," he said with pain in his voice.

"You know what, fuck you!"

"Queen ..."

"No, shut the fuck up and listen to me while I talk. You have one hour to decide what you want. You only get one muthafuckin' chance to kick me to the curb. Make sure that's really what you wanna do," I told him, then walked over to the dresser and got my keys.

"Where you goin'?"

"Home."

"I thought you said you didn't wanna go back there?"

"I thought you said you loved me."

"I do," he whispered.

"You got a fucked up way of showin' it," I spat.

"At least let me drive you home?"

"I can take care of myself." I threw my jeans on with his T-shirt that I was sleeping in and I was out.

He didn't even try to come after me. Fuck him. If it was like that, I was glad I found out then. I didn't want to go home so I went straight to Jennifer's house. I drove my car around back and honked my horn. She stuck her head out of the window. I knew she would still be up.

"What's up, freak?"

"You got company?" I asked, trying to hold back tears.

"What's wrong?" she asked, instantly sensing that something wasn't right.

"I think me and Isiah just broke up."

"Come on up. The door's unlocked," she said.

I went in through the back door. Walking up the stairs I realized that I wasn't wearing a bra. You can't get away with shit like that when you have titties as big as mine. I hoped Jennifer's father wasn't home. He was always looking at me like I was a piece of chocolate cake. I walked down the hall and went into my girl's room. To my surprise, she was in bed with Nate and even though they were under the covers, I could tell that they were both naked.

"Girl, why you ain't tell me you had company?"

"'Cause you're upset. Now what did that nigga do to

Cynthia White

you?"

I just laughed. That was Jen for you. "Fuck that nigga!" I brushed it off. "What's up, Nate?"

"What up, Queen?" He flashed me a quick smile. "My boy trippin'?"

"I don't wanna talk about that nigga right now."

"I got some fire," Nate told me as he showed me a fat-ass fifty bag.

"Well quit talkin' and roll that shit up." I sat down on the edge of the bed.

I rolled one up and so did Jennifer and Nate. Three blunts between us and I was fucked up. I felt so good. That was exactly what I needed. I lay down on Jennifer's floor and tried to keep from thinking. I just wanted to be free, if only for one night. It didn't work. I tried to wipe away the tears quickly before anyone could see, but I failed. Jennifer caught me. She put on Nate's T-shirt and came and sat down on the floor next to me.

"What's wrong?"

"Nothin'," I lied.

"Come on now, Queen."

"I just thought he loved me."

"He does."

"When you love somebody, you don't leave them."

"Look, I'm the last one who should be givin' you advice," she said hesitantly.

"But?"

"But I think you were too good for him anyway."

"Yeah, right."

"I'm serious. Girl, you are smart, strong and beautiful inside and out. If he can't see that, then like you said, fuck that nigga."

I laughed through my tears. Jennifer hugged me and I instantly began to feel better. I loved my best friend so much. Then I felt it. She kissed me on the neck. I felt weird. I thought that maybe I had imagined it. Weed did do strange things to my mind. Then she did it again. She stopped and looked at me. I guess she was trying to feel me out, trying to see if I was cool with it. Tonight I was. She kissed me on the lips and I don't know what happened. Suddenly I wasn't kissing my girl anymore. I was now kissing this fly-ass Puerto Rican chic with a warm tongue and a fat ass.

"Damn!" Nate watched eagerly from the bed.

We had our hands all over each other. She raised the T-shirt I was wearing and began sucking on my breasts. I liked it. I rubbed her soft hair. My pussy was throbbing. I got up and took off my shirt. Next, my jeans hit the floor. I wasn't wearing any panties. I walked over to the bed and climbed under the covers. We all three knew what was about to go down. I crawled over to Nate. His dick was brick. I kissed him hard then went down and started sucking his dick. Jennifer came up behind me and began to eat my pussy from the back. It felt like a dream. It just didn't seem real.

"Your pussy's so good, *mami*," Jennifer professed as she continued to taste me.

My mind was blank. It didn't register that this girl had been my dog since before preschool. All that mattered that night was that she got my mind off of Isiah. I didn't think about him once, not even when his best friend was inside of me.

*****

It was after nine a.m. when I left Jennifer's house. I drove home and took a hot shower. I changed my clothes then went back to the hospital. The first thing I saw when I

Cynthia White

opened the door to Uncle Moe's room was Isiah's face. I turned around and walked in the opposite direction. He followed me.

"Queen, wait."

"What?" I snapped.

"I need to talk to you."

"About?"

"Last night."

"Nothin' to talk about. You said all I needed to hear," I said with serious attitude. That nigga was messing with the wrong one today.

"I'm sorry."

"Too little, too late."

"I didn't mean the things I said," he begged.

"Well, I did. I told you that you had one hour. You didn't call."

"I needed time to think."

"Well how special for you," I said bitterly.

"Come on, don't be like that."

"You brushed me the fuck off last night like I was any ole bitch off the streets and now you want me to bow down to you."

"I was twisted in knots about my father."

"Oh, so now you claimin' him?"

"I always claimed him," he said.

"Lie to yo'self, don't lie to me. You're in now. You don't need me anymore."

"You don't believe that."

"The hell I don't." I started to walk away.

He grabbed my arm. "I love you, Queen," he whispered in my ear.

"Too bad, 'cause I'm over you," I lied then walked away.

I didn't want it to be over, but I needed it to be. He was bad for me. I let down my guard when I was with him. He had me all fucked up in the head.

I sat in the waiting room for three hours waiting for him to leave. I was dying to see my uncle, but I refused to go into that room while he was still in there. I couldn't help but think about how I had fucked up last night. I knew things wouldn't be the same between me and Jennifer. Plus, I had fucked Nate and that was going to create conflict between him and Isiah. Maybe he never had to know? Maybe Nate wouldn't tell him. Yeah, right. When was the last time a nigga had a threesome and didn't brag about it? Never, that's when.

*****

"Hey, baby," Uncle Moe spoke weakly.

"Hey." I tried to smile. I did. Then I cried.

"Come here, baby." He motioned for me to come to him. I did.

"I'm sorry."

"Sorry? I owe you big."

"For what?"

"For saving my son's life."

"It was nothing," I said nonchalantly.

"It was something to me. I know Isiah appreciates it."

"Is that why he dumped me?" I asked in a hurt voice.

"He did that for you."

"For me?"

"He told me that you deserved better than him," Uncle Moe revealed.

"Why would he say something like that?"

"Love makes a man say and do crazy things."

"Love?" I laughed out loud. "Isiah doesn't love me."

Cynthia White

┤ you say that? He changed his entire life for
┐ doesn't do that unless they're in love."
ject. How are you feelin'?"
st had four bullets removed from my chest."
"I'm sorry."
"Why do you do that?"
"Do what?" I asked.
"Apologize for everything like it's all your fault."
"Well, isn't it?"
"Queen, I have been a part of this organization since before you were born."
"Yeah, but you wouldn't have been at the house that night if you weren't stuck with me."
"I'm not stuck with you. I promised your father that I would look out for you. Don't you understand that when you love somebody, you would do anything for that person?"
The question threw me. I guess I really didn't understand love. Where did you draw the line? Where was the cutoff point? Life was complicated enough without throwing love in the mix. I thought that maybe I should just try to forget about Isiah and move on. In a few months I would be starting my senior year of high school. I didn't need all the extra drama. I had a hard enough time trying to decide which college I wanted to go to. I had applied to several schools already, but if I had to make a choice, I didn't know which I would choose.
After I spent a few hours with Uncle Moe, I wanted to be alone. I was feeling kind of low so I needed a pick-me-up. I headed straight toward the mall. Spending money was my favorite form of therapy. My first stop was Ice. Ice was a high priced urban jewelry store that sold hip-hop influenced items. Most of their stuff was diamond and platinum, which

was the only kind I wore. As soon as I saw those earrings, knew I had to have them. They were stunning. The price was sixty-seven hundred dollars and worth every penny. I couldn't take my eyes off of them – big beautiful hoops covered in diamonds hanging from a hinged post, which was also covered in diamonds. The total weight was a little over 8 carats. Daddy would have killed me if he found out I paid that much for a pair of earrings, but daddy wasn't there. Once I saw the bracelet, it was over. It was a modern link with 10 carats of pave diamonds. The heart charm, covered in 3 carats of diamonds, was the cherry on my sundae. It was twelve thousand dollars, but it was so worth it. Any girl in her right mind would have done the same thing. Diamonds truly are a girl's best friend.

After I finished at Ice, I headed to Macy's to check out the new fall handbags. I had to be early if I wanted to wear the hottest designers of the season. They were just fads, but I wanted them anyway. I paid over three thousand dollars for the new Chanel bag. I knew it was excessive, but I continued to shop. I would never have to worry about money as long as I lived. Daddy was a very good business man. He had investments all over town. He was a lot smarter than some people gave him credit for.

My phone rang. I looked down at the screen. It was Isiah. I didn't want to talk to him. I turned my phone off and put it in my purse.

Three hours and thirty thousand dollars later, I decided to head home. At least that was my plan. He grabbed my hand. I stopped. He smiled at me. They had to think of a new word for him because fine just didn't cut it. He smiled. His grill was blingin'.

"You wanna take yo' hands off of me?" I asked sistah-girl

Cynthia White

style with my hands on my hips.

"Not really." He flashed a perfect smile.

"Do you know who I am?"

"My future."

"That's real cute. Now can you let me go?" I asked with attitude.

"What if I don't want to?"

"That sounds like a personal problem."

"At least tell me your name," he persisted.

"Why?"

"So I can know it the next time I see you."

"There won't be a next time."

"Are you sure about that?"

"Positive." I laughed.

"Then why do you look like the woman I saw last night in my dreams?"

"That was the corniest shit I ever heard." I laughed my ass off.

"I knew I could make you smile."

"Now what?"

"Now you tell me your name," he said again.

"Queen."

"Royalty, huh?"

"Something like that. And you are?"

"Xavier."

"That's kind of fly. I like that," I admitted.

"Thank you. Now maybe you'll let me take you out to dinner tonight?"

"I don't know about all that."

"Why not? You got a man?"

"Not anymore," I said.

"Then what's the problem?"

"My life is very complicated right now."

"Isn't everybody's?"

"True, but my issues run deep."

"So do mine. Is eight o'clock good for you?"

He was very persistent. I ended up giving him my cell phone number so that we could possibly hook up later, but I wasn't sure about bringing another man into my life so soon after I broke up with Isiah. The wound was still fresh. I still loved him and I knew that he still loved me, but like I told him, he had one chance. He fucked up, so now it was time to move on.

I went home thinking that I could just chill and be alone for a while but as usual, The Black Mafia was having a meeting. Of course, the prince was there. He looked like he was about to approach me so I ran up the stairs and locked myself in my bedroom. I didn't want to see him. I didn't want to talk to him. I had been thinking about getting my own place for a while. There was really no reason for me to stay in that house. Daddy was gone. Uncle Moe had his son now. He didn't need me anymore.

"Hey, freak." Jennifer answered her phone with her usual greeting.

"What's up, hoe?"

"Shit. What's up with you?"

"Nothin' much, just gettin' ready for my date," I said in an excited voice.

"Spill."

"His name is Xavier, and he is fine as hell."

"He better be with a fly-ass name like Xavier," she joked.

"Girl, he is."

"So where is he takin' you?"

"I don't know yet. He said he wanted to take me out to

dinner."

"That means he wants to fuck you."

"No shit." We both laughed.

"What about Isiah?"

"What about him?" I rolled my eyes.

"Don't you still have feelings for him?"

"I don't want to talk about all that."

"Alright. So, what you wearin' tonight?"

"I was thinkin' about that white leather dress I bought when we went to Atlanta."

"With those white Versace pumps," she added.

"And don't forget the matchin' white Versace handbag. Girl, you have to see these new earrings I brought today from Ice. They are to die for. And the bracelet, girl, you just have to see it to believe it," I gushed.

"Well, I'm on my way."

Jennifer was there in ten minutes. I came downstairs to let her in. I didn't want her to have to deal with the guards. Isiah watched me the entire time I was down there. He was wondering what was going on. He wanted to know why I was so excited. I wasn't telling. Jen and I went up to my room where I showed her my new jewelry.

"Girl, this shit is hot." Jennifer was almost as excited about my new jewelry as I was.

"Ain't it though?"

"You gonna have to let me borrow this some time," she said.

"Any night except tonight."

"Where did you get this necklace?" she asked, holding up a platinum chain with the 12-carat puffed diamond heart pendant hanging from it.

"It was my mother's. Daddy bought it for her right

before he found out what a cheatin', lyin' whore she was."

"This must have cost a fortune."

"Seventy-five grand."

"Damn!" she yelled.

"Yeah, he was generous like that."

"Do you realize you talk about him like he's dead?" she asked.

"Do I?" As I stopped to think about what my best friend had just said to me, someone knocked on my bedroom door.

"Come in!" I yelled. The door opened. It was Isiah.

"Can I talk to you for a minute?" he asked, sounding pitiful as hell.

"I gotta go anyway. Call me when you get back." Jen got up and grabbed her purse.

"I will." I hugged her then she left.

"You goin' somewhere?" Isiah asked me like he would be offended if I were.

"I have a date," I told him, half because he asked and half to make him jealous.

"Anybody I know?"

"I doubt it."

"Who is he?" he asked.

"That's really none of your business."

"You sho do move fast."

"What am supposed to do, sit around lickin' my wounds? You didn't want me, so I found somebody who did," I said with hurt and venom in my voice.

"You know that's not true."

"All I know is what you tell me."

"I never said I didn't want you," he reasoned.

"Don't want me, don't want to be with me, what's the difference?"

Cynthia White

"I do want you."

"Really? Is that why you dumped me?" I asked.

"You really pissin' me the fuck off with all this craziness."

"And what you gonna do about it?" I challenged him.

He came over to my bed. He pushed me back onto it and spread my legs. He entered me like I was still his.

"This how you like it?" he asked me as he took complete control of my body.

I couldn't speak. I tried, but I couldn't. Sex was the one area where we didn't have problems. It was always good between us. He knew just how to touch me to make me react. If his dick was kryptonite, then I was Clark Kent. He made me so weak. Ten minutes later when Xavier called, I was too busy to answer.

We lay in bed together just as we had so many times before. I had a blunt in my perfectly manicured hands. He didn't smoke since he was on duty. I tried to read his mind. I imagined that he was thinking about us. Even if he wasn't, I was. I wanted him back. I was just too stubborn to admit it. I could never admit I was wrong. You would never hear the words "I'm sorry" come from my mouth. Then there was the threesome I had with my best friend and his. I knew that once he found out I fucked Nate, he would never look at me the same way.

"What now?" he turned and asked me like I had all the answers.

"You go back downstairs and finish yo' business and I call my date and reschedule."

"So you still goin' out with him?" he asked.

"Why wouldn't I?"

"Because I love you."

"Isiah, sex and love are two different things."

"I know that," he said.

"Do you? Just because you like fuckin' me doesn't mean that you love me."

"You think I'm that ignorant? I know the difference between lovin' somebody and being sexually attracted to them. You're just lookin' for a way out."

"Don't put this all on me!" I cried.

"If you don't wanna be with me any more, then at least be woman enough to tell me."

"Fine, I don't wanna be with you anymore."

"You don't mean that," he said.

"Well, then why'd you tell me to say it?"

"I wanted to see just how cruel you could be."

"Cruel? No, see, I think you have the two of us confused. You were the one who wanted space. You picked the worst possible moment and you pulled away from me. I needed you." I tried to be strong, but I was on the verge of tears.

"I know."

"Then why?"

"Because that's how much I love you. You deserve so much better than me. Look at you. You look like you should be with 50 Cent or somebody."

"So I'm pretty, get over it. Have you looked in the mirror lately? You don't look so bad yo'self."

"It's not just that you're pretty. You're smart and confident. Shit, you're more mature than people twice yo' age," he said with pride.

"And that's a bad thing?"

"It's intimidating."

"Well, I don't know what to tell you. I can't change who I am. I won't."

"You shouldn't have to."

Cynthia White

"So that's it, just like that?" I asked.

"I don't want it to be."

"Then what? How do we fix this?"

"It's not yo' problem to fix. I just need you to understand how much you mean to me. You've been there for me like nobody else has. After my mother died ..." He stopped himself. He never talked about his mother.

"Tell me about her," I insisted. I took his hand and looked deep into his eyes, letting him know that it was alright to trust me.

"I don't know where to start. She was everything to me. We had a relationship like you and yo' father have. She was always there for me when I needed her. She loved me no matter how many stupid mistakes I made." He laughed as he reminisced.

"Why did she commit suicide?" I asked very cautiously.

I didn't want to upset him anymore than he already was. I knew what it was like to lose somebody you loved, someone you counted on daily.

"She had bipolar disorder. They were always changing her medications. Nothin' really helped. Sometimes she would seem so happy. She'd smile at me and I knew it was gonna be a good day. Then sometimes she was sad and would spend the whole day in bed cryin'. I stayed home from school so that I could watch her. I just wanted to make sure she would be there the next day. She was all I had. Then one day I came home and found her in the bathtub. She had slit her wrists. I called 911, but it was too late. She was already dead. Her skin was pale and cold as ice."

"How old were you?" I asked as I wiped away my tears.

"I was fourteen," he answered with a blank stare on his face.

He looked up at me and his eyes were filled with tears. All I could do was hold him. I couldn't make it better. I couldn't bring his mother back. All I could offer him was my heart and hope that he would be gentle with it. I wasn't as tough as I seemed. Neither one of us were.

*****

The next day, I was still feeling depressed, so I went shopping again. Of course Jennifer and I hit the mall. This was our normal routine. After picking out outfits and accessories for each other, we were going to get our nails done then go out to lunch. I was trying my best not to act as if anything had changed even though I feared it had.

"That's fly," I commented as Jennifer held up a burgundy House Of Dereon skirt and fitted blazer.

"They got some bad-ass Dereon heels to go with it."

"You should get it. It'll look good on you."

"You really think so?" she asked like she needed me to validate her. This wasn't like my girl. She was usually so sure of herself.

"I think we need to talk," I told her as I pulled her to the side, away from all the other shoppers.

"No, we don't. I know what you're gonna say. The other night was a mistake."

"That's not what I was gonna say."

"You don't regret what we did?" she asked, confused.

"No, I don't. Do you?"

"No, but you're my best friend."

"Which is exactly why it was so special. Jennifer, I love you for what you did for me. I was low and you made me feel good about myself again."

"But it can't happen again?" she asked like she was disappointed.

Cynthia White

"It can't happen again," I told her straight out. "I love you too much to mess up our friendship."

"I love you, too, Queen," she told me as she hugged me. "You know you my bitch, right?"

"I know." I laughed. "You my bitch, too."

Though I had said everything I had to say, I felt like she wanted to say more. She didn't. I knew that she loved me just as much as I loved her, but I wouldn't let myself accept the fact that my best friend wanted more from me. I just couldn't.

The remainder of our day together was just like the old days. We flirted with all the fine niggas that passed us. Jennifer even got a few numbers. I, on the other hand, wasn't ready for more relationship drama. Between the two of us, we bought seventeen new outfits, five purses and thirteen pairs of shoes. I was relieved that we talked it out and were still able to remain as close as ever. That one night could have ruined a lifelong friendship. I knew that from then on, I had to be more careful with how I dealt with Jennifer. Something like that could never happen again.

chapter

Six

That summer flew by and before I knew it, I was getting ready to go back to school. Isiah and I did eventually get back together. As difficult as it was to be with him, it was even more difficult to be without him. He spent the majority of his time with his father, learning the ins and outs of the business. Even though I missed him, I supported him one hundred percent. His life was chaotic, mostly because he handled business on the streets. Uncle Moe put him out there to mold him. If he wanted to be a boss, he had to be as tough as he could be. There would be people just waiting for him to slip up.

"Queen, what's wrong?" Isiah asked me as I sat next to him in back of the limo.

I took a deep breath the slowly exhaled. "Nothing."

"Queen ..."

"I'm fine," I lied as I stared out the window.

He had to make a stop in Kansas City and then we were

Cynthia White

off to Chicago for the weekend. I wanted to do some back to school shopping on the world famous Magnificent Mile then spend a little alone time with my man. Nature had other plans. My period was two weeks late. All those times I had forgotten to take my pill had caught up with me.

"You want to stop somewhere and get somethin' to eat?" Isiah asked, snapping me out of the daze I was in.

"I'd rather stop somewhere and get a pregnancy test."

"What?"

I turned to him and looked him in the eyes. "I think I'm pregnant."

"You're serious?"

"You think I would joke about somethin' like this?" I copped an instant attitude. Just saying the word pregnant out loud made my hands start to shake.

"What if you really are pregnant?" He asked the question I had been asking myself all day.

"I don't know," I answered him honestly.

We had the driver stop at Walgreens before dropping us off at our hotel. I was so nervous. This one little test could change everything. All the plans I had for my life were up in the air. I went into the bathroom and tried for twenty minutes to pee on the stick. I couldn't. I was too anxious. Was I ready to be a mother? Was Isiah ready to be a father? Even if we weren't ready, we would have to be if the test came back positive. I drank two bottles of water. That did it.

The worst part was waiting two minutes for the results. I was not a patient person. I walked back into the bedroom with Isiah. The look on his face said it all. He wasn't ready for this. Truth be told, neither was I. I smiled a fake-ass smile and tried to stay strong, while inside I was falling apart. I sat down on the bed and tried to find a way out of

this mess. I told him we should have been using condoms. It was too late for all that now. The damage was already done. How could I fuck up my senior year like this?

It had been over ten minutes and now instead of being impatient, I couldn't bring myself to look at the results. I tried to pretend that if I didn't look at it, the results didn't matter. I was only fooling myself. Isiah got up off the bed and went into the bathroom. He came back a few seconds later with the test in his hands. He didn't look happy. I already knew what it said before he opened his mouth.

"Well?"

"You're pregnant."

"Shit!" I lay down on the bed. Isiah came and sat down next to me. Even though he was so close, I still felt alone. I rolled over and grabbed my cell phone off the nightstand. I had to call the one person I knew would understand.

"What?!!!" Jennifer yelled in disbelief. She was just as shocked as I was.

"I'm pregnant," I told her again.

"You bullshittin'."

"I'm serious."

"Girl, what you gonna do?" she asked in a more sympathetic tone.

"I don't know."

"Where Isiah at?" she yelled.

"He right here."

"Let me talk to him."

"Hold on." I gave Isiah the phone.

He put the receiver up to his ear. "Hello."

"I know you ain't gonna try to play my girl?"

"Come on now, you know me betta than that," he said.

"I know a lot of niggas that claim they love a girl 'til she

Cynthia White

gets pregnant."

"Jennifer, you know I ain't like that," he asserted.

"You betta not be. Don't make me have to come lookin' fo' yo' ass," she warned.

"Yo' friend is crazy." He laughed as he passed me back the phone.

I smiled as I put the phone back to my ear. "Girl, what you say to him?"

"I just told his ass what was real and what was fake."

"You the craziest bitch I know."

"Thank you. You the craziest bitch I know."

"Thank you."

"So, when will you be back?" she asked.

"Sunday evening."

"Stop by here first."

"I will," I said.

"Love you, freak."

"Love you, hoe." I couldn't help but smile as I hung up the phone. That was my girl.

"You okay?" Isiah asked as he wrapped his big, strong arms around me.

"I am now." I smiled.

Somehow that five minute conversation with Jennifer made everything okay. I knew that as long as I had my girl, I would never be alone. Not everybody had a friend like that. I was lucky. She stood beside me when nobody else would. Even when I was in the wrong, she supported me.

Isiah was apprehensive about leaving me, but I assured him that I was fine. He could stay there with me all day and never leave my side, but I would still be pregnant. While he went off to take care of business, I ordered room service then a freaky movie on pay-per-view. It was one of those white movies so you know they did more talking than they did fucking. The young man who delivered my cheeseburger and onion rings looked embarrassed like he was actually in the movie or something. Some people could be such tight asses when it came to sex. Everybody fucks. That's how we all got here. What was the big deal? I sat down on the couch and continued to watch the movie. This tall, blond, white girl came home from work to find her best friend fucking her husband. I just knew it was about to be a big-ass catfight, but I was wrong. She joined them. This was so unrealistic. If I came home and found Jennifer fucking Isiah, I'd shoot them both. I just hoped that they both knew better.

After I finished my movie, I decided to take a long, hot bubble bath. I lay back in the tub trying to imagine myself with a child. I couldn't. I wasn't the nurturing type. I still didn't know what I was going to do, and I still had to tell daddy. I wasn't sure how he was going to react.

Just as I was getting caught up in my deep thoughts, there was a knock at the door. I got out and put on a robe. I remember thinking how soft it was. I tied it up and walked over to the door. I didn't even bother looking out because I figured Isiah had forgotten his room key.

When I opened the door, two guys with guns rushed me. I struggled, but it was no use. I was no match for two fully grown men. They picked me up and carried me out the back of the hotel. Where were all the housekeepers? Where were all the other guests? I tried to fight. Before I knew it, they had me in the back of a van going God knew where.

"Don't worry, Queen. We won't hurt you," the driver said.

I knew that voice from somewhere.

"Who the fuck are you?"

Cynthia White

"You'll know soon enough."

"I want to know now," I said through clenched teeth.

"Spoken just like a spoiled princess."

"Who are you?" I asked again.

"The man who's goin' to rescue you."

"Rescue me from what?" I wanted to know. I got no answer. I didn't know what the fuck was going on, but I did know that I was scared as hell.

We had to have been riding for over three hours when the van finally came to a stop. One of the men came around to the back and let me out. I had been in the dark for so long that the sunlight irritated my eyes. When I finally regained my vision, I noticed that we were parked in front of a big, beautiful house. It was worth at least three or four million dollars. The lawn was huge and the landscaping was impeccable.

"Come on," the taller of the two men instructed me as he grabbed my hand and led me inside the house.

"Can you please just tell me what the hell is goin' on?" I pleaded.

"Come on and I'll show you."

The house was as beautiful on the inside as it was on the outside. I looked around at all the artwork on the walls. Each piece was worth a small fortune. He sat down and motioned for me to come and sit beside him. Once I did, he took off his mask. It was Xavier.

"You crazy muthafucka."

"You don't sound like you're happy to see me." He smiled.

"Probably because I'm not. Are you stupid? Do you know how many people will be lookin' for me?"

"Don't worry. I'm just goin' to keep you for the week-

end."

"Take me back to the hotel right now," I ordered him.

"But I wanted to see you." He smiled.

"Look, I don't know if this is your idea of fun, but it's not mine. I wanna go back to the hotel. I don't even know anything about you. You hit on me at the mall, then you stalk me all the way to Chicago. Who the hell are you?"

"The less you know, the better," he answered. "I'm a very rich young man with the ability to do pretty much whatever I want. And I think you know what I want."

I continued to argue with him, but it was useless. He wasn't about to take me back and he wasn't about to let me go either. I was stuck. For hours I said nothing. I was so pissed off I could've spit fire.

I felt like a kid on timeout. I was given a bedroom as if I were there for a vacation or something. It was beautifully decorated just like the rest of the house. The queen-sized canopy bed was a sight to see. It was made with eccentric plum and lavender satin sheets and decorated with at least a dozen pillows. The fireplace was lit. There were fresh roses on the table and scented candles everywhere. I looked around and noticed that there was no phone. I gave in. I lay down on the bed and within minutes I was asleep.

When dinner arrived, I didn't eat. Even though I was pregnant, I had no appetite. All I could think about was Isiah and what he had to be going through. I just hoped he knew that I didn't leave him on my own free will. I would never do that. Everybody in his life had deserted him in one way or another. He had to be going out of his mind. If he called Uncle Moe, Xavier was in serious trouble.

Knock! Knock! Knock! I jumped. The sound of someone knocking on the door startled me. I was sitting on the bed

Cynthia White

reading a very old issue of "*Sister 2 Sister Magazine*" with Lisa "Left Eye" Lopes on the cover. I looked up just in time to see Xavier enter the room.

"What do you want?" I asked dryly.

"I wanna talk to you."

"What the fuck do we have to talk about?" I asked with attitude. I was getting really tired of this game he was playing.

"Us and our future together."

"Us? Nigga, there is no us." I laughed like he was Bernie Mac or somebody.

"Don't laugh at me." It was more of a warning than a request.

"I'll laugh whenever that fuck I feel like it. You don't own me."

"That's where ya wrong." A sadistic look spread across his face.

He grabbed me and roughly threw me down on the bed. He ripped every last stitch of clothing from my body. I said nothing and looked up into his eyes as he lay on top of me. I didn't want to give him the satisfaction of knowing that he had put fear into me.

"So what, you're gonna rape me now?"

"I don't have to rape you. Even though you'll never admit it, you want me just as bad as I want you."

"Do I?" I asked, even though I already knew the answer.

I did want him. I knew it was sick, but I couldn't help the way I felt. I wanted him to do all the nasty little things I secretly wanted to do. I wanted him to fuck me like I had never been fucked before.

"You want me to fuck you, Queen?" he asked in the sexiest voice.

"Get the fuck off of me."

"Not until you answer my question." He knew what he was doing and he did it so well.

I tried to fight it, but the attraction was too strong. My naked body wanted to be used by him. His hands began to discover my body.

"Uhm ..." I moaned as he played with my pussy. She was dripping wet.

"Tell me you want this dick," he instructed me in a sexy, suggestive voice.

"I want that dick."

"What?"

"I want that dick," I told him again, only this time louder and more powerfully.

He didn't give it to me right away. He made me beg for it. He rubbed it on my clit almost causing me to cum right then and there. He knew when to stop. It was so big and hard. I felt like a slut, but I didn't care. I had my legs spread open as wide as they would go in anticipation of his entrance. Finally, he pushed himself inside me. I gripped his shoulders tight. I let out a powerful moan that was both liberating and imprisoning. I knew he had me exactly where he wanted me. This had been his plan all along.

My head told me to stop this before it went too far. My pussy told my head to shut the fuck up and enjoy the dick. I listened to my pussy. He fucked me so good that I never wanted to leave. Having his big, black dick inside me made me feel more like a woman than I ever had in my entire life. I loved Isiah and it was good with him, but this was more than good. This was once-in-a-lifetime amazing.

"Damn, this some good-ass pussy," he told me as he fucked me like he owned me.

Cynthia White

"Ohhhhh … yes … yes … uhm, right there … right there …" I think I had an out-of-body experience. It was like I was above us watching as we fucked like two wild animals. I enjoyed the show.

"Play with yo' pussy," he commanded me. I slowly and smoothly moved my hand down my chest and stomach.

"Uhm …" I moaned as I touched myself. I moved my fingers around and around in a circular motion. He mirrored my movement. If I went slow, he went slow. When I quickened my pace, he did, too.

"Queen, I want you to give me everything you have." He spoke in a very controlled tone. I knew what he was trying to do. He wanted this to be the best fuck of my life. Well, too late, it already was.

He fucked me for four and a half hours. The things we did in that room should've been illegal. Anything that felt that good had to be bad. The way he licked my pussy made my heart pound like it was about to explode right out of my chest. I had more orgasms than I could count. I felt like I was on something. Whatever it was, somebody needed to bottle that shit. I gripped the sheets and bit down on my bottom lip as he hit me from the back. It was almost too much. Now I understood why Snoop titled his first album *"Doggystyle."* Was there any other style? Jennifer once told me that she didn't like it from the back. I couldn't for the life of me understand why. No woman who truly loves dick could say that she doesn't like that.

*****

The following morning, Xavier dropped me off at the hotel. I couldn't believe what we had done. This mystery man had captured me and had his way with me. It was like a fantasy, except it had really happened. I saw several black limousines and town cars parked in the parking lot of the hotel. I knew The Black Mafia was there. I didn't know what I was going to tell them, but I knew that I had to get creative. I got on the elevator. As soon as the doors closed, I started having flashbacks. I saw myself with another man. I felt so low. I was pregnant with Isiah's child, but I was fucking another man. The worst part was that I did it out of my own free will. He didn't force me to do anything.

"Queen, are you okay?" Jimmy C was the first one to spot me.

"I'm fine," I spoke softly.

"What happened?"

"Where is Isiah?" I asked as I dodged his question.

"He's inside with Moe. Come on, I'll take you to him." He took me by the hand like I was his girl. I didn't protest. I just went along with it. Isiah spotted me immediately. He ran over to me and scooped me up in his arms like he never wanted to let me go. You would have thought I was gone for a year instead of only one night.

"Are you okay?"

"I'm fine," I said softly.

"You sho?"

"Yeah."

"What happened? Where were you?" he fired the questions quickly.

"After you left yesterday, somebody knocked on the door. I thought that you had forgotten your key. I opened the door and two men grabbed me."

"Where did they take you?" he asked.

"I don't know. It was a house."

"Did they hurt you?"

"No."

Cynthia White

"Did you see their faces?"

"No."

"Do you remember anything, the license plate or—"

"No, I don't remember, okay! I don't remember!" I shouted as I lost control and began to cry.

"I'm sorry, baby." He hugged me.

"I'm tired."

"Get some rest. I'll be here." He kissed me softly.

As soon as my head hit the pillow, I was asleep. I dreamed about Xavier. In the fantasy, we were in bed together. Just as we started getting freaky, I noticed Isiah across the room watching us. A look of disappointment dominated his face. He didn't seem mad, just hurt. I was disgraced. I turned my head away from him and my mother was on the other side. She didn't say a word. She just smiled a kind of devious smile then wickedly laughed out loud. Then it hit me. I was starting to become more and more like her. That's exactly what she wanted.

I woke up in a panic. Isiah ran to my side to make sure I was okay. How could I do him like that? I knew better. He climbed into bed with me and pulled me close to his chest. I could feel his heart beating.

"Isiah—"

"Shhhhhh … get some rest," he interrupted me just as I was about to confess all.

"What about you?"

"I'm not tired," he lied. He was exhausted. He just wanted to stay awake in case whoever had kidnapped me came back. I knew better. They weren't coming back.

"I love you so much," I told him then kissed him softly on the cheek.

"Not as much as I love you."

Cynthia White

"And how do you know that?"

"It's not possible. I love you more than anything or anyone. You can't top that."

*****

As soon as we got back home, things returned to normal. Isiah was so involved in the organization that he barely had any time to spend with me. I knew that it was nobody's fault but my own. I had wanted him to join up, so I couldn't complain now. He was only doing what I asked of him. I spent the remainder of my summer shopping and just kicking it with Jennifer. With her father always out of town and her mother doing God knew what, she was just as lonely as I was. Nate got back together with the mother of his thirteen-month-old son, so he didn't have much time to give to her. She tried to act like it didn't bother her, but deep down I knew it did. She wasn't as tough as she wanted everybody to think she was. That was another thing the two of us had in common.

"You like this?" Jennifer asked as she held up an Ecko Red mini-skirt.

"Yeah, if you rock it right," I told her as I examined it thoroughly. We were once again in the mall about to spend way too much money on clothes and shoes.

"What about this?" she asked as she showed me a denim JLO one-piece jumper.

"It's hot. You should wear it with yo' gold Pucci sandals," I suggested.

"And my gold Kate Spade purse?"

"Now you got it, *mami*," I joked.

When Jennifer and I were little, we both wanted to be fashion designers. Our plan was to go into business together and take the world by storm. We were going to be the rawest bitches in the fashion industry. That was before we both realized we couldn't draw or sew. Over the years, I had changed my mind a million different times. I wanted to be a singer, but I couldn't hold a tune. I wanted to be a doctor, but I couldn't stand the sight of blood. I even wanted to be a hairstylist, but I didn't get along with females. I was about to start my senior year, and I still hadn't figured out my future.

After we almost bought the entire mall, we stopped at The Cheesecake Factory for lunch. The only thing I hated about going there was trying to decide between all the different desserts. Jennifer, on the other hand, always got the same thing—the strawberry cheesecake. I wished that my stomach was big enough to have them all.

"You got to taste this," Jennifer told me eagerly as she shoved her fork in my face.

"That's so good," I confessed as I licked the crumbs off my lip.

"This is worth three hours at the gym," she joked.

I hated working out. Obesity ran in Jennifer's family, so she didn't take any chances. She had three aunts who were all well over three hundred pounds and a grandmother who was two hundred and fifty at only five-foot-two. Her mother was one hundred and twenty five pounds heavier before she had her stomach stapled. That was the first of her many procedures.

"So have you talked to Nate lately?" I asked cautiously.

"Girl, fuck that nigga. I ain't got time fo' the baby mama drama. The bitch wants him so bad, she can have him. I keep a spare," she bragged in between bites of her cheesecake.

"Sometimes I wish I could go back to bein' nine years old. It was so simple then."

"It was just me, you, Barbie and Ken," Jennifer joked.

"Can you believe that I got pregnant my senior year of high school? How stupid am I?"

"It's not like you did it on purpose."

"True, but I still should have been more careful. I knew I couldn't just keep on fuckin' without usin' something."

"Well, it's too late to worry about that now. All you can do now is have yo' baby and try to make the best of it," she said matter-of-factly.

"And what about Isiah? He's in so deep now that I couldn't pull him out if I wanted to. What if something happens to him? I can't raise this baby by myself."

"You're not by yourself. I know I don't have a lot of experience, but I know how to change a diaper."

"You do?" I asked.

"Yeah, don't you?"

"No. The last time I was around kids was when I was one myself."

"Why don't you call around and see if any of these hospitals around here have any parenting classes?"

"Will you come with me?"

"You want me to come for real?" she asked excitedly.

"It's not like Isiah has the time. You might end up in the delivery room with me."

"You my girl and all, but that's where I draw the line." We both had to laugh at that one.

Later on that evening, I was lying in my bed reading *A White Man's World*, by my favorite author, Mya Hendrix. It was about her struggles growing up in a small town with a racist stepfather. Her mother was white and her biological father was black. She never met her father. I sympathized with that. I couldn't imagine not knowing my daddy. I was

Cynthia White

about to begin the fourth chapter when my cell phone rang.

"Hello."

"Hey, baby." It was Isiah.

"Hey." I smiled.

"How you feel?"

"I'm fine."

"What you doin'?"

"Reading."

"That's one thing I love about you. You read more than anybody I know."

"It's better than sittin' up in a movie theater for three hours," I complained.

Isiah loved going to the movies. I did not. I had a hard time sitting through an hour of previews then a movie that sometimes lasted two and a half hours. I found books to be much more stimulating.

"I just called to see how you were feelin'. I probably won't be home 'til late."

"What's new?" I joked or at least that's how I wanted it to seem. I didn't want to be one of those chicks who complained about her nigga never being at home, but the truth was, I was starting to get lonely. I could only spend so much time with Jennifer. She had a life of her own.

"I promise it'll get betta."

"And how do you know that?"

"I can't really talk about it right now, but I'll explain it to you when I get home."

"Alright."

"I love you, baby."

"I love you, too." I blew him a kiss then disconnected the call.

I rolled back onto my stomach and continued reading

where I had left off. I got to chapter twelve and fell asleep sometime after midnight. I dreamed about my mother again. In the dream, she was dressed in all white, as if a whore like her had any chance of making it to heaven. She never spoke. She just smiled at me like she knew something I didn't. I wondered what it was. Why was she so damn happy? I woke up at four remembering everything about my mysterious dream.

"What's wrong?" Isiah asked as he stood beside my bed taking the clothes off of his magnificent body.

"Nothin', I just had a weird dream."

"What about?"

"Forget about it. It was stupid anyway."

"I told my father today," he said.

"Told him what?"

"About the baby."

"I haven't even told my father yet. What did Uncle Moe say?"

"He asked me what our plans were. I told him that after you graduated we were gettin' married. Then he started askin' me all these questions I didn't have answers to."

"Like what?" I wanted to know.

"Like where did I see myself in ten years?"

"That's easy."

"It is? Well I wish you'd tell me 'cause I don't have a clue," he said.

"You'll be a boss. Think about it. You're Moe's son, you're marryin' Hershey Aaron's daughter and you're the father of his first grandchild. You're next in line, no questions asked," I explained to him as I closed my book and put it on my nightstand.

He smiled at me. I smiled back. It was when we were

Cynthia White

alone like this that I could speak freely. I let him lead in public, but here I ruled. He would never admit it, but he liked it. He liked when I told him what to do in bed even more. I had become more and more aggressive as I got more comfortable with him. I told him where to touch me and when. I instructed him how hard to hit it and how long to lick it. We were good together that way.

He dropped his boxer shorts then joined me in the bed. His hands were cold. I giggled when he touched me. He lowered the straps of my white lace gown. As the fabric moved down my breasts, I closed my eyes. I liked the way it felt. I wasn't wearing anything underneath and his eyes appreciated that. As he ran his hands down my bare back, my body began to tingle. He kissed my neck softly.

Just as we were really starting to get into it, my cell phone began to ring. I tried to ignore it, but whoever it was didn't want to give up. It continued to ring constantly for ten minutes.

"Hello," Isiah answered in an aggravated tone.

"Can I speak to Queen?" a strange male voice asked.

"Who is this?"

"Xavier."

"Who the fuck is Xavier?" he turned and asked me. This was one question I was not prepared to answer.

"I don't know," I lied. I didn't know what else to do.

"She said she don't know you," he relayed the message back to Xavier.

"She knows me. As a matter of fact, she knows me very well."

"What the fuck is that supposed to mean?"

"Ask her."

"I'm askin' you!" Isiah shouted.

"You sure you really wanna know?"

"Nigga, if you got somethin' to say, just say it."

"I fucked her," Xavier revealed then hung up the phone.

Isiah just sat there with a look of disappointment on his face. I knew that Xavier had told him the truth. That wasn't his place. I was going to tell him eventually. I was mad, but not at Xavier. It was my fault.

"Did you fuck that nigga?" he asked me with tears in his eyes.

"What?" I tried to act shocked and offended.

"He told me he fucked you. Did he?"

"I can't believe you just asked me that."

"Did you?!" He grabbed me by the shoulders.

"No."

"You betta not be lyin' to me," he warned me.

"I'm not." Again, I lied.

Tears began to form in my eyes. I couldn't believe how far I was willing to go to hide the fact that I had been with another man. At that moment, I didn't care. I was taking that secret to the grave.

"I'm sorry." He let me go.

"Isiah, I love you," I pleaded for his affection.

"I know you do." He kissed me softly then wiped away my tears.

We got back to what we had been doing before we were so rudely interrupted. Maybe it was me, but it seemed like Isiah was fucking me harder than usual. Xavier had gotten to him. I couldn't be offended. I cheated on him and I would have to live with that guilt for the rest of my life.

I tried to get in contact with Xavier the next day, but he didn't answer his cell phone. I thought that maybe he just didn't want to talk to me. Maybe he was mad for some rea-

Cynthia White

son. I tried to let it go, but I couldn't. What reason did he have to be mad at me? We fucked, nothing more, nothing less. I didn't even know anything about Xavier. It was almost like it had never happened ... almost. It wasn't until a few nights later that I found out what was really going on.

Isiah had been doing quite a bit of smoking and drinking. He was passed out on my bed when I grabbed my cell phone and headed out into the hall. Once again, I dialed Xavier's number. My heart sank when I heard ringing coming from my bedroom. I disconnected the call. I took a deep breath and went back inside. I put my hand inside the pocket of the Crooked Ink jeans Isiah was wearing and pulled out the contents. There was the phone mixed in with several hundred dollar bills and Xavier's driver's license. My heart sank. I knew that Isiah had killed him. I sat down on the bed and looked at the monster I had created.

chapter

Seven

JENNIFER AND I WOKE UP EARLY one morning with plans to go shopping to get things I would need for the baby. I had been up since five o'clock throwing up. Morning sickness was a pain in the ass. Besides that, I was also having terrible heartburn. It was the first time I had ever had it, and I didn't like it at all. It felt as if there was a small fire in my chest. I took a lot of shit that didn't work until finally I remembered what my father used to do. If you hold your arms up over your head, it goes away within a few seconds. The only bad thing was that as soon as you put your arms down, it comes right back.

"Good morning, Queen." Jimmy C greeted me with a smile as I walked out the front door.

"Good morning, Jimmy." Again I felt his eyes on my ass as I walked to Jennifer's car.

"Hey, freak." That was Jennifer's way of saying good morning.

Cynthia White

"Hey, hoe. What, you think you on the cover of *'Playboy'* or something?" I joked about the way she was leaning against her car.

"Don't hate on my sexiness."

I couldn't help but laugh at her crazy ass.

"Queen!" Jimmy C shouted at the top of his lungs. I turned around just in time to see him flying toward me. I knew something was wrong. I turned in the opposite direction and saw two men hanging out the side of a Hummer with big machine guns in their hands. The bullets roared like thunder. It all happened so fast. Jimmy C tackled me to the ground and fell on top of me. My heart raced as I realized what was going down. This was it. I was going to die. I closed my eyes tightly. I didn't want to see it coming. Then as quickly as it began, it ended.

"Queen! Queen, where are you?" I heard my Uncle Moe call out to me.

"Where is she? Where the fuck is she?" Isiah yelled as he began to panic.

"She's over here," Uncle Moe told Isiah as he saw me crawl out from underneath Jimmy C's body. He was dead.

"Are you okay?" Isiah asked as he searched my body for holes.

"I'm fine."

"No, you're not." He raised my shirt. I was bleeding from the stomach.

"Oh my God." I froze as I noticed that Jennifer was still on the ground. She wasn't moving and she was in a puddle of her own blood. I walked over to her and looked down at the damage. There was no surviving that. She was hit in the head, neck and chest. I began to feel weak. That was the last thing I remembered before I passed out.

*****

I woke up in the hospital confused and disoriented. I did-n't know if I had dreamed the entire ordeal or if it really happened. The pain in my stomach was excruciating. I knew then that it wasn't a dream. No dream could hurt this much. My head was throbbing. I couldn't remember everything, but I did remember that Jimmy C had died protecting me. He'd always said he'd give his life for mine, but I never thought it would come to that. I looked out the window. It was dark. I wondered how long I had been unconscious. When Jennifer had come to pick me up that morning, it was just after eight. I must have been out for a long time. Then it hit me. Jennifer was dead. My eyes filled with tears. The emotional pain hurt a hell of a lot more than the physical pain.

Isiah got up from the chair he was sitting in and walked over to my bed. He looked at me and tried to smile.

"Jennifer's dead?" I asked, even though I already knew the answer.

"Yeah," he whispered softly.

"Did somebody call her parents?"

"My dad did. Her father's flyin' home in the morning. Her mother already started makin' funeral arrangements," he told me as he sat down on the edge of the bed. I tried to move over a little so he'd have more room, but I was so sore. I thought about the fact that in a couple of days I would have to go to my best friend's funeral. I had never been to a funeral in my entire life.

"Did Uncle Moe call Frank?" Frank was Jimmy C's father. He used to be in the game but retired when he turned sixty. He had already lost three of his six sons to violence. This would be his fourth.

Cynthia White

"He's back at the house."

"Why me?"

"What?"

"Why me? Why was I the only one who survived?"

"Because it wasn't yo' time to go," he said.

"But why? What makes me so special?"

"Queen, don't do this to yourself. You already have enough to deal with," he reasoned.

"What aren't you tellin' me?"

He looked down at the floor then back up at me. "You lost the baby." With all that was going on, I had forgotten that I was even pregnant. I didn't know how to feel. How do you mourn a baby you never even got to hold? I don't know why, but I started to cry. I didn't think I was even that attached to the pregnancy, but I guess I was wrong. I realized at that moment that I did love my baby. I wanted him or her to have everything – every opportunity and advantage. I wanted to love my child with everything I had, but now it was too late.

Isiah held me as I cried. No matter what, he was always there for me. He held me down when I thought I was going to lose control. He comforted me when the pain became too much to bear. Up until that moment, I thought I was the strong one. I was wrong. Isiah was strong in ways that I would never understand.

*****

Jennifer's funeral came too quickly for me. It had only been three days. I wasn't ready to say goodbye yet. I looked down at my girl lying lifeless in her coffin. I instantly got upset with whoever did her makeup. It was atrocious. She would have never worn red lipstick. I kept on standing there waiting for her to wake up. She never did.

I felt a pair of strong arms wrap around me tightly. I knew it wasn't Isiah. I knew his embrace like the back of my hand. I turned around and looked up into Mr. Perez's eyes. Jennifer's father was so handsome even when his eyes were red and his cheeks were flushed. I tried to speak, but I couldn't. I wanted to tell him how much his daughter meant to me. I wanted him to know that she was the closest thing I had to a sister. I needed him to know that my life would never be the same without her. Seeing those tears running down his golden cheeks, I knew that he understood. I didn't have to say a word.

After the funeral, I wanted to be alone. I drove down to the riverfront. Jennifer and I used to go there all the time when we were younger. I sat in my car and rolled up a fat-ass blunt. I desperately needed to be high. I smoked the entire thing then rolled up another one. I cried like a baby as I thought about all the fun we had when we skipped an entire week of school our freshman year to be with these two guys we met from Memphis. They were so fine. Jason was twenty-three and in love with Jennifer. He told her that when she turned eighteen, he was going to marry her. I laughed out loud. Then it came on the radio. It was the worst possible song they could have played at that moment. *"Missing You"* off the *"Set It Off"* soundtrack.

> *Who would have known*
> *That you'd have to go*
> *So suddenly, so fast ...*
> *I'm so empty inside*
> *And my tears I can't hide*
> *But I'll try...try to face the pain*
> *Though I'm missing you*

Cynthia White

I thought about us going to the movies to see *"Set It Off"* when we were just little girls. Jennifer said she wanted to be Jada Pinkett because she was the only one who made it. I wanted to be Queen Latifah because she went out like a soldier. I sat in my car and cried for three hours straight. I was worn out. This had been one long-ass day. I drove home with my third blunt between my fingers. The higher I got, the more detached I became. I drove around aimlessly with no destination in mind. I had nowhere to go. I found myself in Jennifer's driveway. I sat there staring at her Lexus, waiting for her to stick her head out her bedroom window and call me a freak. I smiled through the tears. I got out of my Benz and walked up to the back door. I knocked. I knew the door was unlocked but somehow it wasn't alright to just go in anymore.

"How are you, sweetheart?" Mr. Perez asked me as he opened the door in his black satin pajamas and robe.

"I'm uh … I'm just tryin' to get through the day."

"I know how hard this has to be for you," he said with sincerity in his voice.

"It is. She was yo' daughter, yo' only child. I wish it were me and not her."

"Queen, sweetheart, you shouldn't say things like that." He looked at me like I was pathetic.

"She had so much to live for."

"So do you."

"I just feel like God made the wrong choice."

"God never makes the wrong choice." He smiled exuberantly.

"You seem so happy. What do you have to smile about?"

"My daughter is in heaven. She's safe now. She's with God and he'll take better care of her than I ever could have."

"And you just know this?" I asked, amazed by his faith.

"I know this." He smiled proudly.

"I just feel like I lost the only real friend I ever had. We used to talk on the phone every night before we went to bed. Who am I gonna call tonight? Who am I gonna eat lunch with at school and go shopping with on the weekends? I never really had a mother. My father's in prison. I was shot by God knows who, for what reason I don't know. And I had just found out I was pregnant. I was so scared. Jennifer promised me that she'd be there. She promised!" I yelled as the tears began to flow.

"I'm so sorry, Queen. I know how much my daughter meant to you." He put his arms around me and held me like daddy used to. I didn't want him to let me go. If he did, I knew I would hit the ground.

"Please don't let me go," I begged him humbly.

"It's okay. I got you," he whispered in my ear in a strong, masculine voice. I didn't know what I was doing. I looked up into his eyes and we connected. No sense in wasting my high. We kissed even though we both knew it was wrong. Nothing made sense at that moment. We were two desperate people searching for something that we were never going to find in each other. He was old enough to be my father, but that didn't stop either one of us.

We had sex in the same house where I used to play dress-up with his daughter. He treated me like I was made of glass, being extra careful like I might break. He kissed me everywhere and touched me softly like only a man his age could. I never wanted him to stop. I wanted him to take me deeper and deeper into his fantasy. I knew that he had had his eye on me for a while now. The hardness between his legs confirmed that. He sucked my breasts like they fed his hunger.

Cynthia White

I liked the way he touched me. I felt more mature with every stroke of his hand. He pulled my black satin panties from under my dress. I felt the heat building up between my legs.

"Uhm ..." I moaned as he touched my pussy with authority. He was telling me that I was his for the night, and I didn't mind. He spread my legs open. I felt so sexy. His long, thick tongue licked me meticulously. Not one single inch of my softest place went undiscovered. He was a god among men and tonight I was his goddess. He ate me so good. I arched my back as he grabbed me by my thighs and pulled me down farther into his mouth. He couldn't get enough. His craving was vast. I didn't know if I was enough. I closed my eyes and enjoyed what he was giving me.

"Cum in my mouth, Queen," he ordered me.

"I'm cummin' daddy ... ooooooh ... uhm ... I'm cummin' ... yes ... ooooooh ... yes." I completely lost control as I came harder than I had ever come in my life. I fought to catch my breath. My chest heaved up and down as Mr. Perez looked at me and smiled. I couldn't help but smile back. I felt so, so good.

"Did you like that?"

"Yes, sir." I licked my lips, signaling to him that I wanted more.

"I'm only going to ask you this one time."

"What's that?" I asked, barely able to keep my eyes open. Between the chronic and that marvelous face he had just broke me off with, I was high as a kite.

"Do you want me to stop?" This was my last out. I had a chance to stop this now before it went too far. If I just got up and put my clothes back on, we could act like it never happened. We could chalk it up to the two of us hurting and not knowing how to deal with that hurt. I looked up at him, and

I knew what I wanted to do.

"I want you to fuck me," I told him flat out. There was no question about it, I wanted him. I watched as he took off his pajama bottoms. There was a sexiness about him. He was so confident and self-assured. I knew that I could learn a lot from him. I studied his facial expressions. He seemed to have something on his mind. Maybe he was thinking about how wrong this was. Why did things that were supposedly so bad for us feel so good?

"You are so beautiful." He spoke to me like I was the most important thing in his life. I believed that at that moment, I was. I felt so special. I tensed up once I saw what he was working with. Mr. Perez had the biggest dick I had ever seen in my life. I didn't know if I was ready for him. I tried to act calm, but I think my nervousness came through. He kissed me softly on the belly. It made me smile and I relaxed a little. I knew that if I could just hold on long enough to get used to his size, I would enjoy it a great deal. I closed my eyes as he slowly pushed himself inside me.

"Ssssss ..." I hissed like a snake as the pain and pleasure merged together. I felt him in my stomach. The discomfort was soon replaced with desire. It got better with every stroke. He filled me up entirely. I gripped the sheets tightly as he moved inside me vigorously. I had to hold onto something. The ride was a little dangerous, but I liked it. I knew that if I didn't play by the rules, I could get hurt. He was in complete control of my body and we both knew it.

"You feel so good, Queen." He looked down on me with a sex appeal that I had never seen before in real life. This was the kind of thing I thought only existed in movies or in my books. I never knew there were really men like this in the world. Even though he was old enough to be my father, I

Cynthia White

wanted to be his completely. I wanted to be his lover and his woman. I wanted to marry him and give him children. I wanted to cook him dinner and serve it to him wearing only a pair of red Salvatore Ferragamo pumps with a five-inch stiletto heel. I wanted my body to belong to him and only him. I had temporarily forgotten all about Isiah. He wasn't my primary focus at the moment. The fact was, he didn't understand what I was going through and Mr. Perez did. He had lost his daughter, who was also my best friend and my sister. We dealt with it in different ways, but we both understood one another. I helped him and he helped me.

It was a strange way of grieving, but it worked for us. I could feel he needed me and that felt so good to me. I couldn't explain it, but I was whole at that moment. I, too, had just lost a child. Just as I was coming to terms with becoming a mother, the opportunity was ripped away from me. That pissed me off. I just wished I knew who to blame. I knew I would find out one day. I just had to be patient. It might take months or it might take years, but what was done in the dark always came to light.

After taking that big beautiful dick for two hours, I lay there half dead. How I survived was a mystery even to me. I felt like I would have to go in for emergency surgery to repair the damage. The pain remained excruciating between my legs. I wasn't sure if I could get up and walk. I heard that taking a warm bath helped. Jennifer told me that. Strange that the advice she gave me was exactly what I needed to recover from a night of passion with her father.

I went into the master bathroom and took a long soak. The water was hot, but my memories were even hotter. I reminisced for an hour. I saw his face as he worked it out inside me. I closed my eyes and longed to be with him again.

It was the first time I was ever glad that my father was behind bars. If he ever found out what went down, he'd kill Mr. Perez, literally. I couldn't think about that. My mind was fixated on the man who turned my world upside down. I knew I was setting myself up for failure but I continued to fantasize. If I had any sense at all, I would've just forgotten about the night and never saw him again. I would've taken my scandalous ass home and gotten in bed with my man.

"Mind if I join you?" Mr. Perez asked as he stood there looking glorious in nothing but the flawless skin God gave him. He was holding a bottle of champagne in one hand and two glasses in the other.

"Come on in." All I could do was smile. He placed the glasses on the side of the tub then popped the bottle of champagne. It quickly rose to the top and some of it fell into the tub. I had always wanted to bathe in champagne. He poured us both a glass then sat down in between my legs. He seemed to be at home there.

"You take a very hot bath," he remarked as he lay back on me. My breasts felt good pressed up against his back. He was heavy, but in a good way because his weight was firm. His wavy, coal-black hair smelled nice. I wasn't sure, but I think I recognized the fragrance. His hair smelled like Jennifer's. They must have used the same shampoo. I raised my glass and took a sip of the chilled champagne. It was the best I had ever tasted.

"This is good."

"Not as good as you." His comment made me blush. I was glad that he wasn't facing me.

"If I tell you something, will you promise not to hold it against me?"

"Proceed."

Cynthia White

"I have never in my life felt as good as I did with you. The way you touched me and kissed me was just so explosive. Just thinkin' about it now gives me chills." I ran my free hand across his muscular shoulders and down his ripped chest.

"Queen, you are an amazing young lady. You make me feel like I'm twenty-one again." I could tell by the way he was breathing that the way I was touching him was turning him on.

"I just want to give you all of me. I want to taste you and lick you and suck you." I poured the rest of my champagne down the back of his neck and licked it off like a dog in heat. His skin was yummy. My hands feverishly roamed his body. Just touching him was addictive. I stood up. The water in the tub was low enough so that when he sat back, his hard dick stood above the water like a periscope. He leaned against the tub and waited for my eager mouth.

I licked the head ever so softly. I could tell by his reaction that he liked my approach. I teased him with my tongue. I began sucking it in a very tender, delicate manner. This was only a preview of what was to come. I went down farther and gave his nuts some attention. I licked them, then sucked them pulling them in and out my mouth using only my tongue. He reached down and grabbed a handful of my hair.

"You make me feel sooooo good, Queen," he said and then let out a powerful moan. I liked making him happy. Sucking his dick turned me on. We were like magnets being drawn together with such a powerful force that it was impossible to resist. I hungrily took his entire eleven inches into my mouth. I provided so much suction you would have thought my last name was Hoover. I felt him trying to hold back. He didn't want to cum too fast. The more he tried to control himself, the harder I sucked. He finally came in my mouth and I loved every nasty, skanky moment of it.

*****

I didn't get back to Isiah's townhouse until seven that morning. I thought about what to tell the man I had promised to spend the rest of my life with. I decided on the truth. I was with Mr. Perez all night. We were helping each other get through this tragedy, end of story. He didn't need to know everything. I was impulsive, not stupid.

I went upstairs and found Isiah in bed. He was knocked out. He looked so peaceful. If he only knew what I was out doing all night.

I felt a little guilty when I saw the gift he left me on the nightstand. There was a card with my name on it attached to a rectangular-shaped black velvet box. I already knew what was inside. The week before, I had showed him a 10 carat baguette diamond bracelet in the Tiffany's catalog. He remembered. He could be so thoughtful at times. I opened the box and sure enough, there it was. I never questioned him about it, but I knew he was getting paid. The bracelet was thirty-seven thousand dollars and he bought it like it was nothing. Being down with The Black Mafia did have its perks.

Cynthia White

chapter *Eight*

STARTING SENIOR YEAR WITHOUT JENNIFER WAS depressing. School was once an escape for me, but now I didn't even want to be there. We had so many plans for the year, things I didn't want to do alone. Everybody walked on eggshells around me. They all knew about what happened. I guess they thought that if they asked me about it, I would fall to pieces. Instead, they just whispered and talked behind my back.

The first day was the worst. I felt like I was an animal in the zoo on display. I got so tired of being stared at and gossiped about that I couldn't even make it through the entire day. I left at a quarter to noon. I jumped in my Benz and headed straight to the mall. Shopping was the one thing that was always the same. You go in a store, find something you like and give them money. It was so simple like everything should be.

"Queen..."

I heard his voice and almost got whiplash I turned around so fast.

"Hi, Mr. Perez." I smiled and batted my long eyelashes.

"Please, call me Marc," he suggested as he touched my arm softly.

I felt a spark. He was like fire. I knew that if I kept playing around with him, I was going to end up getting burned.

"Okay, Marc."

He looked so good in his gray Armani suit. The bright red tie he was wearing really brought it all together. It had been a few weeks since I last saw him. I didn't want to come off as some nerdy little girl with a crush.

"How have you been?" he asked as he looked me up and down, no doubt reliving in his mind the last time we saw each other.

"I'm good. Today was the first day of school. It really hit me hard that Jennifer wasn't there. We had all these plans. For the last three years, her locker has been right next to mine. Now it's empty. I keep waitin' for her to show up places. I keep expectin' the phone to ring and for it to be her on the other end. I guess I just don't know how to get over that."

"It's okay." He put his arms around me and I damn near fainted. I know he felt it. How could he not? I looked up at him. He brushed my hair out of my eyes.

"Do you have to be somewhere?" I asked, hoping like hell the answer was no.

"I'm exactly where I need to be." He took me by the hand and led me out of the store. We walked through the parking lot without saying a single word. He opened the door to his bright red Ferrari F430 2-door coupe and I got inside. We drove to the Hilton not too far from the mall. As

Cynthia White

soon as we got inside our suite, we went at each other. It was more passionate and intense than the first time.

A couple hours later, we were finished. I felt incredible. This time, we showered together. He washed my body with such care. We ordered room service and before we knew it, we had again spent the entire night together. It was after five a.m. when he drove me back to the mall to get my car. We stood in the parking lot for twenty minutes kissing and caressing each other like he wasn't married and I wasn't engaged.

*****

This time, when I got to Isiah's townhouse, he was wide awake.

"Where have you been?" he asked seriously, like he had a bone to pick with me.

"I was with Mr. Perez."

"Until five in the mornin'?"

"Yeah," was all I said as I sat down on the edge of the bed and began to take off my school uniform.

"So what did you and Mr. Perez do all night?" he asked.

"We talked," I lied.

"About what?"

"I had a hard day at school today. I cut out early and went to the mall. He was there. I got to tellin' him about how much I missed Jennifer and one thing just led to another. We talked and talked and then all of the sudden it was five o'clock."

"And where did all this talkin' take place?"

"What?"

He caught me off-guard. He didn't usually ask me this many questions. It wasn't his style.

"The mall closes at what, ten or eleven o'clock? Where

did you go after that?"

"What's with all the questions?"

"Just askin'."

"We went to his house. Mrs. Perez was there, too. She made dinner." I lied my ass off.

"Was that before or after she came by your house and returned these?" he asked, pulling my black satin panties from his pocket.

I was wearing them the first night I spent with Mr. Perez. I neglected to wear them home. "Those aren't mine," I lied through my teeth.

"Yes, they are."

"No, they're not."

"Queen, I paid for them."

Yes, he did. Damn, there was no way out of this one. I didn't know what to say. I didn't know what to do. I was caught up in a lie that led to an even bigger betrayal.

"Fine, you want the truth? I'll give you the truth." I took a deep breath then slowly exhaled, "I fucked Jennifer's father."

That's not the way I wanted it to come out. It sounded so cold. I sounded so cold. I figured that I might as well just confess before I got so caught up in my lies that I made a bigger mess out of things. Isiah just stood there and looked at me with disgust. I felt low. I let him down, but worst of all, I hurt him. I never wanted to do that.

Isiah slept in the guest room that night. He didn't even want to be in the same room as me. I was disappointed, but I understood. I was once let down by somebody I loved. When I found out that Gauge was a pig, I was crushed. I felt used. I was angry and all I wanted to do was to hurt him back. I just hoped that Isiah wouldn't deal with me the same way I dealt with Gauge. I apologized, but somehow "I'm sorry" just didn't seem to be enough.

I didn't know what the future held for us, but I did know that he would never trust me again. I could do everything by the book and stick to his side like glue, but he would always think I was out doing wrong. The truth was, I had no intentions of ending my affair with Marc. For me to say I loved him would be idiotic, but I did love the way he made me feel.

*****

The next morning was brutal. Isiah hadn't talked to me all night, and my guilt kept me from sleeping. I tossed and turned all night trying desperately to think of a way to make things right for everyone involved. I didn't find one.

"Isiah, I know you don't wanna talk to me right now, but when you do, please call me. We really need to discuss this entire situation," I told him as he sat at the kitchen counter eating a bowl of cereal.

I had two duffle bags in my hands filled with all the things I had over at his place.

"Where you goin'?" he asked without so much as looking up at me once.

"I don't know yet. I'll probably just go stay at a hotel for a couple of days. I don't wanna go back home. That house just has too many bad memories for me."

"You don't have to leave," he told me, even though I could tell by the tone of his voice that he didn't mean it.

"Yes, I do."

"Well at least let one of the guys follow you just to be safe."

"Okay," I agreed, not wanting another fight on my hands.

"Call me whenever you get where you're goin'."

"I will."

I took one last look at him then turned and walked out the door. I felt a pain in my gut that I had never felt before. There were so many things about myself I didn't understand. How could I do this to Isiah after what my mother had done to my father? I walked over to my Benz and opened up the trunk. I threw my bags in then went and slid behind the steering wheel. I started the ignition and immediately the radio blasted *"Burn"* by Usher. That was so not what I wanted to hear.

> *It's gonna burn for me to say this*
> *But it's comin' from my heart*
> *It's been a long time comin'*
> *We done been fell apart*
> *When I'm hurtin' baby, I ain't happy baby*
> *Plus there's so many other things I gotta deal with*
> *I think that you should let it burn…*

That was the first time I really got that song. I had to let it burn. It hurt, but this was the best thing for both of us. Deep down, we both knew we were too young to be talking about getting married. Maybe losing the baby was our way out. Even so, it still hurt like a son of a bitch.

Raymond and Gino followed me to The Hyatt Regency hotel. When the lady at the front desk asked me how long I would be staying with them, I froze up. I had no idea. All I knew was that I didn't want to go back home, and Isiah damn sure didn't want me back at his home. I told her I'd start off with a week and let her know if I needed to extend my stay. She just smiled and looked at me like she felt sorry for me. Maybe she knew that nobody wanted me around. Her silver

Cynthia White

hair and glasses made me want to hug her. I never knew my grandparents. Nothing about my family was normal. I was on my own, alone once again.

*****

"I don't know why I'm callin'," I confessed to Mr. Perez when he answered his cell phone.

"Where are you?" he asked like he was concerned about me.

"I just checked into The Hyatt Regency at Union Station."

"Did Isiah kick you out?"

"Technically, I left voluntarily, but I knew he didn't want me there."

"I'm coming to see you."

"You don't have to do that."

"I want to," he assured me.

That made me feel a little better.

"Do you need anything?"

"No, I'm good."

"I'll be there in half an hour," he promised.

He was there in twenty minutes. As soon as I opened the door, I fell into his arms. He held me like I was his woman – at least that's how it was in my mind. I tried anything to justify our relationship. Nothing worked. It was unexplainable. Nobody would ever get it. I wasn't really sure if we got it. It just felt good and we both desperately needed that. He cradled the back of my head in his hands. If he only knew the effect he had on me. I took a step back to try to get some perspective. It didn't work.

"What's that?" I asked, noticing the Bloomingdale's bag in his hand.

"This is for you."

"What is it?" I asked, my curiosity getting the best of me.

"Open it," he suggested as he raised the bag to me.

I took it from him and sat down on the bed. He shut the door behind him and joined me on the bed. The first thing I saw when I looked inside the bag was a gorgeous Gucci handbag. It was the same one I was admiring at the mall. I smiled.

"Thank you, but ..."

"No buts. Keep going," he ordered.

I liked that about him. He told me what to do and I did it. I took out the Gucci shoe box and immediately knew what was inside. I opened it, and I was right. I couldn't take my eyes off the black and silver Gucci high-heel sandals. I was going to buy them but got distracted when we bumped into each other. I was so flattered. The sandals were seven hundred and ninety-five dollars and the handbag was almost four grand. I hugged him enthusiastically, not knowing there was more to come.

"I can't believe you did this."

"Keep going," he instructed me.

"More?"

"One more." He smiled slyly.

I wondered what else he could have done. This was already too much. I searched inside the bag for whatever was left inside. I found a small box. No, he didn't. It was from Ice, my favorite jewelry store. I opened up the box and my mouth almost hit the floor. A 5 carat flawless, heart-shaped diamond mounted on a platinum setting. I had seen this particular ring in the showroom at Ice, and I knew that it was priced at almost two hundred thousand dollars. It was too much. I didn't know what to say. No words were enough, so I did the one thing I knew would convey my gratitude. I hit

Cynthia White

my knees and sucked him off like he deserved.

*****

He stayed with me that night. We had evolved from having sex to making love. It was tender and passionate. I never wanted to leave that room. If we could have just stayed there forever I knew everything would be fine. I knew that the outside world would never accept us. How could they understand something that neither one of us could explain? All I knew was that I didn't regret anything, though I could have gone about it differently. I wished I would have handled things with Isiah better, but I was happy when I was with Marc.

"Where you goin'?" I asked him as I woke up at seven the following morning to find him sitting on the side of the bed, tying his ostrich shoes.

"I have a meeting I need to get to."

"This early?"

"It's very important."

"More important than me?" I asked like the brat I was.

"It's just business."

"Yeah, right," I pouted.

"Queen, I have obligations. I have to do things that at times I don't feel like doing. I know what you're thinking, but there is no one else."

He seemed to be reading my mind.

"Are you comin' back?"

"As soon as I wrap things up."

He pulled the comforter from my naked body, leaned down and kissed my pussy. Now I was awake. Instead of being suspicious of where he was going, I just wanted him to hurry up and get back.

As soon as he walked out the door, I missed him. I had

promised myself a long time ago that I wouldn't be one of those chicks. I was never one to sit at home waiting on nigga, but this was different. I wished I could explain it, but I didn't know the right words. It was like something was missing in my life until he came along. Then it hit me. The thing that was missing was my father. Marc was filling the void. He was strong and powerful just like daddy. He was cold with everyone except me, and he demanded the best from everyone. I knew that I could never get away with doing him the way I had done Isiah. I liked my men strong and he was. He let me know that he didn't take any bullshit without the need to say it out loud.

My cell phone rang. I looked the caller ID. It was Uncle Moe.

"Can we talk?" he asked more seriously than I would have liked.

I knew that Isiah had told him what was up.

"What do you wanna talk about?" I rolled my eyes even though he couldn't see me.

"Queen, you already know that."

"My personal life is not up for discussion."

"You're in over your head here."

"I know what I'm doin'," I said with big attitude.

"Are you sure about that?"

"Positive," I answered assertively.

"I just don't want you getting hurt."

"No offense, Uncle Moe, but it's really none of your business."

"You are my business and you always will be."

"I appreciate yo' concern, but I'm fine. I'm not sayin' I want to marry him or anything like that, but I'm havin' fun. When the fun ends, more than likely so will we."

Cynthia White

"And what about my son?"

"Uncle Moe, you didn't want me to get involved with Isiah in the first place."

"And this is exactly why!" he yelled.

He was obviously upset with me.

"Why, because I'm just like my mother?"

"No, because you're selfish. You don't consider other people's feelings. You just do whatever makes you happy and say fuck everybody else."

"I can't believe you think that about me."

"Am I wrong?"

"Yes!" I yelled at him in frustration.

"Look, I know you've been goin' through a lot lately. You were shot, you lost your baby and your best friend. You and Jimmy C were cool for years. Your father's being executed—"

"What?!!!" I yelled in disbelief.

The silence on the other end of the phone told me that he knew he had fucked up. As far as I knew, my father was serving life in prison. This was the first I had ever heard of an execution.

"I don't know where that came from. What I meant to say was ..." He tried to cover it up but it was no use.

"Uncle Moe, don't you lie to me. Is my father bein' put to death?"

"Yes," he answered like it hurt him to say it.

"When?"

"We don't know yet."

"When?" I asked him again, hoping that this time he would tell me the truth.

"Within the next two years."

"Oh my God." I fell to my knees.

"Queen, don't get upset."

"Don't get upset?" I asked in a very confused manner.

How could I not get upset?

"We're still working on an appeal."

He tried to give me some kind of hope, anything that I could hold onto.

"Uncle Moe, you know as well as I do that he's not gonna win any appeal. They want him dead. They want him out of the game. I can't believe this shit." I rubbed my head, which had suddenly started to ache like crazy. The room seemed to be spinning. Nothing was as it should have been.

"Queen, I just don't want you to do anything—"

"I gotta go." I interrupted, then hung up on him.

I didn't feel like hearing a lecture. I didn't want to talk to anyone. I didn't want to see anyone. I needed to be alone. I needed time to sort through my thoughts. It seemed that any time I started to think that things could be getting better, something knocked me flat on my ass.

I didn't go to school that morning. How could I concentrate on my assignments when I had so much on my mind? I rolled up a blunt and thought about how to handle the entire situation. I was so mad at daddy for not telling me. I had to wait two days before I could go and see him, but when I did, I fully intended to give him a piece of my mind. I thought we told each other everything. Now I was being the hypocrite. I knew damn well that I didn't tell my father everything. There was so much about me he didn't know, things I would kill to keep from him.

*****

"Hello, beautiful," Marc greeted me as he walked through the door of my suite.

"You're done already?" I asked, never taking my eyes off the spot on the ceiling that I had been staring at for God knows how long.

"I've been gone for six hours. Are you okay?"

"Not really."

"What's wrong?" he asked me as he took off the jacket of his tan Armani suit and sat down on the bed next to me.

"I just found out today that my father's bein' put to death."

"When?"

"I don't know. Uncle Moe said sometime in the next two years, but he's not exactly sure."

"Why didn't they tell you?"

"Because apparently I'm too young to handle something of this magnitude."

"That's bullshit. They should have told you. He's your father and you deserved to know."

"That's what I thought, but evidently what I think doesn't matter."

"It matters to me." He leaned down and kissed me softly on the lips.

"Thank you." I smiled for the first time since he left that morning.

"I have something I think might make you feel a little better."

"What?"

"Get dressed."

"For what?"

"It can't come to us, so we have to go to it."

"Okay, if you say so." I thought it was a little weird, but I still got up and put on my clothes.

We jumped in his Ferrari and were on our way. I was quiet for the majority of the ride. He kept looking over at me, but he never said a word. I tried to remain positive, but it was hard. I was facing a life of loneliness and loss. I didn't know what to expect from one day to the next.

We stopped at a red light. I looked over into the black Chevy Suburban beside us. A sistah was driving. She looked to be in her mid-thirties. She was talking to a man who I assumed was her husband. They made a nice couple. In the back they had two little girls and two boys. They looked exactly how I pictured a normal, happy family would. I imagined that they were going to Chuck E. Cheese or somewhere like that. I was never allowed to go to Chuck E. Cheese when I was a kid. There were too many people there who could hurt me or kidnap me. That was my childhood.

"Here we are," Marc announced, snapping me out of my fog.

"Where?" I asked as I looked up at the tall glass building.

"Come on."

He got out of the car and I followed him. We walked up to the building. It was beautiful.

"Good afternoon, Mr. Perez," the older white doorman greeted Marc.

"Good evening, Thomas. This beautiful young lady on my arm is Queen."

"Nice to meet you, Miss Queen." He bowed his head politely.

"My pleasure." I smiled sweetly then batted my eyelashes.

I had never been called Miss Queen before. It had a nice ring to it.

"Come on." Marc laughed at me then escorted me to the elevator.

"What's so funny?" I wanted to know.

"You."

Cynthia White

What?"

"Flirting with that old man like that. You could have given him a heart attack."

"I wasn't flirtin'. I was just bein' polite," I said innocently.

"Oh, is that what you call it?"

"Yes, it is. This is flirtin'."

I reached up and slowly ran my hands up his chest and behind his neck. I kissed him in a way that let him know he was the only man I was interested in flirting with. I was about to show him just how dirty I could get when the elevator door opened to the twenty-first floor. I was surprised that we were already inside the apartment and not in the hallway. I had never seen a place quite like it before. Everything was white, from the carpet and the drapes to the sofas and the chairs. It was magnificent. Whoever decorated truly knew what they were doing. There were vases of fresh white lilies all throughout the living room, kitchen and dinning room. The windows stretched from the fifteen-foot ceilings all the way down to the floor.

"This is amazing."

"I'm glad you like it."

"Like it? I love it."

"Good, because I bought it for you."

"What?"

"You heard me. It's all yours."

I ran and jumped up on him with my legs wrapped around his waist. I kissed him for what seemed like an eternity. I couldn't believe that fly-ass place was mine. He actually bought me a nine-hundred-thousand-dollar penthouse. It had two levels. The downstairs was for entertaining. That's where the pool table, seventy-inch LCD TV and the home theatre system were located. There was also a full and a half bathroom. Upstairs, there were three bedrooms and three more bathrooms. The master bedroom was extraordinary. It was so big that there was room for a big bedroom set and a couple of chaises. There was a double-sided fireplace that went from the bedroom on one side to the master bathroom on the other side. I felt like I was in a palace. The bathroom was all white with ash gray marble and a huge step-up tub. I climbed the four steps and sat in it with all of my clothes on.

"I take it you like the tub?"

"I love the tub. I just can't believe you did this. Why?"

"Because I want you to have it," he said.

That was good enough for me. I looked around at the shower, which was big enough for ten people, the two enormous walk-in closets and to my satisfaction the separate shoe closet, which held five hundred pairs of shoes. That did it. I was on cloud nine.

We ordered dinner from the restaurant on the main floor of my new building. The lobster was juicy and flavorful but the filet mignon was to die for. Marc made me taste his asparagus and it was surprisingly good. I had never tried it in the past because usually I didn't like green vegetables. Asparagus wasn't bad though. Lately I was revising a lot of my policies. Here I was laying up with a married man. That's something I never thought I would do in a million years. Never say never. I just couldn't get over the way he made me feel. How many men would buy you a penthouse within the first week of seeing each other? Only one I knew.

"How's your dessert?" he asked as I took a bite of my white chocolate truffle cheesecake.

"Uhm, uhm, uhm," was all I could say.

Cynthia White

"Can I have a bite?"

"I don't know. What you gonna do for me?"

"I'll make you a deal. You give me a bite of that cheese-cake and tomorrow I'll buy you a new car. Any one you want."

"Even a Bentley Continental GT?" I asked as a joke.

"I have a friend who owns a Bentley dealership. I'll give him a call."

He whipped out his cell phone and called his friend before I had a chance to tell him that I was just kidding around with him. I was taken aback, but I was no fool. If a man wanted to buy me a Bentley, who was I to turn it down?

Once he finished talking to his friend, we decided to go back to my hotel. I wanted to stay at my new place, but I had to wait until we went shopping and got a bedroom set. There was no way I was sleeping on those snow white sofas. I would probably never even sit on them. They were too pretty and far too hard to clean. I watched him the entire time we were in his Ferrari. He tried not to smile because he knew I was looking. He couldn't help it. I was glad to see him smile so much. That meant I was making him happy. That's all I wanted.

"I don't know how to thank you for everything you've done for me," I told him as we stood so close to each other that I could feel his heart beating.

"I have an idea."

"I bet you do."

"Tell me that I'm the only one," he commanded.

"You already know that. Isiah and I are through."

"And there's nobody else?"

"Nobody."

"I find that hard to believe. How can a young lady as

beautiful as you not have fifty men waiting?"

"Because I don't want fifty men," I said and looked him in the eyes.

"Then what do you want?"

"I think you already know the answer to that."

"Just say the word."

"I wanna be with you, Marc," I confessed as I looked up into his dark brown eyes. Suddenly, his hands were all over me. I couldn't tell where I stopped and he began. He picked me up and set me down on the dresser. I started unbuttoning his crisp, white shirt. He had my turquoise JLO halter top off within seconds. His tongue felt like warm lotion on my breasts. I leaned back on the mirror. It was cold. He worked me over so good.

By the time he pushed himself inside me, I was just about ready to cum. My head was somewhere in the clouds. I couldn't figure out what it was about him that made me feel this way. I felt high. It was so intense and incredible. I held on to him tightly as he fucked me hard while he grunted and moaned. He came inside me. We stayed still for a few minutes, both too weak to move.

My cell phone rang. I didn't know what to do.

"Go ahead." He knew I wanted to answer it so he gave me permission.

He went into the bathroom, and I went to retrieve my phone.

"Hello," I answered, half out of breath.

"Can we talk?"

It was Isiah.

"I didn't think you ever wanted to talk to me again."

"You're the one who walked away from us, not me."

"Is this why you want to talk, so you can make me feel

Cynthia White

bad about myself?"

"Queen, I miss you. Don't you miss me?" he said pitifully.

"I can't talk about this right now."

"Is he there?" he asked with so much pain in his voice that it was hurting me.

"Isiah, please don't call back here," I begged him then hung up before he could respond.

I put the phone down then walked over to the bed. I felt tears welling up in my eyes and quickly wiped them away. I still cared about Isiah, but things with him were too hard. As soon as my ass hit the comforter, my phone began to ring again. I knew it was him calling back.

"Who is that?" Marc asked as he came out of the bathroom.

"Somebody I don't wanna talk to."

"Allow me." He picked up my phone. "Hello."

"Where's Queen?"

"Excuse me?"

"Muthafucka, did I stutter? Where's Queen?" Isiah yelled.

"Look, little boy—"

"Little boy? Man, you got me fucked up! Don't get yo' bitch ass knocked!"

"Don't get my bitch ass knocked?" Marc laughed.

I jumped up and grabbed the phone out of his hand.

"Isiah, I asked you not to call here again."

"It's like that? You gonna just play me like that? After all we been through?"

"Isiah, please, you have to let me go," I begged.

"Fuck that!" he yelled then hung up in my ear.

I get an uneasy feeling. I didn't think that Isiah was the

type to do anything stupid, but he was a member of The Black Mafia. There was no telling what they had taught him. I turned the ringer off on my phone and put it down on the nightstand. I sat down on the bed and wrapped my arms around a pillow.

"Don't worry, I won't let him hurt you," Marc assured me.

It wasn't me I was worried about.

*****

The next day, we did as Marc had promised and went to see his friend at the Bentley dealership. He was a fine man named Sonny with dark hair, dark eyes and beautiful skin. He was very well put together. His suit told me that he sold a lot of Bentleys. Then again, I guess all it takes is one two-hundred-thousand-dollar car to make his week. He kind of reminded me of my Marc. He was probably in his mid to late thirties.

"You must be Queen? Marc's told me a lot about you. It's very nice to meet you."

"You too." I smiled and batted my long eyelashes.

Marc shot me a look. I just ignored it. I wasn't flirting. I was just being me.

"So I hear you're interested in the Continental GT?"

"Yes." I smiled.

"We have a few in stock, but if you don't see one you like, I can order it."

"Okay."

"Just follow me." He led the way.

Marc grabbed me by the hand and held it the remainder of the time we were there. I hoped he wasn't the jealous type. I didn't need any more crazy men in my life.

"I want that one," I announced as I pointed to the white

one sittin' on chrome.

"How about we take her for a test drive?" Sonny suggested.

"That won't be necessary," Marc told him as he pulled out his black American Express card and handed it to Sonny.

He was smooth. You had to give him that.

I sat in my new car and played with all the controls while Marc and Sonny dealt with the paperwork. My cell phone rang. I looked at the caller ID. It was Isiah's cell phone number. I didn't want to answer, but I knew he would just keep letting it ring.

"What?"

"It's like that now?"

"Isiah, what do you want?" I asked in a tired voice.

"I want to know when you got to be such a cold-hearted bitch?"

"When I got with a punk-ass bitch like you," I shot back at him.

Now I knew I shouldn't have said it, but he should have never called fucking with me first.

"I knew you was a hoe the moment I met you."

"That makes two of us, you lil hoe-ass bitch!" I shouted into his ear then hung up.

If a bitch don't want to be with you, a bitch don't want to be with you. Calling her all kinds of bitches and hoes is not going to change that. My phone rang again.

"What, bitch?" I asked, not even looking to see who it was calling.

"Excuse me?" Marc asked.

"Baby, I'm sorry. I thought you were Isiah."

"Is he still playing on your phone?"

"Yeah. He just called."

"First thing tomorrow morning we're calling and getting your cell phone number changed," he said.

"Good idea. So, what were you callin' for?"

"I need you to come in and sign a few papers so you can have the car in your name."

"Alright, here I come."

I got off the phone and turned the car off. I took the keys out of the ignition then got out. As I turned around to walk toward the building, I saw the limo sitting across the street. I knew who it was. Those niggas had some nerve. I walked straight over there and knocked on the bulletproof glass. The window came down. It was Raymond and Gino.

"What the fuck do you think you're doin'?

"We're just doin' our jobs, Queen," Gino told me, knowing I was about to clown.

"Since when is it your job to follow me?"

"Since the boss told us to," he replied.

"Uncle Moe told you to follow me?"

"No, Isiah did."

"Isiah's not the boss."

"He is now," Raymond informed me.

"Did something happen to Uncle Moe?" I panicked.

"He's out of commission at the moment."

"What's wrong with him?"

"No offense, Queen, but maybe you should call and ask him that."

"What, I ain't family no more?" I asked with a little bit of an attitude.

"You still my girl, I just have orders to follow."

"This is real fucked up." I rolled my eyes then walked back across the street.

I couldn't even concentrate in Sonny's office. I wanted to

call and check on my Uncle Moe, but I knew that's what Isiah wanted me to do. I had something for his ass.

After signing my name on a zillion documents, I told Marc that I had some business I needed to handle and drove right over to my house. I didn't give a fuck who had set up shop there. It was still my house. I would close that bitch down if I so desired.

As soon as I got out of my new Bentley, I felt sick. I was standing right where it had all gone down. I tried to keep my composure, but it was hard. I looked down at the concrete and saw Jennifer's body lying there. She was covered in blood and riddled with bullet holes. Jimmy C was just a few inches away from her. He was the worst. Half of his head was gone and his leg was almost completely torn from his body. I didn't belong there anymore.

A car pulled up into the driveway. I didn't recognize it. It was a brand new BMW 760Li. Isiah got out of it. We just stood there looking at each other. I loved him so much. That was one thing I never wanted to feel again as long as I lived. Love was not for me. I just felt confused all the time. I couldn't do what I needed to do because I was always so worried about him. It wasn't like that with Marc. I loved being with him, but I wasn't in love with him and I didn't plan on falling.

"Nice car," he said as he admired my Bentley.

"Yours too."

I admired his BMW. It was alpine white with beige leather interior, sitting on some rims that looked like they cost at least eight grand.

"Why are you here?" he asked coldly like I didn't belong there anymore.

"This is still my home."

"I heard you have a new home now."

"I wonder who could have told you that?" I asked sarcastically as I threw my hands up on my hips.

"Doesn't matter. What matters is that we've both moved on."

My heart sank. Even though I was in a new relationship it hurt me to know that he was, too.

"If you moved on, then why the fuck have you been playin' on my phone like an idiot?"

"I'm sorry. Will you accept my apology?"

He seemed to be sincere, but I still wasn't buying it. It was too easy and if there was one thing we didn't do, it was easy.

"No, I don't accept yo' apology."

"Why not?" He smiled like he was getting the best of me.

"Because you don't mean it."

"Who are you to tell me what I do and don't mean?"

"I'm the bitch who knows you better than you know yo'self," I said with confidence. It was true. I knew him better than anyone ever could.

"Hey, I tried." He threw up his hands like he was giving up and started to walk away.

I quickly grabbed ahold of his Rocawear jacket and stopped him from bailing.

"You need to make up your mind. Either you want me or you don't," he told me directly.

"It's not that simple."

"Maybe not, but you're makin' it ten times harder than it has to be."

This time when he tried to walk away, I let him. I had no right to try to hold onto him while I was involved with

Cynthia White

another man.

I sat outside for a while. I needed the fresh air. Earlier that day I had been so sure of myself and now I was back to where I had started. I put aside my feelings long enough to go inside and see about Uncle Moe. He was in bed when I made it upstairs. It seemed that Raymond wasn't lying. He had seen the doctor the other day to make sure that he was healing properly from when he was shot. The doctor found a problem with his heart.

He had Hypertrophic Cardiomyopathy, also known as HCM. Unbeknownst to any of us, Uncle Moe had been having symptoms for a while. He had chest pain and pressure, fatigue, heart palpitations and shortness of breath. He also revealed that he had almost fainted several times. The doctor wanted to operate, but Uncle Moe refused. Why men had to be so stubborn all the damn time was beyond me. We talked for a while. It was starting to get late and he was starting to get tired, so I decided to leave.

Outside, I found Officer Jenkins in the driveway.

"Well, well, well, if it isn't the Queen of The Black Mafia." Officer Jenkins smiled smugly like he had something on me.

I knew he didn't. We both knew that I murdered Gauge, but he couldn't prove it, and that killed him.

"Good evening, Officer Jenkins." I smiled right back at his slick ass.

"How have you been?"

"Wonderful, and yourself?"

"Terrific. And how's Isiah? I hear he's the head nigger now."

"What the fuck did you just say?" I asked, totally disgusted by his cavalier racism.

"I'm sorry. I didn't offend you, did I?"

"Would it offend you if I called you a fat, greasy, cracker pig?" I asked in my sweetest, most innocent voice.

"You're walking a thin line," he threatened.

"So are you. Consider yo'self warned."

"Was that a threat, Ms. Aaron?" he asked.

"No, that was warning."

He took a few steps closer and bent down so that he could whisper into my ear. "It felt so good when I slapped those cuffs on your father." His breath was almost as vile as he was.

"You arrested my father?" I asked, fuming.

"You're damn right I did, and I enjoyed every moment of it. I thought that busting Hershey Aaron was the highlight of my career, but it wasn't. The day I take you in is going to be ten times better."

I thought before I spoke. This was no time to get sloppy. "You don't have anything on me."

"Not yet."

"Not ever."

"You're a smug little bitch, you know that?"

He was pissed. I had him exactly where I wanted him. People did stupid things when they were angry and pigs were no exception. He grabbed me by the arm.

"Take yo' muthafuckin' hands off her!" Isiah yelled as he appeared from behind the front door.

I knew he would be watching me on the security camera.

"I'll be seeing you," Officer Jenkins told me as he loosened his grip on my arm.

"I can't wait." I smiled, never once letting him see me lose my cool.

He got into his car and drove off. He knew he was out of

Cynthia White

line. He had no reason to be there and certainly had no reason to put his hands on me.

"You okay?" Isiah asked me as he came over to check on me.

"Yeah. Thank you." I hugged him.

It was a reflex. He smelled so good. We both sensed that the hug was going on too long, but neither one of us pulled away. My eyes were closed the entire time. It wasn't until I heard a car door slam shut that I opened them.

"Nigga, no you didn't!" some loud broad yelled as she snaked her neck and put her hands up on her hips.

"Nikki, get back in the car," Isiah told the classless broad.

"You told me you didn't fuck wit' her no more!" she yelled.

That's when I remembered that Isiah told me earlier that he had moved on. All of a sudden, I was having pains in my chest. I realized my heart was breaking. I turned around and walked toward my car. Normally I would have jumped stupid and fought the broad, but he was no longer my man to fight over.

"Queen, wait a minute." Isiah ran and caught up to me.

"I gotta go. I shouldn't have come anyway."

"This is still yo' home."

"No, it's not." I kissed him on the cheek then got into my Bentley.

I had a new home now with a new man. I had to live with the choices I made. I still loved Isiah and I probably always would. Sometimes if you love something, the best thing you can do is release it.

chapter

Nine

IT WAS A WEDNESDAY EVENING. I was sitting on my brand new California king sleigh bed watching this show called *"America's Got Talent."* Brandy was one of the judges. All of a sudden, the wind started to blow heavily. At first I thought it was nothing, but the longer it lasted, the harder it got. I got out of bed and ran over to my window. I pulled back the curtains to see trees being ripped out of the ground. I got a little scared. Then it started to rain like crazy. I reached for the phone to call Marc just as the power went out.

My penthouse was pitch black. I felt my way around to my nightstand. I opened up the top drawer and took out a strawberry scented candle. I struck a match and lit it. At least I could see a little bit. I owned all cordless phones, so they were completely useless to me now. I found my cell phone and as usual, I had forgotten to charge it. I was fucked.

Cynthia White

The storm only lasted about fifteen minutes, but it managed to shake up the entire city. Five hundred thousand people were without power. I was cool at first, but once it started to heat up, I couldn't take it. Outside it was well over ninety degrees. There was no breeze and no electricity to even plug in a fan. An hour passed. I felt like I was stranded on a deserted island. My elevator wasn't working and there was no way I was climbing twenty-one flights of stairs. I was stuck. I just knew that they would have the power up and running soon. I was wrong.

The next day was much the same. No air conditioning and no telephones. My refrigerator was warm. I was dying for a glass of ice water. No such luck. The ice had melted along with all of my ice cream and popsicles.

"Who the fuck is this?" I asked myself out loud as somebody banged on my door like they were the police.

I was surprised when I saw that it was Isiah. He was holding two plastic shopping bags.

"Can I come in?" he asked, out of breath.

"Yeah, come on." I stepped aside and let him in.

"Damn, it's hot in here."

He put the bags down on the counter and removed the red Cardinals baseball cap from his head.

"What are you doin' here?"

"I just wanted to check on you. I brought you some ice and some snacks."

"Thank you." I smiled.

It was good to know that through all the bullshit, he still cared about me.

"Do you have a cooler?"

"Yeah, it's in that closet over there." I pointed it out to him.

He went over and retrieved it. The two bags of ice he brought almost filled it completely. He went over to the refrigerator and took out several bottles of water. After he finished putting them in, he put in a few cans of soda. I couldn't wait to drink some cold water. My mouth felt like it was filled with cotton.

"Well, I'm gonna go."

"You don't have to," I blurted out.

"You sho?"

"Yeah."

"Won't Marc get mad?"

"Marc's not here."

"He hasn't been to check on you?" He sounded genuinely shocked.

"Not yet. Is the power off at the house?" I asked, trying to change the subject.

"Yeah, but they were workin' on it when I left. The guy told me it would be at least a couple more hours."

"I ain't even see anybody workin' over here."

I walked out onto the terrace. There was a nice breeze blowing. I leaned over the railing and threw my head back. My hair blew wildly in the wind. I stood there with my eyes closed, feeling free and uninhibited. I felt Isiah come up behind me. His body was warm. I let him touch me even though I knew it was wrong. He ran his hands up my thighs. I felt his dick grow hard, pressed up against my ass. He pushed up my pink Baby Phat mini-skirt. I wasn't wearing any panties, so his fingers entered me with ease.

"Uhm ..." I moaned in pleasure.

He always knew how to touch me in the right spot at just the right moment. My pussy was so wet that I was sure if I looked down, I would be standing in a huge puddle.

Cynthia White

"I missed this pussy, ma," he whispered in my ear as he kissed and sucked my neck. Things were getting out of control very quickly. Neither one of us was strong enough to stop. The next sound I heard was the zipper on his Polo jeans coming down. He pushed himself inside me and I swear I had never felt that good in my life. The sensation was intense. I raised my right leg up on the railing so that he could murder the pussy. It hurt so damn good. I wanted to tell him to stop but I would have been a damn fool to do that. He worked it out like it still belonged to him. Maybe in his mind it did. I didn't once think about Marc. He wasn't there. He didn't care enough to come and check on me. Isiah was there when it mattered. Anybody could be there during the good times but it's the ones who stay during the bad times who are true.

We did our thang on the terrace for almost an hour before the heat and humidity began to get to us. I knew that my new neighbors were probably watching us, but I didn't care. Maybe they learned something.

We both went inside and grabbed a cold bottle of water. I felt like I was about to pass out. I knew I was dehydrated, but I refused to drink warm water. It just didn't sit well on my stomach. I hopped up on the kitchen counter and continued to drink my water. As I lowered the bottle, I noticed the way Isiah was smiling at me.

"What's funny?" I asked as I narrowed my eyes at him.

"You," he smirked.

"What about me?"

"You really wanna know?"

"I asked, didn't I?"

"The only reason you fucked me was because you know I got a new gal." He laughed.

"A new gal? First of all, I don't give a fuck about that bitch. You can dress her up all you want to, but she still ain't me. Second, you was the one all up in my ear talkin' about how much you missed this pussy so don't get it twisted. I fucked you because I wanted to, not because I'm jealous of some nothin-ass bitch. There's only one Queen and you're lookin' at her."

I was arrogant at times, but I felt I had a right to be. Obviously, so did he. He came over and stood between my legs. I was still a little sore, but I didn't mention it to him. I didn't want to blow up his big head any more. He looked me in my eyes. I hated when he did that. I felt like he could see into my soul, like he knew all my secrets, insecurities and fears.

"You know I still love you, right?" he asked me as he kissed me on the neck.

"I know."

"And no matter how much you deny it, I know you still love me."

I smiled. It felt good to hear him say it. He kissed me on the forehead. I felt safe and protected.

"I gotta go," he told me, completely ruining the moment.

"Why?"

"It felt good bein' with you again, but I can't do this. You got a man. I wish I could say it doesn't bother me, but it does. I want you all to myself. I don't wanna share with anybody else."

"So you just gonna leave me, too?" I asked, feeling abandoned by everyone who claimed to care about me.

"You left me, remember?"

"Isiah, I'm sorry if I hurt you," I said as I looked up at

Cynthia White

him with tears in my eyes.

"I know you are." He kissed me on the cheek then left out the front door.

I had so much time to think. I had screwed things up so bad. I wished I was more controlled and patient like my father. Unfortunately, I had inherited my mother's irrational ways. I hated admitting that I was anything like her, but I figured that coming clean to myself was the first step.

My power was off for a full week. Seven days without any of the luxuries and amenities I was so used to having was pure hell. I realized just how pampered and spoiled I really was. I had to clean out my refrigerator and throw everything out. Almost two hundred dollars worth of meat and produce was ruined. I just sucked it up and went grocery shopping again. There was nothing else I could do.

Later that day, I went to the prison to see my daddy. I was still extremely upset with him for not being honest with me.

"Hey, baby."

That smile wasn't going to work this time.

"Don't 'hey baby' me. Daddy, I am so furious with you right now. Why didn't you tell me you were gettin' executed?" I asked him with tears in my eyes.

Just saying the word "executed" hurt.

"I'm sorry, baby. I just didn't want to put you through anything more. Your life shouldn't be this complicated."

"But isn't that my decision to make?"

"Queen, when a man has a daughter, the only thing he wants to do is protect her. I've always tried to do what's best for you. Sometimes I fail, but I still must continue to try."

"Daddy, I know you love me and you know I love you, but I'm a big girl now. I can take care of myself."

"I know you can. You are so strong and independent. I knew that if I told you about the execution, you would just worry and get yourself all stressed out. You're a young woman. You should be out living life."

"I feel like I don't even know you right now."

"Well, that makes two of us because sometimes I feel like I don't even know myself."

"What now?"

"Now you move on with your life."

"What about you?"

"Baby, this is my life now. I'm never getting out of here."

He was honest with me for the first time since he had gotten locked up. I stayed at the prison as long as they would allow me. I wanted to spend as much time with my daddy as possible before he was taken away from me.

I was walking to the restroom when a fine young corrections officer approached me.

"You must be Queen." He smiled.

"And you are?"

"My name's Patrick. Your father and I have become good friends."

"Well any friend of my father's is a friend of mine." I shook his hand.

"He talks about you all the time."

"We're very close."

"Yeah, he told me."

"What else has he told you?" I asked suspiciously.

"Just that you're a good girl who's been dealt a fucked up hand."

"That's my daddy. He's always tryin' to justify the fucked up shit I do."

"He loves you. Besides, that's what fathers do."

Cynthia White

"Do you have any children?"

"Just one, a little girl. Her name is Dominique. She's four," he said with pride.

"I used to want a little girl."

"And now?"

"Now I don't."

"You don't want a girl or you just don't want kids at all?"

"Not at all."

"I'm sorry to hear that."

"Why?"

"I love my daughter to death. I can't imagine my life without her. Even though things didn't work out with me and her mother, I don't regret having her. She makes my life worth livin'. I can't imagine anyone missin' out on that feeling."

"I don't need a baby to make my life worth livin'," I said with attitude.

"That's not what I meant."

"It doesn't matter. What was your point?"

"My point is I have a lot of respect for your father."

"And?"

"And, so do a lot of people in here." He gave me a look that told me to search for the hidden meaning.

I got it. He was basically telling me that there were people inside who wanted to help my father.

Patrick and I exchanged phone numbers. If there was any chance that my father could get out, I had to explore it. I knew that it was a long shot, so I didn't get my hopes up. I had bigger problems at the moment. I decided that I no longer wanted to be in a relationship with Marc. I did care about him, but that was as far as it went. It wasn't that I wanted to break up with him so that I could go running back

to Isiah, it was something I had to do for myself. I was prepared to give back all the gifts he had bought me, even the Bentley and the penthouse. It was time for me to figure out who I was without a man. I was either Hershey Aaron's daughter, Isiah's fiancée or Marc's young girlfriend. I just wanted to be me.

*****

When I went back to my penthouse, Marc was there.

"Hey, baby." He had the nerve to greet me like nothing was wrong.

For days I had sat in the place with no power, no air conditioning and no water, and he didn't even think to come and check on me.

"Marc, we need to talk."

"About?"

"About us. This isn't workin' for me."

"In what way?"

"Well, for one, you're still married."

"I told you, if I divorce her, she'll take half of everything I own."

"So, she already has half of everything you own. Just be man enough to say that you want us both."

"Fine, I want you both," he confessed.

"You can't have it like that. You can't have me like that. I know you love her and I understand. I don't want you to leave her for me. I'm goin' to be mature enough to leave you for her sake. She deserves betta."

"So this is your way out? You're going to act like you care about her?"

"I do care about her. She was my best friend's mother. I've known her since I was a little girl. I should have never slept with you, but I did and I can't take that back. All I can

Cynthia White

do is walk away and hope that you two can work things out."

"You got everything you wanted out of me and now you're done, huh?"

"Is that what you think this is about? Marc, I appreciate everything you did for me, but it's not like I had nothin' when I met you. I'm only leavin' with what I came with. You can keep this place and you can keep everything else."

I tried not to end things on a bad note, but that seemed impossible. It was what it was. We both knew it wouldn't last forever. Everything has its season and ours had come and gone.

I moved back home that night. Uncle Moe was excited to have me back, but Isiah was overjoyed. He still had a girlfriend, so I had no plans on getting involved with him all over again. I had to learn to think before I acted. That was my biggest fault. I was emotional, and I had a very hot temper – a very dangerous combination.

"I'm glad you're back." Isiah smiled at me as he watched me hang my clothes in my closet.

"Thank you. It's good to be back."

"How did Marc take it?"

"Not too well."

"I can imagine," he said.

"He'll be fine. He still has his wife."

"You don't get it, do you?"

"Get what?"

"The effect you have on men. No man wants to just fuck you and move on. They want to stand by you and be yo' king. Queen, you don't realize the power you hold. If you want something done, it gets done. You want someone dealt with, they get dealt with. You are one of the most influential women in the entire world, and you're not even eighteen yet. Can you imagine how things will be when you're twenty-five or thirty?" he asked with a spark in his eye.

It was then that I saw my future clearly for the first time.

That night, Uncle Moe arranged a special dinner to celebrate me coming back home. The entire Black Mafia was there. I was the only female in attendance. Even Isiah's new girlfriend wasn't there. I'd be lying if I said that didn't make me feel special. I scanned the room, looking at the face of each man who had put in crazy work. Even though Isiah was the newest member, he had done enough to earn their respect. Being Uncle Moe's son didn't make things easier for him. If anything, it made things harder. He knew that he had to work twice as hard and twice as much as anyone else.

"I'm so glad to have you back, baby." Uncle Moe smiled proudly as he put his arm around me.

"I'm glad to be back. I missed you."

"Your father told me you came to visit him."

"I did."

"How was it?" he asked.

"Betta than I expected. I was pissed off at him for not tellin' me he was bein' executed, but I understand why he did it."

"What about me? Do you forgive me?"

"I'll let you know when I'm done with this." I raised the fat-ass blunt that was in between my perfectly manicured fingers.

"So if that's some heat, I'm off the hook?"

"If? Come on now, Unc. You know I don't smoke no bullshit."

We both laughed. He knew I wasn't lying. I had been smoking weed ever since I was fourteen years old.

Cynthia White

"Have fun, baby. I have some work to do, but I'll see you later."

"Work? We suppose to be partyin'."

"Y'all don't need me to party. Besides, I need to go over the books with a fine-tooth comb. I think my accountant has been rippin' me off," he said in an irritated voice.

"If he's been rippin' you off that means he's been rippin' daddy off, too."

"Exactly." He kissed me on my cheek and went into daddy's office.

The celebration went on for hours. I had a great time with everyone, especially Isiah. It was well after three in the morning when I finally went upstairs and got into a hot tub of water. My cell phone rang. I wondered who it could be calling me at this time. I got up and walked my naked body over to the vanity where I had left my phone. I looked at the screen. I didn't recognize the number. I decided to answer it anyway.

"Hello."

"Hello, Queen. This is Patrick."

"Hi, Patrick." I don't know why, but I smiled.

Something about him gave me hope. Maybe it was him believing in my father or maybe it was just him not being involved in our lifestyle. He worked a regular job and had a normal, everyday life.

"Can you talk?"

"Yeah, what's up?"

"I need to meet with you in person to discuss some things."

"How about tomorrow?" I suggested.

"I get off work at eight. Meet me at my place."

"That's cool."

He proceeded to give me his address and home telephone number. I put all his information in my phone and tried to be patient. It was hard. I tried not to get overly excited, but that was also hard. I had so many things on my mind that I couldn't sleep that night. I kept thinking about daddy and how this might be his last chance. I had to find a way to make something happen, I just had to.

*****

The following day, I met Patrick at his place. The plan was simple. My father would be in bed pretending to be sick. Early the following morning, Patrick would notice that my father wasn't feeling well and take him to the infirmary. A struggle would break out. Patrick would end up getting knocked unconscious and daddy would escape, passing three guards who were all in on the plan. They would then wait twenty minutes before setting off the silent alarm. Patrick knew the system well. He also knew that many of the alarms were faulty and that many officers just ignored them systemwide.

We would pay them all off, of course. Five hundred thousand dollars was a lot of money to anyone, but to men who supported wives and children on less than forty thousand dollars a year, it was worth possibly losing their jobs.

*****

Everything went down as planned. I was outside waiting in a black Chevy Suburban with dark, tinted, bulletproof glass. I was more than a little nervous. What if this didn't work? What if something went wrong and daddy was killed trying to escape? I was delighted when he opened the door and climbed inside the truck. I hugged him so hard he could barely breathe. He didn't complain though. He just hugged me back and told me how much he loved me.

Cynthia White

As soon as he got into the truck, I went to work on changing his appearance. I shaved off all his hair. He had been growing it out for a few years now, and it had gotten quite long. Then I shaved off his goatee. I put all the hair into a plastic Ziploc bag.

"Put these in," I told him as I handed him a pair of bright green contacts.

Daddy's eyes were dark brown, so this was a complete change. He already looked like an entirely different person, but I wasn't done yet. I had daddy strip down to his boxers then I sprayed him down with my instant tan. Within minutes, his light skin was golden brown. He would blend right in with the native Mexicans. Next, I had daddy put on a fat suit that I had purchased online using an alias name and a prepaid credit card that could not be traced. It made daddy look sixty pounds heavier. I laughed out loud at the finished product. If I hadn't done it myself, I would have never believed it.

I dressed him in a pair of khaki shorts, an olive green button-down shirt and a pair of brown leather sandals. My father would never wear something so common, but that was the point. He was usually dressed in Armani suits and gator shoes but if this was going to work, we had to be smarter than law enforcement. We had to stay one step ahead of them at all times.

We crossed the border with no problems whatsoever. After switching from the Suburban to a Denali then to a Navigator, we finally settled in a plain black '96 Impala. It was just me and daddy now.

I was now wearing a short blond wig that was cut in a cute little bob. I had in a pair of pale blue contacts and more makeup than I had ever worn in my entire life. I, too, was

tanner than normal. My skin looked as if I had already been in Mexico lounging on the beach for the last two weeks. I wore a tiny red halter top, a pair of skin tight shorts and a pair of silver Baby Phat sandals with a five-inch wedge heel. I looked like a prostitute. The guard at the border even congratulated daddy on landing such a hot piece of ass. If he only knew.

It took us about two hours to get to the safe house. Daddy pulled the Impala into the garage. The door came down behind us then daddy cut off the engine. We had done it. I looked over at daddy. He was completely still. I wondered what he was thinking. He closed his eyes. I knew he was talking to God. Exactly what he was saying to him, I didn't know.

When his eyes opened, they were glassy. I knew he was fighting back tears. He turned and looked at me. I smiled at him.

"I love you so much, daddy." I reached over and hugged him.

"I love you, too, baby."

"Can you believe we pulled this off?"

"No, you pulled this off. This was all you. The more I get to know you, the more amazed I become. You're not a little girl anymore, are you?"

"No, daddy, I'm not."

"You're so much like me that it scares me."

"I didn't think anything scared you, daddy."

"Queen, I want you to promise me something."

"Anything, daddy."

"If we get caught, you let me take the blame," he commanded.

"But daddy..."

Cynthia White

"Queen, please? I need to know that if they come for me, you'll let them take me quietly and go along with whatever story I tell them."

"Okay, if that's what you want." I gave in.

"It is."

It didn't take us long to get settled. The heat in Mexico was absurd, but once we turned on the AC, it didn't take long for the house to cool off. There were five bedrooms and seven bathrooms. Daddy and I chose rooms right next to each other. We talked for a while about any and everything. I lay on the sofa just watching him as he sat across from me on the loveseat. Even though he looked drastically different, he was still my daddy at heart.

I closed my eyes briefly and fell into a deep sleep. I was exhausted. It wasn't just the events that had transpired that day. The past few years had been very trying. So much had changed. So many people were no longer there. I had done things I never imagined I was capable of doing.

I didn't dream, or at least if I did, I didn't remember. I just know that when I woke up, I felt so serene. I figured that it was just having my father there with me, but it was more than that. Something told me to look in my purse. I got up off the couch and retrieved my Fendi bag. I began to look through it even though I had no idea what I was searching for. Then I found it. There was a plain white envelope with my name beautifully written on the front in cursive. I recognized it immediately. It was Jennifer's handwriting. Then I realized that this was the first time I had carried that bag since I let her borrow it three years ago when she went to visit Rico in New York. I was nervous but I opened it anyway. Inside there was a letter. I began to read it.

Dear Queen,

New York is fabulous! The shopping is to die for and the niggas are fine as hell. I'm sitting here in my hotel room missing you like crazy. Things didn't go as well with Rico as I had hoped. He told me that he still loves me but that he can no longer commit to me. Just what the fuck that means I'm not sure but I do know that I wish you were here. I feel silly calling all the time. I've only been gone for two days. I shouldn't have come. I feel so stupid. I knew deep down that we were over but I still continued to hope. He was my first love. I wonder if he ever really loved me? Was I just some stupid little girl who he used then threw away when it was no longer convenient? Did he use me? On second thought, I don't think I really want to know. The only thing that brings me comfort right now is knowing that tomorrow I'll be on a plane flying back home to see my best friend. I don't know if I'll ever give you this letter, but I had to write it. You are the only person in my life who I can really count on. You have always been there for me and I know that you always will. I love you so much that I can't imagine my life without you. I'm a better person just for knowing you.

Your best friend for life,
Jennifer (AKA Jenny from the block)

I didn't know whether to laugh or cry, so I did a little of both. I knew that Jennifer was looking out for me. I folded the letter back up and put it back inside the envelope. I put the envelope inside my purse so that I could take it out and

Cynthia White

read it whenever I needed to be reminded of how lucky I was. Even though I had lost my best friend, I was lucky to have her in my life as long as I did. That day, my whole outlook on life changed. None of us knows how long we'll be here. Every day that we wake up is a blessing. From that moment on, I fully intended to treat each day as if it were a gift from God.

I got my ass off the couch and cooked breakfast for daddy and me. I made French toast, scrambled eggs, sausage and turkey bacon. I poured us two tall glasses of orange juice then we headed outside. We sat down at the table next to the pool and ate. Time seemed to be moving slower than normal. I watched my daddy smile and laugh and knew that no matter what, no one could take these memories away from me.

chapter

Ten

WE HAD BEEN IN MEXICO FOR seven weeks with no contact from the outside world. There were no telephones in
the house, and I was forbidden from bringing my cell with
me. We didn't even have a TV. Luckily, I had packed enough
books to keep my mind occupied for a while. Daddy didn't
have anything, so we just talked a lot. He told me about the
old days when he and Uncle Moe were just getting started.
He told me about all the women who came before my mother. One name that kept popping up was a woman named
Theresa. I could tell by the way that daddy talked about her
that she was once the love of his life. She had walked away
from him when she found out what he really did for a living.
That was back before The Black Mafia, but daddy was still a
gangsta. Some women couldn't handle the life. It's stressful
and dangerous, but worst of all it's the fact that you'll more
than likely lose the man you love.

Daddy also told me about Isiah's mother, Iesha. She was

Cynthia White

the love of Uncle Moe's life. She accepted him for the man he was, flaws and all. Unlike most women, she had no problem with his line of work. All that mattered to her was that he was faithful to her and treated her well. He was, and he did. Daddy said that Uncle Moe never even looked at other women. Iesha was his heart and soul. They were together for two years before Isiah was born. That's when things started to change. It was around that time that daddy and Uncle Moe were becoming large. They were seeing more money than they ever had. They were also becoming bigger targets. Big money came with big problems. There was always another crew out to take you down.

Isiah was only five years old when three men came into his family's home in the middle of the night. Uncle Moe was out of town so they had the perfect chance to prove their point, which was that they could get to his family. They held a gun to Isiah's head while Iesha watched. She cried and pleaded with the masked men. Then they began to beat her. It was so bad that she had to have reconstructive surgery on her face and nose. When Uncle Moe returned home, he found out who did it and put them to sleep. Still, he couldn't live with the fact that his woman and his son would constantly be in danger because of what he chose to do with his life. He walked away from them right then and there. He provided for them financially, but that's where it ended.

"Why doesn't he just tell Isiah?" I asked daddy like he had all the answers.

"I don't know, baby. Your Uncle Moe is a very complicated man."

"All the men in my life are complicated."

"Even Isiah?"

"Especially Isiah." I laughed as I recalled some of the shit

we had been through.

"You love him, don't you?" daddy asked with a glimmer in his eyes.

"Very much."

"So why aren't you with him?" he asked.

"Daddy, do you really want to go there?"

"I'm just curious."

"I love Isiah, but it's a very different kind of love than I'm used to."

"How do you mean?"

"He's the first thing I think about when I wake up. I wanna be with him all the time. I think about him all day. I worry about him constantly," I gushed.

"That's how you know you're really in love with him."

"Well, I don't wanna be."

"You can't control your heart," he advised.

"Oh, believe me, I know. I've tried. I've done everything in my power to try to get myself to stop lovin' him, but I can't. I've even done some horrible things to get him to stop lovin' me."

"And did it work?"

"I don't know."

As I sat there thinking, I heard knocking at the back door. I looked over at daddy. He put his finger up to his mouth to signal to me not to make a sound. He got up and walked toward the back door. He peeked through the blinds then let out a loud laugh. I got up and walked over to him just in time to see Uncle Moe and Isiah come through the door. I stood there frozen as Isiah wrapped his arms around me. That was the answer to daddy's question. It didn't work. He still loved me and no matter how much I protested, I damn sure still loved him.

Cynthia White

We left daddy and Uncle Moe to talk in private, and went into my bedroom. I shut and locked the door behind us. We sat down on my bed. For a while, neither one of us said a thing. I just wanted to look at him. Seven weeks had felt like an eternity without him. I took a deep breath and inhaled his aroma. He smelled good as usual. He smiled at me. I knew what he was thinking. I blushed. I don't know why, but I felt so special at that moment. He reached for me but I pulled back.

"What?"

"Last time I checked, you had a girlfriend."

"Things have changed," he said.

"You broke up with her?"

"I had to."

"Why?"

"I didn't love her," he confessed.

"Do you still love me?" I asked, not sure if I really wanted to hear the answer.

"Don't ask me a silly-ass question like that. I've always loved you."

"I've always loved you, too," I admitted.

"Why didn't you tell me that you were breakin' yo' father out of prison?"

"I didn't have time. Everything just happened so fast. Patrick called and—"

"Who's Patrick?"

"One of the guards at the prison."

"I see," he said angrily.

"It's not like that."

"Did you fuck him?"

"No," I answered in a way that let him know he had offended me.

"I'm sorry."

"No, I'm sorry. After all the fucked up shit I did to you, you have every right to be suspicious."

"I just want things to go back to the way they were."

"So do I."

I looked up at him with tears in my eyes. It was all worth it for that one perfect moment. He reached over and touched my face softly. I closed my eyes. I remembered our first time together. It was good then, but this time would be even better. As we kissed, my heart began to beat faster and faster. I felt like a virgin anticipating her first time. His hand fell from my face to my neck. I knew where he was going next. My breasts were in his hands, my leg was on his lap and my tongue was in his mouth.

It didn't take long for him to get my shorts off. His tongue was just as warm and as soft as I remembered. I rubbed his head as he licked and sucked me. I arched my back and rolled my hips becoming completely lost in ecstasy. By the time our bodies joined together, I was gone in the head. His dick pushed inside me like it knew it belonged there. I didn't want to stop but even if I did, I couldn't. We were back where we had started. I wasn't sure if that was a good thing or a bad thing. Only time would tell. For now, I was just grateful to be loved by such a strong, powerful man.

Uncle Moe and Isiah couldn't stay long. They didn't want to draw more suspicion to the family. But for the five days they were in Mexico, I forgot about all the bad things that awaited me back home. I wasn't for sure if I would ever return home. My daddy was with me and that's where we needed to be, at least for the present time. I knew that I couldn't be separated from Isiah for the rest of my life, but what I didn't know was that it wouldn't be long at all.

Cynthia White

*****

Eleven weeks after my father escaped from prison, he was captured. I was devastated. I fought the pigs with everything I had. They picked me up and threw me in the back of an unmarked car, and I cried as I watched them beat my father. He never resisted, yet they brutalized him over and over again. I tried not to panic, but I knew it was the end. It was over. We had lost.

I was taken to jail, but I wasn't locked up. They put me in a holding room where I sat and waited for two and a half hours. I was bored out of my mind. All I could do was think, and I was tired of doing that. The only thing on my mind was my daddy's execution. I tried real hard not to cry. It was time for me to be strong now. I had to keep it together.

"Your father told us that you were unaware of his plan to escape from prison," my court appointed lawyer told me.

"Did he really?" I asked sarcastically.

"Yes, he did. He also informed us that he took you against your will." He looked over at me like he was waiting for an answer.

I offered him none. I had nothing to say. I wasn't about to sell my father out.

"Does your line of questioning have a point, Mister ..."

"...White."

"Mr. White, of course." I laughed.

His white ass just looked at me like a deer caught in the headlights. He had no clue. This was the man they expected me to confide in. He didn't give a fuck about me, and he damn sure didn't give a fuck about my father.

"Ms. Aaron, do you have a problem with me?" he asked as he ran his hand through his over-gelled hair.

"Yes, I do."

"Why?"

"I would never expect you to understand."

"Why, because I'm white?"

"That's a big part of it," I told him honestly.

"I assure you that the color of my skin has no bearing on my—"

"Look, I really don't give a fuck! You wanna do somethin' for me, call 555-7010 and ask for Isiah. Tell him to call my lawyer."

"Your lawyer?"

"Yes, I'm sure you've heard of him, Buck Malone."

"Buck Malone? He's the one of the best lawyers in the country."

"I know. That's why I hired him." I smirked.

Buck got me out in a matter of hours. There was nothing he could do for daddy. His fate had been sealed.

Isiah picked me up at the police station and drove me home. We didn't talk much in the limo. I wasn't really in the mood to socialize. I had so much on my mind. I was glad to see him, but I was also looking forward to taking a long, hot shower. Just being around all those pigs made me feel dirty.

"You wanna stop and get something to eat?" Isiah asked me as we rode in the back of the limo.

"Nah, I'm not hungry."

"You have to eat, Queen," he pleaded.

"I know. I'm just not hungry right now."

"You just wanna go straight home?"

"Yeah."

I stared out the window and thought about my father. I wondered if they were still beating him. I wanted to see him. I wanted to talk to him. I just needed to make sure he was alright.

Cynthia White

"What are you thinkin' about?"

"Same ole, same ole."

"Yo' father?"

"Yeah."

"He knows how much you love him."

"And I know how much he loves me, but I still miss him," I said sadly.

"I know you do, baby, but at least you had these last few months together. That's somethin'."

"Yeah, that's somethin'." I continued to stare out the window.

The first thing I did when we made it home was take that shower and wash my hair. When I got through, I lay on my bed completely naked with my bedroom window open enjoying the night air. Isiah joined me a few minutes later. He lay down beside me and fired up a fat-ass blunt. It felt good to be high again. I didn't get blowed once in Mexico. Daddy didn't know that I smoked, and I wasn't about to let him find out. I had done a lot of scandalous shit, but I was still his daughter. No matter how old I got, he would always think of me as his little girl. I wouldn't have wanted it any other way.

"I'm goin' out of town tomorrow," he told me as he exhaled a thick cloud of white smoke.

"Tomorrow? Can I go?"

"Not this time."

"So you're just gonna leave me here all alone?" I instantly copped an attitude.

"You won't be alone."

"I'm always alone," I whined then turned my back to him.

Naked or not, I was taking a stand. If he thought he was

going anywhere without me, he was sadly mistaken.

"Queen, baby, don't be like that."

He rubbed my back. I didn't respond. He kissed me soft-ly on the shoulder. Still I said nothing. He ran his hand down the curve of my hip then between my legs. He played with my pussy and though I moaned, I still said nothing. He couldn't make it better with sexual favors. I appreciated the face he gave me, but I was still mad.

*****

The next morning, we boarded daddy's private plane and flew to South America. If Isiah thought he was going any-where without me, he had me all fucked up. Even though I hated to fly, I was packed and ready to go. Once we got in the air, I was singing a different tune. I had my eyes closed the entire time. My stomach was in knots. I was trying to be a soldier, but the princess inside me was screaming to get out. To make things worse, it was an extremely long, turbu-lent flight. As soon as the plane landed, I ran out and put my feet on solid ground.

Brazil was gorgeous. Rio reminded me a lot of Miami. Daddy had taken me and Jennifer for our fourteenth birth-days. We thought we were so grown up because he got us our own suite. Even though he was right across the hall, it was very liberating. We stayed up all night eating junk food and watching scary movies. Jennifer told me all about her sex life. I had nothing to tell. My first and only time had been against my will. Even then, I knew that I would carry it with me for the rest of my life.

"Welcome to Rio de Janeiro," some fine-ass, young Brazilian tender greeted us at the small airport.

"Thank you." Isiah shook his hand.

"And who is this beautiful young lady?"

Cynthia White

"This is Queen."

"Nice to meet you, Queen." He kissed my hand.

"Likewise." I smiled and batted my long eyelashes.

"Have you been to Rio before?"

"Yes. My father loved it here."

"Your father was a traveling man?"

"Yes, he was." I smiled politely.

Back at the house, I got to meet the head of the South American cartel. I didn't get his name and I knew better than to ask it. He was an older man with dark skin, dark hair and cold dark eyes. He was not somebody I would ever want to get to know. There was something evil in his stare. I didn't like the way he looked at me when he didn't think Isiah was paying attention. One thing I knew about Isiah was that he was always paying attention.

"I'm sorry to keep staring at you like that young lady, but you look so familiar to me. Are you from California?"

"No, I'm not. I'm from St. Louis. I stayed in California for a few months with my father. That was a couple of years ago."

"What was his name?"

"Hershey Aaron."

"*The* Hershey Aaron?"

He, too, had heard of the legend.

"The one and only." I smiled.

"How is he? I heard that he murdered his wife." He actually had the audacity to say it out loud.

I couldn't believe how poor his manners were. You would think that a man that rich would have a little class. I guess money can't buy everything.

"No offense, but we really have to be gettin' back home." Isiah stepped in, realizing how uncomfortable I was getting.

"Of course. I didn't mean to overstep my bounds. I apologize. That was very insensitive of me. I know it must be hard to talk about your father."

"Yes, it is," I admitted.

I just sat there and watched him for the remainder of the meeting. They were speaking business, and I was supposed to be ignorant to all of that. What does a woman know about running a multi-million dollar organization? They didn't give me an ounce of credit, but I didn't care. I was just there for decoration. It was my job to simply smile and look pretty. They weren't as smart as they thought they were. I made a mental record of everything that was said. If those fools could run an empire that large, so could Isiah. All he needed was a little help from me.

*****

We returned a week and a half later, glad to be back home. Although the United States had its problems, I wouldn't want to live anywhere else. A limo awaited us and drove us home. I hugged Uncle Moe then went up to my room to allow he and Isiah time to talk business. I sat down on my bed and reached for the phone, but I stopped myself. I was about to dial Jennifer's number. I was so used to calling her after every trip and dishing all the dirt. I had nobody to call. I don't know why, but I found myself dialing Patrick's number. He answered on the third ring.

"Hello."

"Hey, it's Queen."

"Queen, how are you?" he asked, sounding glad to hear from me.

"I'm good."

"I'm glad you called."

"You are?" I asked.

Cynthia White

"Yeah, I wanted to talk to you, but I didn't know if I should call."

"Why?"

"Things are complicated. They transferred me and all the other guys who were on duty the night your father escaped."

"I'm sorry. I never meant to get you in trouble."

"I'm fine. I'd really like to talk more, but I can't really get into this over the phone. You doin' anything later?"

"Not that I know of."

"I get off at nine. Can you meet me at my place around nine thirty?"

"I'll be there."

I hung up the phone not knowing why exactly I had agreed to meet him. Our business was finished. He no longer worked at the prison where my father was being held; therefore, he was no use to me anymore. Still, I made plans to be at his apartment at nine thirty.

When I got to Patrick's apartment, he was sitting in his Ford Expedition smoking a blunt. I got out of my Benz and joined him. For being a corrections officer, this nigga sure did love to break the law. If he wanted to be a renegade, he was hanging around the right bitch. His weed was fire and soon I was high as a kite. We went inside and sat in his living room. It was nicely decorated, which told me that even though he claimed to be single, there was a woman in his life.

"So did they question you after my father escaped?"

"For damn near twelve hours."

"I'm sorry. I should've never involved you."

"I wanted to be involved. I approached you. Remember?" he asked.

"I remember."

"I don't want you to blame yourself for anything."

"Easier said than done."

"Queen, why are you so hard on yourself?"

"I have to be," I said.

"Why?"

"You would never understand."

"Try me."

"I owed my father. This was my one chance to make things right, and I fucked it up."

"You didn't fuck it up. He got to be free for eleven weeks. That's a lifetime for a man in your father's situation," he reassured me.

"I just wish I could have been a betta daughter to him."

"Could he have been a betta father to you?"

"Not in a million years." I smiled as I thought about all the time I had spent with my father.

He was more of a parent than my mother ever was. He was the one who took me shopping on the weekends. He helped me with my school projects and came to parent-teacher conferences. He took me and Jennifer out for ice cream every Saturday after ballet class. He even tagged along on boring-ass field trips. There was no way he could have done anything better or been more attentive. I knew that perfection didn't exist, but if it did, it would have lived inside my daddy.

Patrick and I talked for a while. We got to know each other better than we did during our first few encounters. He told me how he never knew his father. Growing up, it was just him, his mother and his younger brother. They lived in poverty until Patrick was old enough to help out. To my surprise, I found out that he used to hustle when he was

Cynthia White

younger. He started when he was fourteen and didn't stop until his baby brother got murdered when he was twenty-two. I could tell by the sadness in his eyes that it was still very painful for him. They must have been very close, probably as close as Jennifer and I were. If losing his brother hurt half as bad as losing Jen, he must have been in agony. Jennifer wasn't my sister in blood, but I couldn't have loved her more if she was.

I stayed at Patrick's place for a few hours. It was nice to talk to someone who wasn't part of the family. I could see us developing a very strong friendship. Even though I thought he was sexy, I would never pursue anything sexual with him. I had already hurt Isiah enough. I promised myself that this time would be different. I was going to focus all of my energy on being the woman I wanted to be. I wanted Isiah to be proud to be my man. I wanted other men to envy him and not just because I was the princess of The Black Mafia, but because I was loyal to him and I honored him. I wanted to cook him dinner and run his bath. I giggled as I pictured us in our mid-thirties, married with kids.

It didn't strike me as odd when I pulled up into the driveway of my house and saw four police cars sitting there. What the fuck did they want? I parked my Benz and took a deep breath. I grabbed my Kate Spade handbag and got out the car. I walked up to the front door and greeted Gino. He was posted at Jimmy C's old spot. I guess that was the circle of life. You die only to get replaced a short while later.

I got a chill as I walked through the front door. Something was wrong. The only thing I heard was the sound of my three-inch heels clicking as I rushed to daddy's office. My heart sank when I saw Isiah in handcuffs. I looked over at Officer Jenkins. He smirked at me. How could I hate someone so much that I barely even knew? He was arrogant and not in a good way. I knew then that something had to be done about this nuisance. He was quickly becoming a major pain in my ass.

"Good evening, Ms. Aaron," his ugly ass greeted me, pretending to be polite. He was no gentleman.

"It was."

"Not happy to see me?"

"Officer Jenkins, is anybody ever happy to see you?"

"Nobody in this house," he said icily.

"Or yo' own for that matter."

"How does such a pretty girl end up with such an ugly attitude?"

"I'm sorry," I apologized. "If I've been rude, I truly am sorry. My allergies have really been bothering me a lot lately." I put my hand on my head and softened my body language.

"I understand. I have allergies myself. What are you allergic to?"

"Pork," I spat at him.

He wasn't amused, but everybody else in the room was. The laughter was infectious. Even the other officers were game.

"You think you're so funny, don't you?"

"I don't *think* anything." I smiled sweetly. Ever since I first laid eyes on that swine, I knew he was going to be trouble. There was something deeper there. Something I had to get to the bottom of.

"Your fiancé was just telling me how you had nothing to do with your father's escape."

"How do you know he's my fiancé?" I wanted to know. I was suspicious on a good day, but lately I was downright

Cynthia White

paranoid.

"I know a lot of things."

"Yeah, about me and my family."

"Family?" he asked sarcastically then laughed as if he was auditioning for the role of an evil villain in some cheesy movie. "Queen, I hate to be the one to inform you of this, but you have no family. Your mother is dead and your father is about to join her."

"You watch yo' muthafuckin' mouth!" I shouted as I jumped up in his face, ready to go to jail if need be.

"You know what I wonder? Why is it that when I mention your mother I get no reaction at all, but the moment I bring up your father, you're ready to risk your own freedom to defend him?"

"It's called loyalty. I would never expect you to understand."

"Why no loyalty to your mother?"

"Why are you so interested in my life?"

"Just making conversation." He tried to breeze by me. It wasn't happening. I knew he had it out for me, but I didn't know why.

"I'm getting' real sick of yo' bullshit, Officer Jenkins. I've tried to be nice, but you don't appreciate that. I've even tried to ignore you and your idiotic comments, but you don't appreciate that either."

"Is this where I'm supposed to get scared? Little girl, you don't frighten me."

"No, because you don't have the good sense to be frightened. I might be a little girl, but I'm a very well-connected little girl."

"Do your worst."

"Is that a challenge?" I narrowed my eyes at him.

He gave no response, but I could tell by the look in his eyes that he wanted a war. So be it.

I called Buck. He was there in twenty minutes. I knew it was going to cost me, but at that point I didn't care. Buck informed Officer Jenkins that if he did not take the handcuffs off of Isiah and leave the house at once he was going to sue the department for harassment. I didn't even know you could do that. Apparently you could because the cuffs came off of Isiah and Jenkins and the other pigs got gone. They had entered our home without a warrant. They had no reason to cuff Isiah and really no reason to even be there. They were just fishing and unfortunately for them they were using the wrong bait.

"Where were you earlier?" Isiah asked me when we were finally alone.

"I went to see Patrick."

"The nigga who works at the prison?"

"Yeah."

"What the fuck you go see him for?" he asked angrily.

"He wanted to talk."

"About what?"

"Everything," I said.

"So what, y'all friends now?"

"Yeah, we're cool."

"Cool, huh?"

"Don't start that shit!" I yelled.

"I don't want you seein' that nigga, and I damn sure don't want you at his place."

"Why not? I told you we're just cool. There's nothin' else goin' on." He was really starting to piss me off. I was really telling the truth.

"Like there was nothin' goin' on with Marc?"

Cynthia White

"That's not fair."

"It may not be fair, but it's true." He grabbed his jacket off the chair and left.

I knew I had hurt him, but I didn't know how bad. I realized that just because I said I was sorry didn't mean that all the damage was washed away. I still had a lot of work to do if I wanted to get back what we had lost.

*****

Isiah was gone all night. I woke up just about every hour expecting to see him on the other side of my bed, but I never did. I finally gave up all hope at seven in the morning.

I had to get up and get ready for school. I didn't really want to go, but I had missed way too much already, and I had to pull it together if I wanted to graduate on time. I had applied to several colleges, but so far hadn't heard back from any of them. I was starting to get a little nervous. What if I didn't get into any of my top schools? I knew it was no time to panic, but I did it anyway. At the rate my life was going, I'd be lucky to get into community college. That wasn't exactly my dream scenario, but I was willing to do whatever it took.

I put on my uniform, grateful that these were the last few months I would have to wear it and jumped in my Benz. I turned my radio up as Beyoncé murdered some song about being dangerously in love with some nigga. They could say what they wanted to say about that girl, but she could out-sing ninety-nine percent of most broads in the industry. I looked in my rearview mirror and as usual my makeup was flawless.

I looked up just in time to see the light turn red. I jerked to a stop. The white lady in a Pontiac Bonneville screamed as I missed her car by mere inches. My heart was pounding.

That was the closest I had ever come to having an accident. The old bitch gave me the finger. I returned the gesture and I laughed at myself. I had some nerve flipping her the bird after I had almost wrecked the car that she was probably still paying on. I was wrong and I knew it.

I heard a horn honk and I turned my head to the right to see who it was. I didn't recognize the nigga in the candy-apple red Chevy Monte Carlo but he was fine. He was at a complete stop, yet his rims continued to spin. Most chicks hated it when their men pimped their rides, but I admired a man who took good care of his possessions. His system sounded professionally installed. The latest Jadakiss CD bumped as he continued to try to get my attention. I was locked on something else. The moment I looked up, I saw Isiah's BMW in the parking lot of the Amoco at the intersection of Natural Bridge and Kingshighway. The muthafucka had the nerve to be standing there talking to that bitch Nikki. It was the same bitch he told me he had broken up with.

"HE GOT ME FUCKED UP!!!" I managed to get out through clenched teeth.

As soon as the light turned green, I made a quick right in front of ole boy in the bad-ass Monte Carlo and pulled up on the Amoco parking lot. You should have seen that nigga's eyes.

"Queen, it ain't what you think," he tried to explain as I ran up on him and that bitch and dropped her with two quick rights and a hard left.

All I could see was red. I continued to swing even when he picked me up and carried me away. I was kicking him all up in his chest. I did everything I could to bring him pain. I was hurting so bad. It must have been like how he felt

Cynthia White

when I was with Marc. "Let me go, Isiah!" I yelled like a crazy woman.

I was entertaining the entire neighborhood, but I didn't give a fuck. I was wounded so I did the only thing I knew how to do in that situation. I fought.

"Queen, listen to me!" he yelled.

"Fuck you!" I yelled back at him.

"Queen, I didn't lie to you. I broke up with Nikki."

"Then what the fuck are you doin' here with her?"

"She called me and told me she needed to talk to me. Queen ... she's pregnant."

He still had a hold on me, but it didn't matter. I had stopped fighting. It was over. She won. She was having his child. The Hershey Aaron in me told me not to give up, but the little girl who missed her daddy told me that this was a battle I couldn't win. If he was having a child with her, then he had to be with her. Life didn't always turn out the way you wanted it to, and slowly but surely I was learning that lesson the hard way. When he let go of me, it felt horrific. We were about to go our separate ways once and for all. As soon as my size six-and-a-half feet hit the pavement, I turned and headed back toward my car. He called my name, but I didn't respond. There was no point. I got in my car and drove away.

*****

For the next two weeks, I was completely useless. I couldn't eat, I couldn't sleep and functioning at school was absolutely out of the question. I finally understood what a broken heart felt like. I knew that because of business, Isiah would constantly be at the house, so I mostly stayed in my room. When I did run into him, I found an excuse to rush out of the room. We didn't talk. He tried, but I just couldn't. Every time I looked at him, I saw Nikki's face. It was one thing to have a meaningless fling, but to bring a child into the world with that broad was unforgivable. That was definitely the end for us. I needed something, someone.

"Hello." Marc answered his cell phone on the first ring.

"Hey, it's me."

"Queen, how are you, baby?"

"Not so good," I said sadly.

"What's wrong?"

"I don't really want to talk about it."

"How can I help if I don't know what's wrong?"

"Just make me forget."

"Tell me when and where and I'll be there," he said in a serious voice.

"Wherever you want me you can have me."

"How about your penthouse?"

"It's still mine?" I asked.

"It always has been."

"I'll be there in half an hour." I hung up the phone.

I knew from this point on there was no turning back. I couldn't have cared less. I knew that I had hurt Isiah first, but I was never stupid enough to get pregnant by another nigga. How could he fuck that bitch with no rubber? Forget about me, how could he have so little respect for himself?

I met Marc at my penthouse just as I told him I would. He was a sight for sore eyes. He looked so damn good in his olive Armani suit. All I could do was smile. I started to remember all the good times we had shared. If it hadn't been for Isiah's meddling, we probably would have still been together. This time would be different. Even though I knew he would never leave his wife for me, I was prepared to ded-

Cynthia White

icate myself to him and only him. He could keep wifey, but he would still be my man.

"Hi." I raised my arms and wrapped them around his neck as I hugged him tightly.

"Hey, baby." He hugged me back.

"It feels good to be in your arms again."

"I'm glad you feel that way. I've missed you."

"I missed you, too."

"Come on."

He took me by the hand and led me inside. Things heated up on the elevator. We kissed like we were addicted to each other. Our hands and heavy breathing only added fuel to the fire. He slid his hand down my ultra low-rise jeans and rubbed my clit. I gripped his shoulders and purred like a kitten. My pussy was talking to me. She told me to forget about Isiah and fuck this fine-ass man. She had steered me wrong in the past, but I decided to give her another chance.

I listened to her and for once she was right. That was exactly what I needed. Marc fucked me long and hard for two and a half hours straight. My body was relaxed and my mind soon followed. Marc and I smoked four blunts together then had a few glasses of wine with our lunch. He had to leave to get to a meeting but promised me that he would be back in a few short hours to spend more time with me.

When I turned my cell phone back on, I had thirty-four messages from Isiah. Fuck him. I had no plans to call him back.

You could buy me diamonds
You could buy me pearls
Take me on a cruise around the world
Baby you know I'm worth it

I was doing my best rendition of *"A Woman's Worth"* by Alicia Keys as I lathered my body in the shower. I was fighting a losing battle with my mind. Every time I let my guard down, I found myself thinking of him. I wondered what he was doing. Was he thinking about me? Did he miss me? Was he sorry for hurting me?

"Snap out of it, Queen," I told myself, trying to regain my composure.

The fact was that he was having a child with another bitch, and I couldn't handle that. I knew myself, and I knew that I could never be with him ever again.

After my not-so-relaxing shower, I crawled my naked body under my Fendi sheets and tried to get some rest. I lay there for an hour and didn't get a wink of sleep. I was so tired, but my brain just wouldn't let me relax. I just stared up at the ceiling wishing that I could make it all go away. Things seemed so simple in Mexico with daddy. I knew right from wrong, and I was going to live my life in a way that made him proud. Now I was back to my old self, looking out for me and only me. If I didn't do it, who would?

"Hey, baby." Marc greeted me with a kiss on the cheek.

"Hey. What's that?" I asked, referring to the Macy's bag in his hand.

"Something for my baby."

"Marc, you know you don't have to do that."

"I know, but I enjoy it. I like seeing your face light up when I buy you something pretty."

"You're a special man, you know that?"

"Only when I'm around you." He smiled a very charismatic smile.

I knew it was game, but as long as I got something out of it, I didn't care.

Cynthia White

"So, what is it?"

"Open it." He handed me the bag.

As soon as I saw what was inside, I threw my arms around him and hugged him the same way I used to hug daddy when he bought me something new and expensive. I almost had a heart attack when I saw the fierce pair of Valentino sandals. They were zebra print and trimmed in brown leather with a four-inch wedge heel. I flipped them over and saw the six hundred and ninety dollar sticker. As if that wasn't enough, he also brought me the matching bag at a cool three grand. The man had taste. I had to give him that. He was about to get the shit fucked out of him. I turned around to kiss him and got the shock of my life. Marc was down on one knee holding in his hand the biggest diamond I had ever seen in my life. I froze. I had to be dreaming.

"Marc, what are you doin'?"

"I love you, Queen. I lost you once, and I never want to go through that again. These last few months without you have been unbearable. I know that our time together was short, but sweetheart, you made me happier than I have ever been. Please, will you marry me?"

"What about your wife?"

"I already filed for divorce." He looked up at me, and I knew that now I had a way out. He was about to rescue me. I was safe.

"Yes, I'll marry you, Marc."

It was so surreal. I had just agreed to marry my best friend's father. The same man who yelled at me for talking in church when I was ten years old. He put that gorgeous ring on my finger and still I didn't believe it was real. I had been engaged twice before, and I wasn't married yet. Even if it didn't happen, I was happy if only for that moment.

chapter

Eleven

THE FOLLOWING WEEK, MARC AND I were married in a very small church that he used to attend when he was a little boy. It was a very simple ceremony. The only guests were a few of his business associates and their wives. No one was there to support me, not even good ole Uncle Moe. I was on my own. When I said, "I do," I got a pain in the pit of my stomach. That should have been my first clue. Still, I continued on with the charade, not willing to admit I was wrong.

"Marc, we need to talk." I was prepared to tell him that we had just made the biggest mistake of our lives, right in the middle of our reception.

"What's wrong, sweetheart?"

"Can we go somewhere private?"

"Is something wrong? Are you okay?"

"I'm fine. I just think ..."

Just as I was about to drop the bomb, some drunken, fat

Cynthia White

Hispanic man stood up and clanked his butter knife against his champagne glass.

"I would like to propose a toast. To Marc and Queen, may life grant you all the happiness ... all the love ... and all the sex. There's only one reason a man would marry a woman more than twenty years younger than him, and we all know what that reason is. Marc, you are one lucky, lucky man." He looked over at me and blew a kiss.

Everyone laughed. I didn't think it was funny. I was mortified. I couldn't wait for this day to be over. What was supposed to be the most incredible day of my life was a disaster.

*****

Marc and I didn't have much of a honeymoon. I was busy packing and getting all my affairs in order, and he was busy setting up shop in California. A week later, we were there. Marc got us a nice house that wasn't too far from my new high school. It had four bedrooms and five bathrooms with a gorgeous lagoon pool in the backyard. It was big enough that we wouldn't crowd each other, but not too big that we would lose ourselves in it.

"Where are you going dressed like that?" Marc asked me when I came out of the bedroom dressed in a bright red DKNY bustier and a pair of skin tight DKNY jeans.

"To a school party," I told him as I primped in the mirror over the marble accent table.

"I don't think so."

"Why not?"

"Because you're my wife, and I'm not letting you leave the house dressed like that."

"Every girl my age dresses like this." I threw my hands on my hips. I was tired of his bullshit when it came to my wardrobe.

"But every girl your age isn't married to me."

"What's wrong with what I'm wearin'?"

"You look like a hooker."

"More like a high-priced call girl." I laughed.

"I don't see anything funny. Go change."

"Fine."

I stomped and pouted my way back into our bedroom. I stripped down to my bra and panties then threw my white fluffy robe over them. I went back into the living room and sat down on the couch.

"What are you doing?"

"I'm stayin' home."

"I didn't say you had to stay home."

"I don't have anything else to wear," I pouted.

"Queen, you have more clothes than most department stores."

"Nothin' as fly as what I just took off."

"Fine, you want to go out dressed like a hoe, then you be my guest. When some psycho snatches you off the street and rapes you, don't come crying to me."

I couldn't even respond. I was so pissed. I was raped before and he knew that. I couldn't believe he was insinuating that a woman deserved to be raped because of the way she dressed. I got up off the couch and walked outside. I had nothing more to say to him. I sat down on the side of the pool, put my feet in the water and stared at my reflection. Here I was in another fucked up situation that I brought on myself.

*****

A few months had passed and things weren't going so well. Marc and I were constantly arguing, and it was starting to affect my grades. I couldn't concentrate at school and the

Cynthia White

chaos at home was making it hard for me to do homework. I felt like every choice I had ever made in my whole entire life was wrong. I wasn't happy. Marc bought me expensive presents, but that's as far as he went. He never once said he was sorry. Two stubborn-ass people could not make a relationship work. Neither one of us was willing to admit our mistakes. At some point, we just stopped communicating. Even our sex life was starting to suffer. If I got broke off once a month I was lucky.

"I'll be back," Marc told me as he put on his jacket.

I was sitting at the computer trying to get some work done, but as usual I couldn't. I had a fifteen-hundred word paper due the next day, and I was stumped.

"Where are you goin'?" I asked him, barely looking up from my laptop.

"I got some business I need to go handle."

"Business. Why am I not surprised?"

"Is there a problem?"

"Why would there be?" I asked him sarcastically.

"Queen, I have an organization to run."

"So did my father, but he always managed to make time for me," I complained.

"Well, I'm not your father."

"Obviously."

"I know you think that your father's perfect, but he's not. Nobody is. No man will ever live up to your expectations."

"One did."

"And who was that, Isiah? If he was so wonderful, then why aren't you still with him?"

"I ask myself that every day."

"I don't have time for your bullshit right now." He turned his back to me then proceeded to walk right out the

front door.

I didn't care. I had no desire to be with him that night or any other that followed. It just so happened that my nineteenth birthday was coming up, and it was also the day before my father's execution. I didn't feel like celebrating.

*****

Marc and I flew in to St. Louis so that I could talk to my father one last time. I got out of the limo and walked inside the prison. Marc stayed put. He knew how my father felt about him. I was beginning to feel the same way.

"Hi, baby." His deep voice penetrated my soul.

"Hi, daddy." I forced myself to smile.

"How are you?" he asked, concerned.

"I'm the one who should be asking you that."

"Baby, I'm fine. Your old man's tough." He stuck out his chest proudly.

"I know but—"

"But nothing," he interrupted me. He knew what I was about to say. It was my fault he was in this situation. I should've been the one behind bars. Not him.

"I miss you, daddy," the little girl in me whined as my eyes began to fill with tears.

"I miss you, too, baby girl." He closed his eyes in an attempt to hold back his own tears.

"I'm goin' to go talk to your lawyer tomorrow."

"You will do no such thing," he scolded me.

"But you don't deserve this. You don't deserve to die." I put my hand up to the glass.

"Baby, I'm at peace with God." He put his hand up to the glass as well. His was twice as big as mine. He smiled at me. I wanted to hug him so badly.

"I just don't know what to do," I confessed.

"You live your life. I know it hurts, baby. It's okay to be sad sometimes. You don't always have to be so strong."

"Yes, I do." I looked back up at him.

"That's why you have a husband."

"Barely." I laughed out loud as I thought about the problems my husband and I had been having lately.

"What's wrong, baby?"

"We're just driftin' apart."

"I'm sorry to hear that. You'll work it out."

"I doubt it."

"Are you saying that he's done something to you? If he has, I'll ..."

"Daddy, no. I can handle my own problems. It's not that serious. You said you're at peace with God so don't do anything to mess that up."

For a while we just stared at each other. It was almost time. We knew that this was the last chance we would ever have to speak to one another.

"I don't want you to come tomorrow." Now he was the one who couldn't look me in the eye.

"But daddy—"

"No!" he shouted.

"Fine. If you don't want me to come, I won't come." A single tear fell from my face on to the JLO jeans I was wearing.

"It's not that I don't want you to come. I just don't want that to be the last image you have of me stuck in your head."

"Okay." I lowered my head as I began to cry uncontrollably.

"Queen, baby, please don't cry," he begged.

"I'm sorry, daddy." I tried to control my emotions, but I just couldn't get ahold of myself.

"I love you, baby." His words were so simple, yet they meant so much to me.

"I love you, too, daddy." I wiped away the tears.

*****

That was the last conversation I ever had with my father. The next day, as I sat in my suite at the Adam's Mark Hotel, I cried from the time I woke up until I got the phone call.

"It's over. He's gone, baby," Uncle Moe told me.

"Did he suffer?"

"No. It was over real quick."

"That's good."

"Are you okay?"

"No," I told him honestly.

"Is Marc there with you?"

"No. He had to fly back to Cali for a business meetin'."

"Would you like me to come over and sit with you?" he asked.

"No. I think I just wanna be alone for a while."

"Okay. Well call me if you need anything."

"I will. Thanks, Uncle Moe."

"You're welcome, baby. You know how much I love you, right?"

"I know. I love you, too."

"I know."

When I hung up the phone, I felt a strange sense of peace. I felt my father's presence. It was as if he was right there in the room with me. I knew he was in a better place. I was happy for him. I couldn't be selfish anymore. I had to let him go.

So many memories of the two of us together came to me all at once. I thought about the water balloon fight we had in Mexico. I almost slipped and fell in as I ran around the

Cynthia White

pool trying to get away from him and his dead-on aim. Every time I threw one at him, I missed. The only time daddy missed was when he did it on purpose. Then, when I finally did fall into the pool, he jumped right in behind me.

"Did I ever tell you about the day you were born?" daddy asked as he wrapped a towel around me.

"No." I smiled at him even though I was shivering and my teeth were chattering.

"The umbilical cord was wrapped around your neck so they had to perform an emergency c-section." He sat down in the lounge chair next to me. "When you came out, you didn't cry. You didn't make a sound. The nurses took you away immediately. I was so afraid. I had only known you for a few seconds, but the thought of losing you was unbearable."

"What was wrong?" I asked, a little confused. I had never heard about me having any type of health problems.

"Nothing was wrong." He laughed. "You just didn't cry. The nurse brought you over to me and placed you in my arms. That was the most powerful moment of my life. You looked up at me like you knew who I was. You weren't scared."

"That's because I knew you were gonna take care of me."

He smiled at me and took my hands in his. "Queen, I know I tell you this all the time, but you are a very special young lady. I truly believe that God sent you to me for a reason. Baby, you have brought so much joy into my life. I loved your mother, but she was never really mine. I never had her heart."

"You have my heart, daddy."

"And you have mine, baby. You always have and you always will."

That short conversation brought me so much comfort now. I went from crying to laughing then back to crying again. I tried to be strong. I knew that's what daddy would have wanted, and all I ever wanted to do was to make my daddy proud.

I got up and went into the bathroom. There she was again. I knew it was me on the inside, but on the outside I looked just like my mother. She was the one who had hurt my father. This was all her fault. "I hate you!" I yelled.

Then I thought about my father, and the anger started to dissipate. "You still have my heart, daddy," I cried. "You always have and you always will."

*****

A few hours later, I sat on the chaise trying to follow some dull-ass movie with Julia Roberts. She was one of my favorite actresses but this movie was not one of her best. Maybe it was just me. I was in no mood to watch a movie where everyone was happy. I picked up the remote and changed the channel. Nothing was on. Someone knocked on the door. I jumped. I wasn't expecting anyone. I got up and answered it.

"Isiah ..."

"Hey, beautiful." He smiled at me.

He was the last person I was expecting to see.

"What are you doin' here?"

"I came to check on you."

"How did you know I was here?"

"My father."

"Of course."

"Why didn't you tell me you were in town?"

"I don't know. Everything just seems so complicated these days. Do you want to come in?" I offered.

Cynthia White

"I'd like that."

He came in. His aroma instantly filled the entire room. He always smelled so damn good.

"You look good," I complimented him.

"Thank you. You look as beautiful as ever."

"Thank you. So, how have you been?"

"You don't have to do that."

"Do what?"

"Pretend like everything's alright."

"Sometimes I forget how well you know me. I've missed that. California is a big place," I said as I looked away.

"You know you can always come back home."

"Marc doesn't want to. Things are good for him there."

"What about you?"

"I'm lonely. I miss Uncle Moe. I miss the family. Marc would probably kill me if he heard me say this, but more than anything or anyone else, I miss you."

"You don't know how glad I am to hear you say that." He grabbed me and kissed me passionately.

It felt like every kiss should feel. I was his again. My body surrendered to him. All the things we had done to each other no longer mattered. He was always there when I needed him. He still loved me. His body proved that. We made love like addicts, getting higher with every kiss and every stroke. He moved inside me like he had a secret treasure map. He knew what to do to make me feel so sexy. If it was wrong, then maybe there was no right. Maybe there was just us, Isiah and Queen. Maybe it wasn't meant to be any other way.

We lay there exhausted, but not too exhausted to pass a blunt back and forth. It felt like old times. I was back with the one person who always got me. Isiah understood all my mood swings and my erratic behavior. He was there for me at times when I wasn't even there for myself. He loved me through all my ups and downs and here he was, loving me even though I was married to another man.

"Know what I was thinkin'?" he asked me as he passed me the blunt.

"What?"

"How am I supposed to just let you go again?"

"I don't know."

"Do you still love me?" he asked as his eyes peered into my soul.

"Of course I do. I always will."

"Then I guess the question is, who do you love more, me or your husband?"

"You have to ask?"

"I need to hear you say it."

"You, I love you, Isiah, only you," I said honestly. We both knew that I could only love him.

"Then stay here with me."

"He'll never let me go that easily."

"He won't have a choice."

I didn't have to ask what he meant by that. I already knew what he was willing to do to keep me.

*****

Isiah stayed the night with me in my hotel suite. I felt right at home in bed next to him. He was my king and I was his Queen. It was all perfect up until five o'clock the next morning when my husband called and Isiah answered the phone.

"Hello." His voice was groggy and raspy.

"I'm sorry, I must have the wrong room."

"Right room, wrong time."

Cynthia White

"Who is this?"

"The nigga who's takin' yo' place."

"Isiah?"

"Got it right on the first guess."

"Where's Queen?"

"Layin' right next to me asleep."

I wasn't asleep. I was just pretending to be.

"Let me talk to her."

"Talk to me."

"This has nothing to do with you."

"That's where ya wrong. Queen's mine. She always has been and she always will be."

"Did you sleep with my wife?"

"A gentleman never brags."

"I'll kill you," Marc threatened.

"You know where I am," he spoke calmly then hung up the phone.

I turned over to let him know that I was, in fact, awake, and had heard the whole thing.

"It had to be done," he told me as he ran his fingers through my hair.

"I know."

"This is what you want, isn't it?"

"Yes."

"Then from now on, you belong to me, and I belong to you."

"Sounds good to me." I moved my hands up his big, muscular arms and wrapped them around his neck.

I kissed him passionately. Soon his hands were all over my body. He made me feel so good. By the time he forced his dick inside me, I was begging him to fuck me. Any way he wanted it, I was down. I didn't care. As long as it was me

he was fucking, I was cool. There was nothing I wouldn't do for him, sexually or otherwise. If he wanted me to stand on my head I would have. I had it bad and I knew it, but luckily for me, he had it bad, too.

*****

I moved back into my childhood home. Things just seemed to fall into place after that. Uncle Moe was still in poor health so Isiah was running the day-to-day operations. He was busier now than ever but he still made time for me. He was sitting at the head of the table. It was exactly what I envisioned for him just a few short years ago. He was so much more confident than he was back then. I guess all that power helped.

I watched him order men twice his age around. Whatever he told them to do, they did. If he said a muthafucka had to go, all they said was how many bullets. He was "that nigga" and everybody knew it. Nothing went on in St. Louis without him knowing about it. He only allowed a few other organizations to continue to do business and that was only because they paid him a hefty percentage. I guess they figured that forty percent of something was better than one hundred percent of nothing. Isiah made the rules, everybody else just lived by them.

I came home from shopping one afternoon and was completely surprised by what I saw. Marc was sitting in daddy's office. Isiah was standing next to him holding a gun to his head. A few guys stood there watching. Nobody was doing anything to defuse the situation.

"Isiah, what are you doin'?" I asked as I walked into daddy's office.

"I caught this muthafucka out back tryin' to climb over the gate," he told me, full of rage.

Cynthia White

"I had to see you, Queen." Marc tried to move toward me.

I took a step back.

"Shut the fuck up!" Isiah yelled, then hit him across the face with his 9mm. Blood flew everywhere. I gasped. I had seen a lot of violence in my life but this was different. I felt responsible for this.

"Isiah ..."

"Leave," he ordered me.

"But ..."

"I said *leave*."

I knew that I had to do as he said. Even though I knew what was about to happen, I turned and walked out of the room. I could never question Isiah in front of the men who worked for him. That would most likely cause dissention among the ranks. They were never to see him show even the slightest hint of weakness. I turned around and left the room. I heard the gunshot as I walked up the main stairs. I didn't even flinch. I continued to walk until I got to our bedroom. I had been so desensitized to the sound of gunfire that hearing it was normal for me.

I fell asleep trying to wait up for Isiah. I hadn't been sleeping much lately and it was finally starting to catch up to me.

"Queen, wake up." Isiah shook me lightly.

"Huh?"

"I need you, baby."

"What's wrong?"

"Nothin's wrong. For once everything is right," he told me as he joined me under the covers.

"I know that I'm not supposed to ask you about business, but is he ..."

"He's no longer a problem."

"Good."

He kissed me and I went with it. On one hand, I was relieved. This was our second chance. We could be together with no one trying to tear us apart. Isiah and Nikki were over, and Marc was out of the picture. On the other hand, I was kind of sad. I did care for my husband. He did so many wonderful things for me. When Jennifer was killed, I didn't know how I was going to go on. He was there for me. He comforted and consoled me. I would have to mourn him silently. I could never let Isiah see me distraught over him. I could never even let him hear me speak his name.

Cynthia White

chapter *Twelve*

UNCLE MOE WAS NEVER THE SAME after daddy's death. He tried to be strong for the rest of us, but the truth was, he was probably taking it worst of all. They had been friends since way back before I was born. I knew what losing Jennifer was like for me. No matter what, I couldn't get her out of my head.

"Uncle Moe, are you okay?" I asked him as I sat down next to him on the couch.

He was watching old reruns of *"Sanford and Son."* That was their favorite show.

"I'm fine, baby."

"Seriously?"

"Seriously." He smiled the fakest smile I had ever seen in my life.

Now I really knew something was wrong.

"I'm worried about you," I confessed.

"I'm fine. I promise." There was no sincerity in his voice.

He could barely even look me in the eye.

"I know that losin' daddy was hard on you, too. He was your best friend, and I should have been here for you."

"You were out living your life."

"That's no excuse."

"Queen, don't be so hard on yourself. It's not your job to watch after me."

"You're my family."

"And I couldn't love you more if you were my own daughter, but you still don't owe me anything."

"I owe you everything. You know what I did, but you've never held it against me."

"I have no idea what you're talkin' about."

"Yes, you do. You know it was me who killed my mother, not daddy."

"You don't have to talk about that if you don't want to."

"I know. I want to. I wasn't thinkin' clearly that night. I was so mad at her. I wanted her to suffer. I wanted her to hurt the same way Hector hurt me."

"Hector, what does that piece of shit have to do with anything?"

"Daddy didn't tell you?"

"Tell me what?"

"When I was thirteen, Hector raped me."

"He what?" Uncle Moe asked, filled with rage.

"I can't believe daddy didn't tell you." I smiled.

That was my daddy. He knew how ashamed I was, so he kept it to himself, not even telling his best, most trusted friend.

Uncle Moe and I talked for a little while longer. I tried to get him to open up to me, but a black man is the hardest puzzle to put together. Now I finally saw where Isiah got his

Cynthia White

stubborn streak. He was more like his father than he would ever admit. They were both strong and bold, but they could also both be withdrawn and introverted. It was hard to get close to a man like that, but once you did, you were stuck. They'd pull you in and make you care. I loved the both of them so much.

After we ate lunch together, I kissed Uncle Moe on his cheek and told him that I would see him later. I did see him later, but it wasn't how I thought I would.

Isiah came home later that evening and found his father dead. I was the first person he called. Apparently, he had been suffering from depression for the last few months. He was taking anti-depressants and this time had taken a few too many. He followed that with half a bottle of whiskey and passed out, never to regain consciousness. Isiah was an absolute wreck. Just when he was starting to get close to his father, he lost him.

*****

Uncle Moe's funeral was more depressing than most. It was hard on me to see Isiah in such agony. His heart was broken. I tried my best to be there for him every way I knew how. I held his hand the entire time, only letting go briefly to put a long-stemmed white rose in Uncle Moe's casket.

He looked so handsome in his all-white Stacy Adams suit. He even had on matching white Stacy Adams loafers. It reminded me of the time he and daddy threw a White Ball for all the members of The Black Mafia and their families. They looked so fly as they posed for pictures together. I was only around six or seven, but I still remembered it vividly. I had on my pretty little white dress with my hair done up all in curls. Daddy showed me off like I was his prized posses-sion. Uncle Moe told everybody there that I was his niece. It

wasn't until I got older that I figured out that we weren't related by blood.

That night when we got home, I let Isiah take his frustrations out on me. He fucked me so hard that I almost cried. I just bit down on my bottom lip and endured the pain. I knew that my man was hurting far worse.

"I'm sorry," I told him as I stroked his back lovingly.

"For what?"

"I know how hard it is to lose yo' father."

"Queen, I don't wanna talk about this shit right now."

"Then when? It's never gonna stop hurtin'."

"I said I don't wanna talk about this shit!" he yelled.

"Isiah, you need me just like I need you. Don't push me away. I love you, and I'm just tryin' to be there for you. Let me help you through this."

He pulled me close to his chest. I could hear his heart beating. I closed my eyes and just listened. I felt something wet on the side of my face. Even though I never opened my eyes, I knew that Isiah was crying. He wasn't weak, and he damn sure wasn't soft, he was simply mourning the father he never really got the chance to know.

*****

I could never forget all the people I lost, but I had to find a way to go on. The same went for Isiah. He never really got over his father's death, but he managed to go on. He had to step up to the plate in a major way. Whether he was ready or not, The Black Mafia needed a leader. He had to be so many things to so many people. His strength amazed me. His power enticed me. I watched him go from serving under his father to running the entire operation. There was so much more to oversee than drugs and guns. We owned businesses and held some very lucrative investments. Isiah had to be

Cynthia White

part businessman and part killer. Nobody ever said that being on top was easy.

My world was threatened when I came home one afternoon and found Isiah in daddy's old office talking to Nate. My heart stopped. It was time. My past had come calling. It was time for me to reap what I had sown. When I saw the look on my man's face, I knew that Nate had told him about that night that we shared with Jennifer. The pain in his eyes was unmistakable. His heart was broken, and once again it was all my fault.

"Isiah ..."

"I don't wanna hear it," he told me as he walked past me. I grabbed ahold of his Coogi shirt.

"Isiah, please..."

"Please what, let you explain?" He looked at me like I was trash.

"Yes."

"Go ahead. I wanna hear this shit. How the fuck can you explain fuckin' my best friend?"

"It was a long time ago."

"So that makes it alright?"

"No, but I'm not that same little girl anymore. I've grown up."

"If that were true, you would have told me."

"It didn't mean anything."

"It means somethin' to me. It means I can't trust you."

"Isiah ..."

"I can't even fuckin' look at you right now." He snatched away from me and walked right out the front door.

There was really nothing I could do. I could have lied and told him that I never slept with Nate. I could have said that he forced me. I was high, but that wasn't it either. The

truth was that I was hurt. It was no excuse, but it was the truth. He hurt me when he pushed me away, and I did the only thing I knew how to do at the time. I turned to someone else for comfort in the form of sex. Ever since I was thirteen years old, sex had been fucking up my life.

After Isiah left, I went upstairs and moved all my stuff out of my bedroom and into one of the guest rooms. Since I had fucked up, I felt that I should be the one to accommodate him. He had enough on his mind without having to deal with me and all my drama.

"What are you doin' in here?" he asked me when he came home and found me three rooms down the hall.

"I knew you probably wouldn't wanna see me, so I moved all my stuff in here."

"You didn't have to do that."

"Yes, I did. This is your house, too. You shouldn't have to share a room with me if you don't want to."

"Go back to your room. I'll move my stuff somewhere else."

"Too late. I'm already here. I might as well just stay."

"Why do you have to be such a pain in the ass all the time?"

"I'm not tryin' to be a pain in the ass. I'm tryin' to be considerate of yo' feelins."

"Why did you do it?"

"It just happened. I was hurt. You hurt me, Isiah. I needed you, and you just pushed me away. Jennifer was the only other person I had. When I got to her house, she and Nate were in bed together. We smoked a few blunts. I started to cry and she consoled me. She kissed me, and things just went from there. It was a mistake."

"Were you two ever together again after that?"

Cynthia White

"No. I never even saw Nate after that night."

"Not Nate, Jennifer. Were you ever with Jennifer again?"

"No. Why would you ask me that?"

"Because she was in love with you."

"What? No, she wasn't."

"Yes, she was."

"You're crazy."

"Am I, or are you in denial?"

"Jen was my girl. She wasn't in love with me. I would know if she was."

"Why?"

"Because she told me everything."

"Maybe she didn't think she could tell you this."

Could he be right? I wondered. Was my girl in love with me? I didn't think so, but maybe I was wrong. She did get very upset when Isiah and I had a threesome and didn't include her. I just brushed that off as her not wanting me to get close to any female in any way. She was my best friend, my sister, the person to whom I told everything.

"Queen, Jennifer came right out and told me that she loved you and that she didn't think that I was good enough for you. It was after my father was shot," he confessed.

"When you told me you needed some space."

"Yeah. You'll never know how much I regret that."

"So do I."

I wasn't surprised that Jennifer had feelings for me. Just surprised that she told Isiah. She must have really cared deeply to have done something like that.

"Come back to our room."

"You ain't mad at me no more?"

"Queen, I wasn't mad. I was hurt. It hurts me to think of

you bein' with another man."

"Especially yo' friend?"

"Any man," he said.

"I'm sorry."

"I know you are, and I know that was a long time ago. I should have never pushed you away like that."

"We both made mistakes," I said.

"Yes, we did, but things are different now."

"I would never do that to you again."

"I hope not."

"Baby, I swear I wouldn't."

"Come here."

I got up and walked over to him. I stood up on my tippy toes and kissed him. He wrapped his arms around me.

"I love you," he whispered into my ear with such sincerity.

"I love you, too."

"If I ever lose you again ..."

"You won't," I told him then kissed him again.

He deserved my best, so that was what I was prepared to give him. I felt like I owed him for all the dirty shit I had done to him. It was justifiable, but I still knew it was wrong. It was in my nature to strike back. If somebody hurt me, I hurt them back. I knew it wasn't very mature, but maturity goes right out the window when you're in pain.

*****

The next few months were amazing. Every day I tried to do something to show Isiah how much I loved and appreciated him. I woke up early each morning to cook him breakfast. I ran his bath water. I ironed his clothes. Every night when he got home, I gave him a full body massage with warm oil. I even rubbed his feet. There was nothing I

Cynthia White

wouldn't do. I just wanted him to know that he was my king. I tried so hard to please him that I started to neglect myself. I had to find a way to balance it all. I had to find a way to make him happy but to also make myself happy.

For once, sex was the solution to all my problems instead of the cause. I knew it wasn't healthy, but it worked. Isiah loved to fuck and I loved to fuck. We were at our best when we were naked. The more we fucked, the better we got along. As a couple we were flawed, but as two sexual beings we were perfect. I couldn't make sense of it, so I stopped trying. I wanted us to work so bad that I ignored everything else. Especially the little voice that told me I was making a mistake. I painted on a smile, turned on some R. Kelly and did what I did best. I fucked Isiah to sleep then sat up the entire night and worried about our future. I never did learn how to turn my brain off.

chapter *Thirteen*

IT STARTED OFF AS JUST ANOTHER DAY. It was quiet and routine. Nothing special was going on. After watching an hour of Martha Stewart, I decided to call on my inner domestic goddess. I went downstairs to the kitchen and began to prepare Isiah and myself a nice, late breakfast. It was already after noon. We had spent the majority of our morning fucking and sucking while we enjoyed a blunt or two or five. I put on a pot of coffee for my man. I hated the stuff but what Isiah wanted, Isiah got. I got the turkey bacon out of the refrigerator and began putting it in the skillet.

"Good morning, Queen," Gino greeted me as he walked in through the back door.

"Good morning, Gino." I flashed him a quick smile.

I was in a good mood. Isiah did things to me in that bed that would make any woman smile.

"That coffee smells so good. I stopped at Starbucks but the line was long as shit."

"Well how 'bout I bring you a cup when it gets done?" I offered.

"That would make my day."

"You gonna be out front?"

"Yeah, I'll be posted up," he joked as he headed toward the front entrance.

I continued to cook all of Isiah's favorite breakfast foods. I made him grits, eggs, fried potatoes and the special toast made in the oven, not in the toaster. It was smelling too good. I knew he would be coming downstairs soon, so I decided to go outside and get the newspaper. He reminded me of daddy the way he sat down and read the entire paper while he drank cup after cup of coffee. That's when I learned to make it. I was around eight or nine at the time, but I knew it was another way to be closer to my father.

I tied my lavender satin robe then went out the front door. To my surprise, Gino was nowhere to be found. I thought that was strange, but I just let it go. I got the paper then turned around and walked back up the steps. As I took my first step inside the doorway, someone came up behind me, put a hand over my mouth and picked me up. I tried to scream, but all I could do was mumble. I struggled, but he was too strong. Within seconds, men rushed in on either side of us. There had to be at least twenty of them. My heart sank. I knew they were coming for Isiah. I closed my eyes and prayed to God that he hadn't gone back to sleep. If they found him in the bed still sleeping, it was over. He had to be awake. I had already lost my father, Jennifer, Jimmy C and Uncle Moe. God couldn't be this cruel.

I heard the first gunshot a few seconds later. I couldn't move after that. Did they get him? Was that it? After all we had been through, did I lose him?

"You can always come with me. I need a down-ass bitch on my team," the coward who was still holding me whispered into my ear.

He started to grind on me. What the fuck was he thinking? I took his mistake and ran with it.

"You would really let me come with you?" I asked, sounding like the naïve little daddy's girl they perceived me to be.

"Yo' lil sexy ass can have anything it wants," he promised me then kissed me on the neck.

My skin began to crawl. He smelled like a mixture of cheap liquor and musty cologne. He put me down long enough to squeeze my breasts with both hands. I knew this was my chance. I let him touch and grope me just long enough to get comfortable. I quickly grabbed the gun he had tucked in his waistband and pointed at him. He looked as ugly as he smelled. I took a few steps back just to make sure that if he tried to make a move, I would have time to shoot him before he got to me.

"You stupid muthafucka!" I shouted at him.

Before he had a chance to respond, I pulled the trigger and watched him fall lifeless to the floor. I had to think quickly. Then it hit me. I ran into the kitchen and got my cell phone. Isiah always put his on vibrate at night. I dialed his number. It rang at least fifteen times then there was nothing. I was about to hang up when I heard someone breathing.

"Isiah, baby, is that you?" I asked desperately. "If it is, push a button."

He pushed a button to signal that it was, in fact, him. I heard a noise behind me. I turned around and fired a shot wildly. Thankfully I missed Gino. He looked like he had just

Cynthia White

seen a ghost. I guess I'd be scared too if some crazy-ass bitch almost shot me. I ran over to him and grabbed his arm, pulling him out of the house.

"Where the fuck were you?" I asked desperately.

"What's wrong?"

"They're in the house."

"Who?"

"I don't know who the fuck they are. Isiah's upstairs alone. Where the fuck is everybody?"

"Hold on."

Gino got on his walkie-talkie and within seconds, Raymond, Dorey, Reid and Carmen were there. I was glad to see them, but we were still out-numbered.

"How many of them are there?" Carmen asked me.

"At least twenty."

"Who took out that one?" he asked as he pointed to the body of the intruder who had gotten a little too close to me.

"I did," I admitted proudly. The muthafucka had no right to come into my house and put his nasty hands all over me. He got exactly what he deserved. They all seemed to be surprised by my admission.

"She's on my team," Carmen joked.

For a second I forgot about the impossible odds we were facing and I allowed myself to laugh. I was glad Carmen was there. He always had a way of making me feel at ease. My laughter was cut short by a second gunshot and then a third. I got a bad feeling in the pit of my stomach. I knew Isiah was in trouble.

Since I knew the layout of the house the best, I led the way. There was a secret opening in the back of my walk-in closet. Isiah and I had discussed that if anything like this was to ever happen, that would be the perfect place to hide.

There were only four people who knew about that secret room and two of them were no longer with us. My father put me in that room purposefully. He knew that if someone came into our home, there would only be a few brief seconds for me to get in and lock the door behind me. I just hoped that Isiah remembered our plan.

I crept up the stairs without making a sound. Carmen was right behind me and Gino was right behind him. Raymond, Dorey and Reid were back there somewhere, but I didn't have time to worry about them. My focus was on Isiah and trying to save his life.

I got to my room. The door was shut. I said a brief, silent prayer before I opened the door. There were three dead men on my floor. None of them was Isiah. I took a deep breath then released a sigh of relief. Then I saw the blood. It was leading from the bed over to the closet. I knew Isiah was inside. I walked over and opened the door quickly. There he was, lying in a puddle of blood. I knelt down at his side.

"Isiah … Isiah, baby, talk to me."

I didn't know if he was dead or just unconscious, but I was terrified. I couldn't lose him. He was all I had left.

"Is he alive?" Carmen asked like I was an EMT or something.

"I don't know. We need to get him to a hospital."

"Stay here and don't make a sound."

"But …"

"Queen, you have to trust me."

"I do."

"We can't carry him out of here until we clean house. If anyone opens this door, shoot them."

"Okay."

"I'm comin' back." He gave me his word.

Cynthia White

"I know you are."

He shut the door. It was dark. I could barely see Isiah. All I could do was hold my 9mm tight and pray for a way out.

I was so scared for those ten minutes. I tried my best to stay calm, but it was hard. I hoped that daddy was watching over me. I needed him so much. Things just kept getting worse. I checked Isiah to make sure he was still breathing. He was. All I could do now was wait on Carmen and the other soldiers to return. I just prayed that they wouldn't be too late.

When the door finally opened, I moved faster than I ever had before. They carried Isiah down the stairs and put him in a limo. The driver ran every stop sign and red light along the way. I made a mental note to give him a raise.

At the hospital, I found out that Isiah was only shot once but that his injury was very serious. He had lost a lot of blood and his pulse was extremely weak. He didn't look like he was going to pull through. I began to panic.

"Please don't let him die," I begged the white doctor who couldn't have cared less about me or Isiah.

"I need room to work," he barked at me in a very disrespectful tone.

"Is he gonna make it?"

"Get her out of here!" he yelled at the staff.

"No, he needs me. He needs me." My eyes pleaded with him as my hands gripped his white jacket tightly.

"Fine, but you have to be quiet and stay out of my way." He snatched away from me.

I did as he told me. I didn't want to do anything to jeopardize Isiah's life. I just wanted to be there. I had to be there. If he died in that room without me, I would never forgive myself. I had enough guilt to live with.

241

It took a few hours to get him stabilized, but eventually I was told that he was going to pull through. It would take a while, but he would make a full recovery. I didn't care what it took, I was going to be there right by his side. Anything he needed I would give him. He needed me.

*****

I wasn't able to see him until the following day. I was so happy to see him sitting up in that hospital bed. I ran over and hugged him. I tried not to cry, but I couldn't help it.

"What's wrong?"

"I almost lost you."

"I'm fine," he tried to reassure me.

I wasn't going for it. It wasn't fine just like I wasn't fine. "This was too close," I told him as I sat down in the chair next to his bed.

"I'll deal with it."

"You'll deal with it? Isiah, take a long hard look at yo'self. You won't be dealin' with anything for a while."

"I'm still runnin' shit."

"Baby, of course you are, but you need someone to take over until you're betta."

"Someone like who?"

"Well, it has to be somebody you trust. They have to be loyal, strong, diligent and most importantly she has to be willin' to get down and dirty."

"She?" He looked at me knowing exactly what I was thinking.

"You know I can do it."

"I know you can do it, but ..."

"But nothing. If the only reason you're gonna tell me I can't do this is because I have a pussy, then I don't wanna hear it," I argued.

Cynthia White

"Queen, you're my woman."

"And you're my man."

"Baby, I don't wanna see you get hurt," he said with pain in his voice.

"Well, that's funny because I just watched you get hurt."

"It's not the place for you."

"And what is, raisin' yo' babies and cookin' yo' dinner?"

"You know I'm not even like that."

"Then what's the real issue, Isiah? You honestly don't think I can do it, do you?" I asked in a hurt voice.

"Baby, I know you can do it."

"Then case closed. You need someone you can trust who can get the job done and even though you hate to admit it, you know that's me."

"Queen, you have to be one hundred percent sure. This is not a game."

"I know that."

"Do you?"

"I lost my father just like you lost yours."

"Exactly, so you know how dangerous my world is."

"Your world? I've been survivin' in this world since the day I was born. Unlike you, I didn't have a choice. This is me. This is my life. Either you give me yo' blessin' and I walk out of this room with nothin' but love and respect for you, or you continue to doubt me and I leave angry and emotional. Either way, I'm doin' this."

"Fine, you have my blessin'," he surrendered.

"Thank you." I kissed him on the cheek then turned to leave.

"Queen ..."

"Yeah?" I turned to face him.

"Be careful."

"I will."

*****

As soon as I got back to the house, I called an emergency meeting. The entire family was there – at least what was left of it.

"You all know what happened to Isiah yesterday." I stood and addressed the soldiers.

"How is he?" Gino asked.

"Not good, but he's gonna make it."

"Queen, I'm so sorry. I thought—"

"Gino, just stop. There's plenty of blame to go around. This is supposed to be a family. What happened to us?"

"What happened to us is we don't have a leader. Ever since Moe died, Isiah—"

"Raymond, you're already on thin ice so I would advise you to think before you speak."

"You're right. I'm sorry, Queen."

"As for the rest of you, if you have somethin' to say, now would be the time to say it."

"Queen ..." Carmen lifted his hand like we were in the middle of a classroom.

"Yes, Carmen?"

"I just want you to know that I'm gonna find out who did this to Isiah, and when I do, the muthafucka's dead."

"Thank you, Carmen. I appreciate that. Just one thing ..."

"Anything for you, Queen."

"When you're done with him, bring me his fuckin' head."

"I'll do that."

"Yo' loyalty will be greatly rewarded."

I walked over to my father's old desk. I ran my hand over

Cynthia White

the cold marble top. I sat down in daddy's chair. I knew that this was where I was supposed to be.

"Today is a new day. All those old, ancient notions you all have about The Black Mafia are over, done with. From this moment on, you answer to me," I told them with nothing but authority in my voice.

I searched the room for reaction but thankfully found none. They all knew this day was coming.

"What took you so long?" Carmen asked with a smile on his face.

"Just waitin' on the right time."

"Well, I for one would be proud to serve under you."

"Thank you, Carmen. Does anyone else have anything to say?"

I waited, but no one said a word. "Good. I will only be in charge until Isiah gets better, but I still ask that you show me the same respect that you show him. I am not as easygoing as Isiah or as patient as my father, but that's just because I know each and every one of you and I know what you're capable of. This room is filled with thirty-four of the strongest and most intelligent men I have ever had the pleasure of meeting. I trust each and every one of you with my life. I want the same things you want. I want you to eat. I want yo' children to eat. I want yo' wives, yo' girlfriends, yo' baby mamas to eat."

"Mine could stand to miss a few meals," Carmen joked.

We all had a good laugh.

"You know what I mean."

"I feel ya, Queen."

"I want you all to be very well taken care of. I want you to be able to provide for yo' families. Now I've gone over the books and we are still in very good financial shape. So as a sign of good faith, I am offerin' you all a ten percent raise." The room erupted into cheers and applause. Money was a universal language. "On one condition," I continued.

"I knew there was a catch," Carmen joked once again.

"No catch, just a condition."

"I was only kiddin', Queen. Go ahead."

"Thank you. I want yo' best. My ass is gonna be on the line twenty-four hours a day, and I need to be able to count on you."

"Queen, I will protect that beautiful ass any day of the week," Carmen told me then blew me a kiss.

"Thank you, Carmen. What about the rest of you, can I count on you?"

They all began nodding their heads and yelling out, "Yes!" and, "Hell yeah!" I couldn't describe the feeling I had at that moment.

After the meeting I went outside for a little fresh air. I needed to be alone with my thoughts.

"Queen, can I talk to you for a moment?" Carmen asked as he pulled out his lighter and fired up my blunt for me.

"Yeah, what's up?"

"I just want you to know that I'm here for you. I know that you've had it rough these last few years, but you handled it like a soldier. You're a very special lady."

"Thank you, that really does mean a lot to me."

"You mean a lot to me."

"Still?" I asked as I searched his face.

"Still," he confirmed.

"It seems like you been in my life ..."

"... Forever." He finished my sentence.

"Yeah, forever and a day." I smiled.

To understand the true meaning of this conversation,

Cynthia White

you would have to understand the history that Carmen and I shared. He first started working for my father when I was only twelve years old. He was eighteen. I had a huge crush on him, and he knew it. He was the finest thing my young eyes had ever seen. He was tall and sexy with a bad-ass body covered in thuggish tattoos. He was half black and half Cuban with the most beautiful skin God ever gave a man.

I would look out my bedroom window and watch him play basketball with the other guys. He would always play without a shirt. I used to pretend that I was his own personal cheerleader. In my fantasy I wore a red and white uniform and had red and white pom-pons. My hair was in two long ponytails with red and white ribbons tied around them. Even in my fantasies I had to match.

One day, Carmen caught me staring out my window at him. I was so embarrassed. I ducked down as fast as I could, but I knew that he had already seen me. I tried my best to avoid him, but that only lasted for two days. At the time, my father and The Black Mafia were at war with The Lopez Family. They were a Mexican drug cartel that was trying to set up shop on daddy and Uncle Moe's territory. My father was very protective of me, so that entire summer, Carmen was assigned to me. Everywhere I went, he followed. Everything I did, he did, too. Everything I ate he also ate.

One night, Jennifer had a party. Her father was out of town and her mother was recovering from one of her many cosmetic surgeries. Jen knew that I had a huge crush on Carmen so when we started to play spin the bottle, she asked him to join. At first he said no, but then she started calling him all kinds of punks so he gave in. I swear Jennifer must have rigged that bottle. I don't know how she did it, but the first time I spun that damn bottle, it landed on Carmen.

When we kissed, I could have died right then and there. I didn't think life could get any better than that. That was my first kiss.

After that day, every time I saw Carmen, we sneaked off somewhere to make out. Kissing him was the climax of my young life. We came so close to having sex, but I never could work up the nerve to do it. That fall he went away to college, and I didn't see him again for four long years, until my sixteenth birthday party. When he got back, he was even finer than he was when he left, and there was still a mutual attraction, but I was with Gauge and his girlfriend Serita was pregnant with his child. It just never seemed to be the right time for us. Then he came back to work for my father. I would catch him looking at me the same way I used to look at him.

I still wanted him, but I was with Gauge. Then after Gauge was out of the picture, I was with Isiah. The thought of cheating on Isiah never crossed my mind, and I would have never done it if he hadn't told me that he needed space.

One night, right after Uncle Moe got shot, I was lonely and feeling abandoned. Carmen didn't take advantage of me, but he was smart enough to know that it might be his only shot so he went for it. We went to the pool house and he did everything in his power to make it special for me. He lit candles and put on an R. Kelly CD. He kissed me affectionately all over my face and body. I felt wanted and appreciated.

By the time he had all of my clothes off, I was practically begging him to fuck me, but he didn't. He made love to me, mind, body and soul. He told me he loved me as he slowly and fluidly stroked my insides. Though I would never admit it to anyone else, that night, my crush on Carmen evolved into love. It was just one more problem that I didn't

Cynthia White

need, so I made sure that it ended there. I told him that it could never happen again.

"Queen, that night we spent together was the best night of my life."

"Why, because you got to fuck the boss' daughter?"

"No, because I got to make love to someone I had been in love with for so long. When you told me that you could never see me again, it broke my heart."

"I seriously doubt that."

"Queen, I've never been so serious about anything in my life."

He took a step closer to me. For a brief moment, I let my head rest on his firm chest. I took a deep breath then slowly exhaled. I looked up at him. His eyes were filled with tears. That's when I realized that he was being sincere.

"Carmen, I won't lie and say that I don't still have feelins for you, but I'm with Isiah now."

"I know."

"I love him and you love Serita."

"I know, and I know it's wrong but I can't stop thinkin' about you."

"Carmen ..."

"You don't have to say anything. I know you're not that same little girl who had a crush on me all those years. Please just let me say what I have to say."

"Go ahead."

"You have my word that as long as I breathe, you will breathe. I'll never let anything happen to you. I want you to relax when I'm with you. I don't want you to have any fears."

He made me feel so much better. I was more confident and focused. I knew what had to be done and I was fully prepared to do it.

*****

Things moved along quicker than I thought they would. Within a few weeks, I was more powerful than I had ever imagined. I was "That Bitch" and everybody knew it. I was truly my father's daughter. The family grew. I brought a few of the older men out of retirement. They were more than happy to assist with the rebirth. The Black Mafia was one hundred members strong and still growing. I only chose men I knew I could trust. My intuition forced me to turn away dozens. I would not be stabbed in the back by some power hungry little boy who had issues with powerful women. I trusted my soldiers and they trusted me. Without that, we were nothing.

The time soon came for their loyalty to be tested. Word got out about my reign. People didn't like the fact that we were expanding. Even more, they didn't like the fact that a woman barely out of high school was driving them out of business. I learned that there was a price on my head. I waited silently for someone to test me. I wanted to see if anyone from my own crew would betray me. I didn't like it, but I had to be prepared to go to war with my own if that was what it came down to.

"Queen, we need to talk to you." Carmen stuck his head in my office.

"Okay." I turned and gave him my complete attention.

I was surprised to see half of my entire organization walk in.

"There's somethin' I think you should know."

"Speak ya mind."

"The Yang Family has placed a price on yo' head."

"Really? How much?"

"Five million dollars."

Cynthia White

"I'm flattered."

"Queen, this is no laughin' matter."

"It wouldn't be if this was the first time I heard about it."

"You knew?"

"I knew."

"Why didn't you tell us?"

"I had to make sure that I could trust you."

"All of us or just me?"

"Don't take it personally."

"How else am I supposed to take it?" he asked, more hurt than upset.

"You know as well as I do that some of you seriously considered sellin' me out."

"Not me."

"I'm not sayin' it was you. The guilty parties know who they are." I looked the entire crew over.

"Is that true?" Carmen turned and asked them with complete disdain in his voice.

"They'll never admit it. The point is, they didn't do it. I appreciate that much, but the fact that I had to wait two weeks to hear about somethin' like this from my own crew does not sit well with me."

"Queen, I swear I just heard about this today."

"I believe you. What about the rest of you, huh? How long did you know before you decided to come to me with it?"

They all stood silent. I knew I had a major problem on my hands.

"Don't you niggas hear yo' Queen talkin' to you?" Carmen asked.

"I don't feel comfortable surrounded by men I can't trust. I put my life in your hands on a daily basis. How am I supposed to do that now?"

"Queen, you have to know I would never do you in like that," Reid promised.

"Then why didn't you come to me?"

"I don't know. I guess I thought it was better that you didn't know."

"And why is that?"

"I didn't want you to panic."

"Well, too muthafuckin' bad 'cause that's exactly what I'm doin'."

"You don't understand," he stressed.

"Make me understand."

"Queen, most of us aren't that much older than you. We came up with you. Mr. Aaron was like a father to us. The last thing we want is to see you get hurt."

"How do you expect me to believe that?"

"Look me in my eyes."

"Okay." I did as he requested.

"Do you really think that I would do you like that?"

"I don't want to."

"Queen, I love you just like every other man here. You're like a little sistah to me."

I knew he wasn't lying, but I was still a little skeptical. I sat back in my chair and started to think. I was between a rock and a hard place. Either I trusted these men completely or I didn't. If I was wrong, I would end up dead. Then again, if I was right, I could also end up dead. It was a roll of the dice.

"If you say you did this to protect me all I can do is believe you."

"Thank you."

"Not so fast. This is just the beginning. The Yang Family

Cynthia White

started this and one way or another I'm goin' to end it. I have to send a message to them."

"What did you have in mind?" Carmen asked like he was intrigued.

"They have to know that we're more powerful than they are. They tried to get to me, but they failed. I have to find a way to get to them. I want them to panic. I want them to feel helpless."

"Jin Yang has a twenty-two-year-old son who just came home from college. Word is that he's groomin' him to take over in a couple of years."

"Can we get to the son?" I asked, already beginning to plot and scheme.

"We can," he confirmed.

"Sit on the house. I want to know everything Jin Yang does. I want to know everybody who comes and everybody who goes."

"Do you want us to get his son?"

"Not yet. I'll let you know when it's time."

Mr. Yang had taken things a step too far. We could have lived peacefully on opposite sides of town. But now I had to show them that underestimating me was a huge mistake.

I had a few of my boys watching Jin Yang and his little crew. They were the second largest family in the entire city. Unfortunately for them, I ran the largest. Everybody knew that The Black Mafia was not to be fucked with, but some people just insisted on learning the hard way. I didn't start the battle, but I wouldn't rest until I was victorious.

I was becoming more and more scandalous with every day that passed. I was worse than daddy, Uncle Moe and Isiah all rolled into one. Nobody could stop me. This was something in which I was determined to succeed. Never in my life had I been so focused and driven.

*****

"Hey, baby." I greeted Isiah with a kiss as I strolled into his hospital room with balloons and roses to brighten the place up.

"Hey," he responded dryly.

"Is somethin' wrong?" I asked as I put the vase filled with two dozen yellow roses down on the table by the window.

"I'm fine."

"Are you sure?"

"I said I'm fine," he snapped.

I stood there just looking at him. Obviously he had lost his damn mind. Here I was taking time out of my busy day to come all the way downtown and spend some time with my man, and I was treated like I did something wrong. I tried to be patient and understanding, but he had been acting shitty with me for days. It wasn't my fault he was on bedrest. I did-n't shoot him.

"I really don't appreciate you gettin' a lil funky-ass atti-tude with me when all I'm tryin' to do is cheer you up."

"I don't need to be cheered up."

"The hell you don't." I snaked my neck and threw my hands up on my hips.

"If you don't like comin' down here, then don't come."

"Fine, I won't." I turned and headed toward the door.

"Queen, wait."

"Fuck you."

"Please don't go," he begged.

I stood there frozen, contemplating what to do next. I wanted to stay and be there for my man, but he had pissed me the fuck off. I thought about Isiah and what he would do if the shoe were on the other foot. I knew there had been

Cynthia White

plenty times in the past where I had done him wrong and he forgave me. I guess I just wasn't used to people mouthing off and getting smart with me. Life as a Queen wasn't all lipstick and Gucci handbags.

"Apologize," I ordered him.

"Baby, I'm sorry."

"Now tell me what the fuck that was all about." I walked back over to hospital bed he was laid up in and sat down next to him.

"I feel like …"

"Yeah?" I urged him to continue.

"I feel like I'm weak."

"Well, baby, the doctor said it'll take some time for you to get your strength back."

"No, you don't understand. I feel like I'm your bitch or somethin'."

"My bitch? Why would you say somethin' like that?"

"You out there in the trenches while I'm up in here loungin'."

"You're not loungin', you're gettin' better."

"What's the difference?"

"The difference is, lazy muthafuckas lounge, and you are anything but lazy. The family understands. They know this is just temporary. As soon as you're back to yo' old self, you'll go back to runnin' shit."

"If I get back to normal."

"*When*," I corrected him.

"Ain't no guarantee that I'll get betta."

"All this negativity is not helpin'."

"I'm not tryin' to be negative. I'm tryin' to be realistic."

"What do you want me to say?"

"I just want you to be real with me."

"Fine, you wanna get real, then nigga, let's get real. I don't need this shit. I have a family to run. I don't have to time to be sittin' up here strokin' your ego. If you have a problem with me, get over it. This ain't all about you. This is about Gino and Carmen and Raymond and the hundred other niggas out there puttin' themselves on the line. They have families to feed. You may not care about your seed, but they care about theirs."

"What did you just say?"

"I'm pregnant, Isiah, almost three months."

"Why didn't you tell me?"

"You have enough to deal with. Look at you. How could I tell you?" He was in no shape to share the burden with me. Emotionally, he was a wreck. Physically, he was far from bench pressing his usual two hundred pounds. He looked fine, but he was in constant pain. His internal injuries were complicated. If he wasn't careful, he could do some serious damage. This was where he needed to be right now. Whether he liked it or not, he would have to spend many more weeks in the hospital room.

We talked about the baby as much as I would allow. It was not an easy decision for me. When I had first found out, I seriously thought about terminating the pregnancy. After losing our first child, I went through a lot. I blamed myself. I thought that because I had been unsure that I deserved to be shot and, as a result, lose the baby. It took me a long time to get over that. What was so different this time? If anything, my life was more dangerous now. A pregnant woman wouldn't exactly be seen as powerful and threatening. I knew that I would lose clout and influence. It was in our best interest if Isiah could recover fast enough to take over before I started to show. If he didn't, then God help us all.

Cynthia White

chapter

chapter *Fourteen*

The next few days were critical. My pregnancy was the last thing on my mind. I decided that it was time to make a move against Jin Yang and I put Carmen in charge. The decision to kidnap his son was a mutual one made by both of us. We agreed that it was our best offense. There was no way I could just ignore what they tried to do to me. They tried to divide my family, and that was a mistake. I had to make them fear us. Respect could only take you so far in this game, but fear could make you or break you. I had to learn to play the cards I was dealt. Luck had nothing to do with it. You had to manipulate your enemies and stay one step ahead of them at all times.

"It's done," Carmen informed me as he called on his cell phone from our warehouse down by the riverfront.

"Did anybody see you?" I questioned.

"Nobody," he confirmed.

"I'll be there in twenty." I hung up the phone feeling

nauseous and sick to my stomach.

It wasn't the pregnancy. I knew that I was about to do something that could never be taken back. My nerves were all over the place, but I hid it well. Even those closest to me couldn't tell when I was panicky. That was my little secret.

I was dressed in all black. My wardrobe mirrored my mood. I knew it had to be done, but still I wasn't completely into it. My maternal side was starting to kick in. Gone now was the impulsive young girl who wanted to take over the entire world. I was starting to think more clearly. Logic was a muthafucka. How could I be a good mother to my child knowing all the lives I had taken?

I pulled up to the warehouse in my Benz. I turned off the ignition and just sat for a while. I tried to clear my head. I looked in my rearview mirror and stared at my reflection. Who was I? Who was I becoming? I wondered what daddy would think of me and the way I was living my life. This was exactly what he didn't want for me. I knew he would be disappointed. Even more so, he would be hurt. I took a deep breath and got out of my car.

"Hello, Mr. Yang," I greeted the bruised and badly beaten young Asian man.

"My father is Mr. Yang. I'm Sun." He smiled through his pain.

I could tell that he was an attractive young man even through his busted lip and swollen eyes. He was well-dressed in an expensive suit and a pair of loafers that must have cost well over a thousand dollars.

"Sun, do you know who I am?" I asked carefully.

"I don't live under a rock. Everybody knows Queen. You're even more beautiful than I was told." He smiled then winced in pain.

Cynthia White

"Thank you. I'm sure you're not so bad yo'self when you're not covered in blood."

"Your men are very thorough."

"They have to be, but you already know that. You're no stranger to the game."

"Unfortunately, I am not."

I sat down in a metal chair across from him. I crossed my legs and leaned forward. His last comment intrigued me. I had to know more.

"You don't approve of yo' father's business?" I asked, wide-eyed, completely enthralled in the conversation.

"No, I don't. What about you?"

"What about me?" I wanted to know.

"You're second generation. How do you feel about it?"

"Some things just have to be done," I told him plainly.

"Bullshit."

"Excuse me?"

"You could have let this bullshit die with your father, but instead you chose to follow in his footsteps."

"This is my father's legacy."

"You're his legacy." He challenged my way of thinking.

"I only do what I have to."

"Is that what you have to tell yourself to get to sleep at night?"

"That's really none of yo' business."

"I'm sorry if I hit a nerve, but I've just had the shit knocked out of me."

"I apologize if my men were overly aggressive, but—"

"Please don't do that," he cut me off mid-sentence.

"Do what?"

"Apologize when you know you don't mean it."

"Fine. I really don't give a fuck how you feel. Yo' father

is an idiot who fucked with the wrong bitch and now you have to pay for that. Now, was that betta?" I winked my eye at him.

"Much. I appreciate honesty."

"So do I."

"Can I be honest with you?"

"If you feel the need."

"You are far too beautiful, too intelligent and too classy to be doing this kind of thing."

"Thank you, but I'll make my own life decisions if you don't mind."

"Are you planning on killing me?"

"If I was, would you really wanna know?"

"Yes. There's someone I would like to say goodbye to."

"Yo' wife, girlfriend?"

"My daughter."

"You have a daughter?" I asked hesitantly. My daddy's face flashed in my mind.

"Yes." He smiled proudly.

"How old is she?" I asked, even though I really didn't want to know. He was becoming too human to me, too real. That was going to make him hard to kill.

"She just turned four."

My heart sank. How could I take away a four-year-old girl's daddy? Could I really be that ruthless? "Do you have a picture of her?"

"In my wallet."

"May I?" I asked before I invaded his personal space.

"Go ahead," he permitted.

I reached inside the pocket of his gray slacks and pulled out his wallet. As soon as I opened it up, there she was. She was precious. She had a smile that could light up an entire room. She reminded me of one of those porcelain dolls with her creamy skin and long, coal-black hair. I turned to the next picture, and there she was again. Every picture in the wallet was of her. She was his world and he was hers.

"She's a doll." I smiled even though it hurt my numb face.

"She takes after her mother," he told me modestly.

"How come there are no pictures of her mother in here?" I asked, now full of curiosity.

"She's no longer a part of my life. She abandoned us when my daughter was just a few weeks old. She was not ready to be a mother, at least that's what her letter said. I haven't seen or heard from her since."

"So you've been raisin' her on yo' own?"

"Just me, myself and I."

"So if I kill you then she'll be all alone?"

"Yes."

And there it was, plain and simple. If I did what I needed to do for the family, I would destroy this little girl's life. If I looked the other way and allowed Jin Yang to get away with what he tried to do to me, I would never again be taken seriously.

"What about yo' father, would he take her in?" I asked, searching for some solution.

"I would rather have her raised by strangers."

I sat back in my seat. "Guys, would you leave us alone for a moment?" I addressed my team. Carmen and the rest of the crew left as I prepared to get down to business with my enemy's son. "What am I supposed to do?" I asked him straight out.

"You're supposed to kill me to send a message to my father." He returned my candor.

"I just recently lost my father, and I could barely handle it. How could I do this to yo' little girl?"

"What other choice do you have?"

I thought for a moment. What could I do to get Jin Yang to do what I wanted him to do? How could I get to him? Then it came to me.

"I could always make yo' father think you're worse off than you really are," I told Sun with a mischievous look on my face.

"What are you suggesting?"

"Hold on a second."

I jumped up from the chair I was seated in and walked outside to my car. I opened the glove compartment and got my digital camcorder. If I could pull this off, I wouldn't have to worry about The Yang Family for a while and best of all, I wouldn't have to carry the guilt of killing that little girl's daddy. I walked back inside the warehouse like a new woman. I was confident and so sure of myself.

"Just play along," I instructed Sun.

He nodded his head to let me know he was on board.

I turned the camcorder on and pointed it at myself. "Mr. Yang, let me first start off by sayin' that I do not appreciate what you tried to do to me and my organization. As you can see, you failed just as so many before you have. You under-estimated me and for that, you must pay." I spoke very seriously with just enough drama thrown in to make it seem real.

I turned the camera on Sun. He was up. Now it was his turn to convince his father that his life was on the line and that if he didn't do as I said that he would lose his only male child.

"Father, please help me?" he begged as he began to cry.

Cynthia White

Raymond and Gino took turns punching and striking him. I told them not to kill him but to make it look real. They did. I cringed as they battered him. He took everything they dished out. It was hard to watch. I closed my eyes as I continued to film for twenty minutes.

*****

The sun set on that day and soon it was night. I sat in my bedroom window and stared at the moon. I had so many things on my mind and no one to talk to. Carrying this heavy load was starting to wear me down. I wished that I had never volunteered myself for the job. Who was I kidding? I could never do this long term. I wasn't my father. Maybe this really was a man's world.

I couldn't sleep, so I decided to get some air. I threw on a pair of jeans and a jacket and jumped into my Bentley. I just drove with no destination in mind. I didn't have anywhere to go. I thought about paying Isiah a visit, but I was too upset. I didn't need to hear him say I told you so. I knew I was wrong. I didn't need him rubbing salt in my wounds.

"Queen, what are you doin' here?" Patrick asked me when I showed up at his place unexpectedly.

"I didn't know where else to go," I confessed.

"Is something wrong?"

"Everything." I started to get choked up.

"Come in."

"You sho? I know I shouldn't have come by so late."

"It's fine. Come in."

I walked inside, and he shut and locked the door behind me. I had no idea why I was there, but for some reason Patrick made me feel safe. Maybe it was the bond we shared through breaking my father out of prison. Maybe it was just as simple as him being the only person in my life who was legit. Yeah, he smoked a little weed here and there, but other than that, he was straight.

I sat down on the couch. He sat down next to me. His stereo was playing very low. I had to listen hard to hear what was playing. It was *"Getting Late"* by Floetry, off their Floetic CD.

It's getting late
Why ya gotta be here
Beside me
Watching, needing, wanting me

I just sat and listened for a moment. I loved that song, and I hadn't heard it in so long. I closed my eyes so that I could live in the melody. I felt him watching me. He was probably wondering what the hell was wrong with me. Lately, I had been wondering the same thing.

"Queen, are you okay?" he asked cautiously, like he didn't want to upset me any further.

"I'm fine. I love this song."

"You like Floetry?"

"No, I *love* Floetry. You seem surprised by that."

"You seem more like a 2Pac kind of girl," he joked.

I laughed. It felt good to laugh again.

"Ah, I love me some Pac."

"Who else do you like?" he asked, like he was really interested in me.

"DMX, Jadakiss, Eminem, Jay-Z …"

"You like that hardcore shit."

"Of course. I like shit I can relate to."

"What about R. Kelly?"

"Everybody loves R. Kelly."

Cynthia White

"True," he agreed. He got up and walked over to his stereo. He put in a CD. R. Kelly came on. His voice always soothed me, but this time it damn near put me to sleep. I just sat and listened as he sang about how some lil fly chic made him love her. *"You Made Me Love You"* just so happened to be my favorite track off of the *"Chocolate Factory"* CD.

"How's Isiah doin?" he asked me as he came and sat down beside me.

"Not too good," I admitted.

"I heard about what happened."

"My life is an open book."

"It must be hard to live like that." He looked at me with empathy.

"It's damn near unbearable."

"I'm sorry."

"It's not yo' fault."

"Do you ever think about sayin' fuck it all and movin' to some far away place?"

"All the time. A few years ago Isiah and I went to Hawaii on vacation. I loved it there," I reminisced.

"Was that yo' first time goin'?"

"No, my father took me a few years before that. Nobody knew us there. Nobody knew what my father did. Nobody knew we were rich. It was paradise."

"Is that where you would go?"

"I'd go right now with only the clothes on my back and the seven hundred dollars I have in my wallet."

"Could you see yo'self livin' there forever?"

"Yes," I told him instantly.

"You don't even have to think about it?"

"What's there to think about?"

"Something's different about you."

"Can I trust you?" I asked desperately.

"You can."

"I'm pregnant," I confessed. It felt so good to get that off my chest. The only person I had told so far was Isiah and he was in no position to be supportive.

"You're pregnant, seriously?"

"Yeah."

"Why do I get the feelin' you're not happy about it?"

"I don't know what to feel. All I know is that I can't bring a baby into my world the way it is right now."

"So what are you gonna do?"

"I don't have a clue," I told him honestly. Before I could finish my sentence, tears started running down my face. Patrick put his arm around me. He held me close the way I so desperately needed Isiah to. He couldn't be there for me right now. I was on my own. He could barely be there for himself.

"I'm sorry." I pulled away from him and wiped the tears from my eyes.

"Queen, you don't have to apologize for bein' human."

"My problems are my own. I shouldn't burden you with them."

"We're friends."

"Are we really?"

"Yes, we are. Why is it so hard for you to trust people?"

"I don't know."

"You have to know that I would never betray you."

"That's what they all say right before they sell you out."

"Look at me."

"I am lookin' at you."

"No, I mean really look at me. Look into my eyes."

I did. When I looked into his eyes I felt something I had

Cynthia White

never felt before in my life. I felt like I was looking into a mirror. There was so much more there than just a corrections officer with a good heart.

"What is it you're not tellin' me?" I wanted to know.

"Can I trust you?" He flipped the script on me.

"Yes, you can trust me, Patrick," I told him as I gripped his hand.

"Queen, I'm yo' brotha."

"What?" I asked, completely stunned.

"I'm yo' brotha." His voice was sincere.

"My brotha, how is that even possible?" I wanted to know.

"My mother's name is Theresa. She and Hershey were together before he married yo' mother."

"Oh my God." I knew he wasn't lying. "Did my father know?"

"Yes."

"Why didn't he tell me?"

"He didn't find out until he came to the prison where I was workin'."

"I can't believe this. I have a brotha. I can't believe daddy didn't tell me."

"It wasn't his fault. I asked him to let me tell you."

"Then why didn't you?"

"Every time I was about to, something happened. You were always dealin' with one thing right after another. I didn't want to force myself on you."

"So that's why you helped daddy escape?"

"I wanted him outta there as bad as you did."

"I have a brotha." I sat there and tried to let it all sink in.

"Only if you want one," he offered.

"All this time I thought I was all alone."

"You're not anymore."

I stayed up all night with my new big brother, just talking and getting to know each other better. We were so alike yet so very different. He loved his mother while I, on the other hand, despised mine. Our birthdays were exactly five days apart. He was very intelligent, something we both inherited from daddy, but unlike me he lived his life on the straight and narrow. He seemed to be content with his life. He was perfectly happy being normal. I couldn't imagine living a "normal" life. I strived to be exceptional and didn't settle for anything less. His normalcy gave me hope. He was daddy's child, too, and if he could live straight, then so could I.

*****

I got back home later that morning to learn that Mr. Yang was ready to make a deal. His son's life would be spared for no less than twenty million dollars. It wasn't about the money, it was about the respect. He had to learn that just because I was a woman didn't mean that he could scare me off. Whether I was running it or not, The Black Mafia was here to stay. He didn't have to know that his son's life was never really in any danger. In addition, he also agreed to stop coming after me and to scale back his business. That had to be a major blow to his over-inflated ego, but I didn't care. I got what I wanted. I was pleased, but I was also no fool. I knew that if he got the chance, he would come after me again. I had to be on point. If I slipped up even once, that could be my ass, literally.

I decided to do a little light shopping to relax. I don't know if most people consider spending forty grand light, but it worked for me. As I went inside the dressing room to try on a stunning sapphire blue Versace dress, I realized just

Cynthia White

how ridiculous things had gotten. Two armed guards stood on each side of the door to make sure that no one tried to harm me. I had to have bodyguards just to go to the mall.

"Leo …" I called out to the bigger of the two men.

"Yes, Ms. Aaron," he answered me without turning around.

"Do you have any kids?"

"No ma'am."

"What about you, Carl?" I asked the smaller, darker man.

"Yes ma'am, two boys."

I don't know what that meant. I wasn't even sure why I asked. Maybe it was just curiosity or maybe I was trying to find somebody, anybody to relate to.

The remainder of my shopping trip I stayed mostly to myself. No matter how hard I tried to pull somebody else in, the fact remained that I was still alone in this. Even my brother didn't fully understand. I knew that there was a lesson in this somewhere. The question was, how much would I have to lose before I figured it out?

I thought about Jennifer and what she would be doing right about now. I wondered if she would have gone to college. The memories I had of her were the hardest to let go. I had spent just about every day of my life with her up until the day she died. I still couldn't get that image out of my head. People tried to make me feel better, but the truth was, she died because of me. That was something that would stay with me my entire life. No amount of time or therapy would change that or take away the guilt that I felt.

After four hours at the mall, I went home and fell into my bed. I was so tired. Being pregnant really took a toll on my body. I never used to get worn out, but now I could barely go an entire day without taking a nap.

"Wake up, baby," Isiah whispered into my ear then kissed me on the cheek, waking me from my sleep.

"Isiah …" I woke up surprised to see my man standing over me.

"Good morning." He smiled.

"What are you doin' here?"

"I came to see my baby."

"Are you okay?"

"I'm good."

"Are you sho? How's yo' …"

"Queen, I'm fine," he reassured me.

I threw my arms around him and squeezed his body tightly. He felt so damn good. He smelled even better. My man was back. Finally, things could go back to normal. I looked up at him, and just like that I knew that I was safe. He was there to take care of me.

I decided not to tell Isiah about Patrick, at least not right away. It was a big revelation, and I wondered if he would get jealous of another man being in my life. Isiah didn't need to doubt himself. Even I was a little skeptical as to whether Isiah had really recovered or not, but he put all my fears to rest that night. He made love to me like never before. It started off slow and tender, but soon it was rough and rugged just like old times.

"Uhm … oooooh … I missed this pussy."

"Ooooooh … I love you, Isiah."

"I love you, too, ma … I love the shit outta you."

"Ooooooh … uhm … you feel so good inside me, daddy … ooooooh it's good."

"Tell me you love this dick," he commanded like the warrior he was.

Cynthia White

"I love it … oooooh … I love my big, black dick."

"You wanna suck it?"

"Yes … yes, daddy … yes."

When I finally did get that muthafucka in my mouth, I sucked on it like there was a prize inside. We were nasty as hell, but we didn't care. I tried my best to carry myself like a lady at all times, but get me behind closed doors and I'd do things to a nigga that should be illegal. He knew that whatever he wanted to do, I was down for. I would never lose my man over some dumb shit. I knew that whatever I wasn't willing to do, ten other bitches were. If he wanted to hit me in the ass I let him hit me in the ass. If he wanted his salad tossed I tossed it. Even if he wanted to skeet, skeet, skeet on my face I let him. You can't just be a down-ass bitch when it's convenient for you. You have to do things that you may not want to do sometimes.

*****

The following morning, I called a meeting to let the organization know that Isiah was back. He stood at my side, ready to get back to business. Maybe it was just me, but the guys didn't seem too enthusiastic. I felt let down. I was so excited to have him back, but to know that they didn't feel the same way saddened me. After Isiah left, I was furious. I decided to address the situation.

"Is there a problem I need to know about?" I asked the entire room flat out.

"It's nothin'." Carmen was the first to speak up.

"What's nothin'?" I wanted to know.

"Some of us feel as if things ran betta with you in charge."

"That was only temporary. You all knew that."

"Yeah but—"

"But nothing!" I shouted. I didn't mean to lose my cool, but I was done. At that point I couldn't have cared less what they wanted. I wanted my man back in charge and he was, end of story.

"Queen, please don't take this the wrong way. We all respect Isiah for steppin' up the way he did when his father died, but he's not a natural born leader," Dorey spoke up.

"And you think I am?"

"We know you are," he told me, like he had no doubt about it.

"Well that's where you're wrong. I thought I could do it, but I was mistaken. It was too much for me to handle. It was only by the grace of God that I didn't get myself killed."

"You didn't get killed because you're smart and clever. No matter what they threw at you— "

"I'm pregnant," I blurted out without thinking.

The silence was complete. No one spoke. They all just looked at each other with bewildered expressions. It was like they didn't even realize that I was capable of having children. Had they forgotten that I was a woman?

As if I didn't have enough to deal with, Gino came in and told me that Officer Jenkins was at the front door. I told him to just let the asshole in. He did. A few seconds later, a dozen cops walked into my daddy's office.

"Good morning, your Majesty." Officer Jenkins tried to be funny as he greeted me, but it was a little too early in the morning for my taste.

"What do you want now?" I asked him impatiently.

"Why must you always be so rude to me, Queen?"

"Probably because I don't like you."

"Well, I love you," he attempted to joke.

"Again, what do you want?"

Cynthia White

"I just came to check on you."

"That's funny."

"I'm serious. I heard you were expecting."

"How did you know that?"

"I have my sources."

"What sources, my gynecologist?"

"Now, why would I need to go to the gynecologist?"

"That's where all pussies go." My soldiers laughed.

"Watch your mouth, little girl," he warned me.

"Why? You watch it enough for the both of us."

"Are you implying something?"

"Are you denyin' something?"

"I'm tired of playing games with you."

"Then get out of my face. As a matter of fact, I didn't see a warrant."

"That's because I didn't show you one."

"You know, when I was younger, I heard a story about a man who had a smart-ass mouth just like you. He talked so much that that he eventually talked himself into some trouble."

"Are you going to tell me what happened to him?"

"Let's just say it's hard to talk without a tongue."

"Are you trying to tell me something, Ms. Aaron?"

"Just tellin' a story."

"Did your father cut this man's tongue out?"

"Don't know."

"What about your Uncle Moe?"

"Again, I don't know."

"Maybe it was Gauge. You remember him, don't you?"

"Vaguely."

"What about your husband?"

"What about him?"

"You use men then toss them in the trash like they're disposable."

"I don't use anybody."

"Keep telling yourself that."

"I will. You keep tellin' yo'self that you're not a power hungry pig and maybe one day somebody else will believe it."

"You know nothing about me or my life."

"I know enough. Let's see, you were abandoned when you were five by a mother who loved her crack pipe more than she loved you. You never knew yo' father. You were bounced around from one foster home to the next. Then when you were sixteen you were finally adopted by a seventy-five-year-old black woman. That's where you got the name Jenkins. Sadly, she died seven moths later. You went back into the system. Then when you were eighteen, you aged out. You got a job at McDonald's until you were twenty-one and then you joined the police force. Did I cover everything?"

"How did you find that out?" he asked, growing very upset.

That's when I knew I had him. It was time to stop playing games. "I have my sources." I smiled like the cat that had just swallowed the canary.

"Did you have me investigated?"

"Why, does that bother you?"

"If I find out you've been snooping around—"

"You'll do what? I haven't done anything to you that you haven't done to me."

"You make sure you really want to—"

"Whatever you're about to say, save it. You don't scare me the least bit. I can make things very uncomfortable for

Cynthia White

you, Officer Jenkins."

"What did you just say?"

"You want me to say it louder so that the bugs you planted in my house pick it up?"

He didn't deny it. He just stood there looking like the fool he was.

"Why didn't you tell me yo' wife was a teacher at my old school? Mrs. Jenkins was a lovely woman. She never talked about you. She had such nice things to say about her son and daughter but never even mentioned her husband. I always wondered who the sorry bastard was who blacked her eyes and bruised her arm. One day she even came with her arm in a cast. Did you do that, too?"

"That's none of your business."

"You made it my business. Now you can either turn around and walk out that door or you can stay here and I can tell yo' fellow officers what else I know about you. It's your decision."

It didn't take long for him to realize that he couldn't beat me. He retreated like all cowards eventually do. I knew that I had either made one of the smartest moves of my life or the dumbest. The law was nothing to play with, especially when you're up against a dirty cop.

*****

Over the next few weeks, things went back to normal. Isiah was holding down the organization while I went back to my routine. I enrolled in college, and come fall, I would be a full-time student at St. Louis University. I wasn't sure how I was going to balance going to school and being a new mother, but I was determined to make it work. Ironically, I had decided to study law. I knew that after four years of college I would have to then go to law school, but I was com-

mitted to making it happen.

"I'm so proud of you," Isiah told me as we lay in bed side by side.

"For what?"

"Goin' to college."

"I haven't even started yet."

"I know, but I'm still proud of you."

"Thank you." I kissed him softly on the lips.

"You know if yo' father was here, he'd be proud of you, too."

"I know." I smiled.

Just thinking of daddy made me happy. Isiah knew that he would always be number two in my life, and he was okay with that. My father was and always would be my first love.

"Remember when we first met?" he asked me as he put his arm around me.

"Of course I do. It seems like a lifetime ago."

"We were at the mall."

"I was with Jennifer." I smiled.

"And I was with Nate."

My smile disappeared. The look on his face changed. I knew what he was thinking. Finding out that I had been with his best friend was probably the toughest thing we had ever been through, and that was saying a lot. Since the very first day we met, we had been faced with one problem right after another.

"Are you ever gonna be able to get over that?" I had to know.

"Over what?" He tried to play it off.

"You know what, me sleepin' with Nate."

"I'm tryin'," he finally confessed.

"Are you really, or are you just gonna hold this over my

head for the rest of my life?"

"I'm not the one who fucked up."

"Not this time." I got up and walked over to the window. There was a full moon out that night. I inhaled a deep breath through my nose then slowly released it out of my mouth. The night air was so fresh. I was a little chilly in my mint-green lace bra and matching boy short panties. I rubbed my arms where I was starting to get goose bumps.

"I love you," Isiah whispered in my ear as he came up behind me and wrapped his big, strong arms around me.

"I love you, too," I told him in a cracked voice. I was glad that my back was to him so that he couldn't see my tears. In my heart I knew that he could never forgive me for what I had done. I couldn't even forgive myself. I knew that he would always look at me differently. His image of me had been tarnished, and no matter how hard I scrubbed, I just couldn't get it back to the way it used to be.

chapter

Fifteen

THAT SUNDAY WAS ONE OF THE longest days of my life. I was so bored and so tired of sitting up in that house. The Black Mafia had completely taken over my entire life. I wanted to do something. I wanted to have some fun. Believe it or not, I was tired of shopping. It just wasn't the same without Jennifer. I missed the way we used to pick out accessories for each other to go with the outfits we were purchasing. We would stop and get our nails done then go to lunch before round two. We could spend eight hours straight in a mall and never get tired or bored. Those days were gone. Now I did most of my shopping on the internet. It was quick and easy, but not as much fun. Shopping with Isiah was torture. After half an hour he was ready to go. I was mostly on my own.

"Baby, I'm bored," I whined to Isiah as we sat in my father's office going over financial records.

"Why don't you have one of the drivers take you shoppin'?" he suggested, not taking his eyes off the computer screen.

"I'm tired of shoppin'."

"You're tired of shoppin'? Should I call a doctor?" he asked, trying to be Cedric the Entertainer or somebody.

"I'm serious."

"Since when don't you wanna go shoppin'?"

"Since my best friend got murdered."

"I'm sorry." He looked up at me for the first time.

"It's fine. I know I should be over it by now, but I'm not, and I don't know when I will be."

"Queen, there is no time limit on how long you can mourn somebody. Jennifer was yo' best friend, the person you were closest to in the entire world. I get that."

"I know you do." I got up and went and sat on his lap. He put his arms around me. "I don't know what I would do if I lost you, too." I confessed my worst fear.

"You won't."

"How can you be so sure of that?"

"I can't really. All I can do is be cautious and alert. Every day when I leave this house, there's a chance that I won't come back, but I do everything in my power to prevent that."

"I love you more than I ever thought I could love a man. I know that things haven't been perfect between us."

"Things aren't perfect between anybody. I love you, and as long as I live, I will always love you. Do you know how special you are?"

"You sound just like my daddy."

"He was a wise man. He knew how precious you are, and I don't blame him for protectin' you the way he did. If we have a daughter, I'll be the same way with her." He smiled as he rubbed my belly.

The following morning I had a doctor's appointment. This was the day that we would find out the sex of our baby. I was so nervous yet excited at the same time. Isiah and I waited patiently as Dr. Josephs adjusted the screen on the ultrasound monitor. It started making all these funny noises. Then I heard it, my baby's heartbeat. I damn near cried.

"How you doing up there, mom?" Dr. Josephs asked as she smiled from ear to ear.

"I'm fine. What about the baby?"

"The babies are fine."

"Babies?" Isiah caught on before I did.

"That's right. You're having twins," Dr. Josephs announced.

"Twins?" Isiah asked like he didn't hear her right.

"A boy and a girl." She smiled.

"Twins," Isiah spoke to himself.

"Isiah, are you okay?" I asked, concerned. If he was half as freaked out as I was, we were in trouble. I stared at Dr. Josephs. She was a large sistah with a kind face. She wasn't fat, just big-boned. I couldn't figure out what she was mixed with, maybe Indian or Puerto Rican. She had beautiful coal-black hair that was naturally wavy. I found myself wondering what kind of shampoo she used. Her dark brown eyes were pretty with a subtle softness. She had lashes for days.

"I know it can be a little overwhelming to find out you're having twins," she said, like she could read my mind.

"A little?" I asked sarcastically.

"What about you, dad, how are you doing?"

"I'm … I'm havin' twins." He smiled.

I knew then that everything was going to be okay. As long as he didn't freak out, neither would I. He was my rock.

Cynthia White

Whenever I needed him he was right there at my side.

After we left Dr. Josephs office, we went out to lunch, just the two of us. It wasn't often that we got to spend time by ourselves, so when we did, I cherished it. There was only one other couple there, so for the most part, we were alone. They were all the way on one side of the restaurant, and we were all the way on the other.

"I can't believe I just found out I'm havin' twins and I'm actually happy about it," I joked.

"I can't believe you're gonna have my child." He looked at me from across the table with nothing but love in his eyes.

"Children," I corrected him.

"Did you ever think that we would end up like this?"

"How could I? When we first met, I was engaged to another man. I was confused and bein' lied to. I knew after our first night together that there was something special there. I tried to deny it, but it was too powerful."

"I love you, Queen." As he looked at me I knew he was picturing our future. His smiles were soon replaced with looks of worry and concern. I recognized those looks. They were the same ones my father used to give me. He was about to become a father. Every man dreams of his firstborn son. His would grow to become a very powerful man with more responsibilities than most. He was also about father to a daughter. She would be constantly guarded and protected. People would want to harm her. Not only was her father a very powerful man, but her mother was a very powerful woman.

"You're thinkin' about her future, aren't you?"

"What? Who?" he asked as I brought him out of his daze.

"Our daughter."

"How did you know?"

"I just did somehow."

"I'm worried for her," he admitted.

"So am I." I shared his concern.

"What are we supposed to do? How do we protect our children?"

"We can't really. We can take precautions. We can put guards on them twenty-four hours a day, but that's still no guarantee."

"What if we walk away?" He asked the question I had been longing for him to ask.

I wanted to walk away so badly. We could finally be free. We could finally be normal. Then reality kicked in. "You know we can't do that," I told him realistically.

"But what if we could? Where would you wanna go?"

I didn't even have to think about it. "Hawaii," I told him almost instantly.

"Hawaii *was* perfect. We had such a good time there."

"Could we really do it?"

"Only if you're sure."

I thought for a moment. I knew it wouldn't be easy but if he was down, then so was I. "I'm sure."

Even if I wasn't completely sure, the events that were about to transpire were enough to convince me. We drove home under a spell. Everything seemed perfect. We had decided that the lifestyle we were living was not an appropriate one to bring two little lives into.

We held hands as we walked from the car to the front door. I went in first. What I saw shattered me. Gino and Raymond were dead. They were hanged to death. It was gruesome. I got sick to my stomach. It was bad enough to have to see two people you were close to dead, but to see two

Cynthia White

black men hanged was a horrible sight.

"Come on." Isiah grabbed me by the hand and tried to get me out of the room.

I snatched away from him. I didn't want to leave. I had to see this. For it to be real, I had to let it sink in. It had to be burned into my memory. I studied every angle. This, I would never forget.

"Isiah …"

"Yeah," he answered in a sad, lost kind of tone.

"We have to go."

"I know, baby. I know." He put his arm around me and tried his best to comfort me.

It didn't work. I was past the point of being able to be comforted. The police were eventually called. They came and went and I paid them no mind. Even the very annoying Officer Jenkins couldn't get me riled up. To my surprise, he didn't even try. There was something different about him that night. Maybe going toe to toe with a pregnant woman wasn't his thing. Whatever the reason, I was grateful. I was too sad to fight.

*****

Isiah and I decided not to tell the family that we were leaving. Eventually we would have to, but not just yet. We had affairs we had to get in order. First we had to find a place to live in Hawaii. I got on the internet and found a few places that I liked. I spoke to ten different realtors before I met Monique Hoskins.

Monique was originally from Detroit. She had moved to Hawaii three years ago and from the sound of things, she didn't regret it one little bit. She was selling a property that was perfect for us. The open floor plan was exactly what I had in mind. The asking price was three and a half million, and that was fine with me. I wanted paradise, so I had to pay a high price for it.

"We have to figure out who we're gonna leave in charge." I brought up the last order of business we had to attend to before we left for good.

"Did you have somebody in mind?" Isiah asked, sitting in daddy's chair.

"What do you think about Carmen?" I suggested.

"That's exactly who I was thinkin' of."

"Really?" I asked, a little surprised that he said that. They had never had words or anything, but there was always a tension between Isiah and Carmen.

"Yeah. He's loyal, and I know he can handle the pressure."

"And the other men respect him," I added.

"That was easy."

"Almost too easy," I added suspiciously.

"What's wrong?" he asked as he gave me a look.

"Nothin' is ever this easy for me. It just feels like a set up."

"You're gonna have to stop bein' so suspicious."

"I can't help it. I've been like this all my life." I knew Isiah was right. Once we were safely in Hawaii, I was going to have to relax. It would be a welcomed change of pace for me. I wanted to be more relaxed. I longed for the day when I could just sit back on my front porch sipping iced tea, exchanging pleasantries with my neighbors.

I couldn't sleep that night. I kept tossing and turning, wondering what was going to happen to shatter my life this time. My intuition was screaming at me, but I couldn't quite hear what it was saying. Was I just being paranoid? Or maybe I was just nervous about moving to a strange place

Cynthia White

where I didn't know anybody. Whatever the case was, I didn't get one hour of sleep.

I went downstairs and sat in my father's office. I closed my eyes and saw him sitting at his desk. I smiled at him. He didn't smile back. I got an uneasy feeling. I reached for the phone and dialed my brother's number.

"Is this a bad time?" I asked him cautiously.

"Queen?"

"Yeah, it's me."

"Are you okay? Did something happen?"

"Not really. I just need someone to talk to."

"Is Isiah alright?"

"Yeah, he's fine. He's upstairs sleepin' like a baby."

"What's on yo' mind?"

"Have you ever gotten that feelin'?"

"What feelin'?"

"The one that makes yo' stomach do flips."

"You sure that's not just the baby?"

"No, the babies are fine."

"Babies?"

"I'm havin' twins," I told him with a smile on my face.

"When you do something you really go all out, don't you?"

"Don't put it all off on me. Isiah had something to do with it, too."

"I'm happy for ya, sis."

"Sis, huh? I like the sound of that."

"So you still haven't gotten to why you're up at three in the morning," he said, reminding me of why I called in the first place.

"We doin' it. We're goin' to Hawaii."

"To stay?"

"Permanently."

"Well, then you should be happy."

"I am, but I have this naggin' feelin' in the pit of my stomach."

"Maybe it's just nerves."

"Or maybe it's a sign."

"You think something bad is about to happen?"

"I don't think, I know. Ever since I was little, I could always tell when something bad was about to happen. It's like a premonition except I don't see it, I feel it."

"Have you talked to Isiah about it?"

"Yeah, and he just thinks I'm bein' paranoid."

"Queen, you know yo'self betta than anybody else. Maybe you should try to lay low until you leave."

"See, that's the thing. I can't lay low. There's too much to do. Isiah and I both have our hands full right now."

"When are you leavin'?"

"In four weeks."

"That soon?"

"Soon? It feels like an eternity to me."

"Just try to stay calm. Talk to Isiah and let him know how deep these feelins really go."

"I don't want to bring him down. He's so excited."

"Well, you know that you can always call yo' big brotha."

"Thanks, Patrick. I really appreciate that." For some reason, talking to Patrick always made me feel better. Even before I knew he was my brother, something about him just put my mind at ease.

Since I was already up at six in the morning, I decided to go to the cemetery and pay my father a visit. It was cool out. The sun was barely up, but for some reason I had the top down on my Benz. My hair flew wildly in the wind. I felt so

Cynthia White

free. This was how a young woman was supposed to feel. I was alive and that had to count for something.

"Hi, daddy." I smiled as I knelt down to place the single red rose I brought my father on his grave site. Before I could say another word, tears overwhelmed me. I promised myself I wouldn't cry. I lied. "I miss you so much. I don't know what to do without you. My life has been a complete mess ever since the day you got arrested. That was my fault. All of it was my fault. I wish I could go back and do it all over. I wish I could bring her back, not because I miss her but because I miss you." I looked up at the clouds. A few cold raindrops hit my face. It was about to storm. It had been raining a lot lately.

"Daddy, I just want you to know that I'm tryin' to be a betta person. It's hard to live right when all you know is wrong. I know you did the best you could with me, and I don't blame you for anything."

After I left the cemetery, I stopped by Jennifer's old house. Mrs. Perez no longer lived there. She had moved in with some old rich guy she met shortly after Marc married me. Finding a man was never a problem for her. Word was that she got fifteen million when Marc was murdered. I remembered how lonely Jen always was in that big ole house. I hoped that wherever she was now, there were plenty of people around her.

"I guess I have to say goodbye to you, too," I said out loud, hoping that my girl could hear me. I didn't know what to say. I searched my heart for the right words. I wanted to be eloquent and articulate. Then I realized that Jen knew me better than anybody. She accepted my foul mouth and my sharp tongue. She knew better than anybody that I wasn't perfect. She accepted all my imperfections. I loved her for

that. "I love you, Jen. I miss you so much. I just hope you're happy. I guess I'll see you when I get there."

Next, it was time to say goodbye to the big man. Uncle Moe was my surrogate father after daddy went to prison. He loved me like only he could. He was stern when I needed discipline. Then when I needed him to be gentler, he was. I could never figure out why he loved me so much. I was just grateful that he did.

"Hey, Uncle Moe." I smiled. "Seems like just yesterday you were yellin' at me, tellin' me how selfish I was. I didn't realize it then, but you were right. I was selfish. Thank you for bein' honest with me when nobody else would. I miss you. I can't imagine how I'm gonna make it without you." I wiped the tears from my eyes. "Goodbye, Uncle Moe. I love you."

I drove home doing at least eighty on the highway. I just wanted to get home.

"Hey, baby." Isiah greeted me with a soft kiss.

"Hey."

"Where you been all day?"

"Sayin' goodbye to a few people."

"Yo' father?"

"And Jennifer and yo' father."

"You okay?"

"I am now."

"I'm glad. I know how hard these last few years have been on you."

"Yeah, but they've been hard on you, too. In a perfect world we wouldn't have to go anywhere. We could stay here and raise our children with the people we love. Jennifer would be their godmother, and they would have both of their grandfathers in their lives. This isn't a perfect world."

Cynthia White

"Not even close."

"It's up to us to pick up the slack. Our children won't have grandparents. They won't have anyone but the two of us, so we have to do the best we can."

"You're gonna be a great mother."

"I hope so."

"You will."

"If not, at least they'll have you. No matter what was goin' on between us, it was always you who kept me grounded." I wrapped my arms around him and held him tightly. Everything else drifted further and further away. Isiah and the two children inside me were my world now. Everything I did was for them.

*****

We decided that it was time to approach Carmen. I called him on his cell phone and told him to meet us at the house. He agreed. I didn't know what I was going to say. I hoped that he didn't need too much convincing because I was in no mood to sell this life to anyone.

"Carmen, we need to talk to you," Isiah took the lead.

"We? This must be serious. Did I do something wrong?" he asked with a worried look on his face.

"Actually, it's the exact opposite. You did something very right."

"Well, in that case." He sat down and gave us his undivided attention.

"What we are about to discuss must stay between the three of us for the time bein'."

"Understood."

"Queen and I are leavin' town soon."

"How soon?"

"A couple of weeks."

"What, are you goin' on vacation or something?"

"No, we're leavin' permanently."

"Permanently?"

"Yes."

"I don't get it."

"Things have just gotten out of hand lately. We are about to bring two children into the world and we don't feel like we can protect them here."

"Queen, you're havin' twins."

"Yes, I am." I smiled proudly.

"Congratulations, mama."

"Thank you."

"Carmen, I'm not gonna beat around the bush. Queen and I feel that you would be the best replacement while we're away."

"Me?" he asked like he couldn't believe his ears.

"Yes, you. Carmen, the men respect you. They'll follow yo' lead."

"I don't know. I'm just a worker. I'm not a boss."

I got up from my seat and went and sat next to him. I took his hand in mine and looked deep into his brown eyes.

"I wouldn't ask you to do this if I didn't think you were ready. This means a lot to me. You're the only one I want," I told him passionately.

"There's nobody else?" he asked me as he stared deep into my eyes.

"No, nobody," I told him honestly.

"Then I'll do it for you, Queen."

"Thank you so much. You don't know how much this means to me." I hugged him. The hug must have lasted too long because when I finally looked up, Isiah was giving me a very dirty look.

Cynthia White

I said goodbye to Carmen. I didn't want him to leave because I didn't want to face Isiah. I wasn't ready for this.

"What the fuck was that all about?" he asked, pissed.

"What was what all about?" I tried to play it off.

"You know what I'm talkin' about."

"It was just a hug, Isiah."

"The hell it was."

"Carmen and I are just friends."

"Did you fuck him?"

"Does it really matter?"

"It matters to me."

"Isiah, we are about to leave all this bullshit behind. Please don't ruin this for me."

"For you, what about me? How am I suppose to feel knowin' my baby mama fucked every nigga I know?"

"That's not fair."

"Did I hit a nerve?"

"Fuck you." I turned to walk away but he grabbed me and prevented me from leaving.

"I asked you a question, and I wanna hear the answer."

"Yes, I fucked Carmen. Are you happy now?" I asked coldly.

"When?" he wanted to know.

"It doesn't matter."

"When?!" He shouted at me with enough anger to send a chill through my body.

"When you needed yo' *space*."

"The same time you fucked Nate. You were a busy girl that day."

"I didn't fuck them both the same day."

"At this point, I wouldn't believe a muthafuckin' thing you told me."

"And at this point, I don't give a fuck. You said you needed yo' space and that's exactly what I gave you. What was I supposed to do, spend the rest of my life waitin' around for you?"

"We weren't even apart long."

"It doesn't matter. You knew I had nobody else."

"Seems like you had plenty of people to comfort you. Nate, Carmen, even Jennifer couldn't wait to hop into bed with you."

"It wasn't like that."

"Then you tell me what it was like."

"No."

"What?"

"I said no. I've apologized over and over again. You're never gonna forgive me. Maybe what we have isn't worth savin'."

He just looked at me. This time I couldn't tell what he was thinking. It seemed that the connection I once had with him was lost. We were lost. I closed my eyes for only a few seconds, but our entire relationship flashed through my head. The pain, the anger, the passion, the love, it was all there. I could feel it pulsating through me. This time when I turned to walk away, he didn't try to stop me. Maybe this time we were *really* finished.

I spent the next few days alone. I was so tired of trying to justify myself to Isiah. He had made mistakes, too. Mine just seemed to be bigger and have heavier consequences. After the whole situation with Nikki, I forgave him and never once brought it up again. He couldn't give me the same respect. Maybe it's just easier for women to forgive. Men have so much damn pride. I loved him, but I was tired.

I went to Carmen's house to talk to him. I hated to dis-

Cynthia White

turb him. He looked stressed. Maybe asking him to take over was a mistake. I didn't know what else he had going on in his life.

"What's wrong?" he asked as soon as he saw my face.

"Isiah found out about us."

"And let me guess, he's upset."

"More like pissed the fuck off."

"That was a long time ago."

"I tried to tell him, but he wouldn't listen."

"Do you want me to talk to him?"

"No, this is between me and him. I'm just sorry that it came out now when we were so close to bein' happy."

"So are you gonna stay now?"

"I'm not. I don't know what Isiah's doin'. I already bought a house, and if I have to raise both my children on my own, I will. I love him, but I'm not gonna put my life on hold for him."

"I'm sure if he knew—"

"I don't wanna talk about it anymore," I interrupted him.

"I'm sorry."

"What for? It's not yo' fault. Like you said, it was a long time ago. If he's too self-righteous to realize that I'm not the only one in this relationship who's not perfect then too fuckin' bad for him. I am who I am. I've made mistakes, but that doesn't make me a bad person."

"Of course it doesn't."

"I understand where he's comin' from. Even if it was in the past, it hurts to find out that the person you love was with other people. It hurt me when I found out about Nikki, but I got over it. Why can't he just do the same?"

"Please don't think I'm tryin' to take up for Isiah, but I can kind of understand where he's comin' from."

"Carmen …"

"Let me explain. Queen, you are no ordinary woman. You're beautiful and intelligent and feisty. You have more heart that ninety percent of the niggas I know. You fight for what you believe in, and you don't back down to anyone. The night I spent with you was the most intense, passionate night of my life. I felt like I was under a spell. You just have that effect on people, especially men."

"Did you ever want to be with me?" I asked out of nowhere.

"Hell yeah," he admitted.

"Why didn't you tell me?"

"Because I knew it wasn't possible. When I came back you were already with Gauge. Then I met Serita."

"Do you love her?"

"That's what I tell myself for the sake of my son."

"How can you do that? I could never be with someone I didn't really love."

"What about Marc?"

"I loved Marc. It didn't run as deep as it does with Isiah, but I did love him. He was the only one who could reach me after Jennifer died. If it wasn't for him, I think I would probably still be in that deep, dark place."

"What about me?"

"You know how I feel about you."

"Actually, I don't."

"Seriously?"

"Seriously."

"Carmen, I have been in love with you since I was a kid. You were the first man to ever have my heart. I'll never be completely over you."

"I wish things could have been different."

Cynthia White

"But they can't. Maybe you and I could have worked out. Maybe we could have had somethin' real, but we'll never know."

"What if I go with you?"

"What?"

"If Isiah decides to stay, then I'll go in his place."

"I can't ask you to do that."

"You didn't ask. I offered."

"What about Serita? What about yo' son?"

"I'll bring my son. As far as Serita goes, she's betta off without me. She knows I don't really love her."

"You think she'll just let you take her son like that?"

"What other choice does she have?" He meant that because he was in The Black Mafia there was nothing she could do to stop him.

That's when I realized that he was lost. He was willing to leave with me, but he wasn't willing to give up the life completely. That's not what I wanted. I wanted to be through with this life. I didn't want it ever to touch my children. If I couldn't save myself, at least I could save them.

After I talked with Carmen for a while longer, I decided to go to Isiah and be upfront and honest with him. Carmen rode along with me. I think he was afraid that Isiah was going to do something to me. He waited outside while I went in.

"Is this a bad time?"

"That depends on what you want," he said rudely.

"Damn, it's like that?"

"You made it like that."

"I'm not gonna argue with you. I just came to let you know that if you decide not to come to Hawaii with me, Carmen has offered to come."

"I bet he has."

"What's yo' problem?"

"Wake up, Queen. If you think I'm about to let you leave with my children ..."

"Let me? Muthafucka, you must have forgotten who I am. Nobody *lets* me do anything. I do what the fuck I wanna do when the fuck I wanna do it."

"Queen, don't test me."

"I know you didn't just threaten me."

"You know I would never do that."

"I don't know what the fuck you're capable of. All I know is when it's time to get on that plane and go, I'm leavin'." As I turned to walk away, I felt this pulling pain in my stomach. I doubled over and tried to catch my breath.

"Are you okay?"

"I don't know."

"Is it the babies?"

"I think so." I screamed as the pain got more intense. My legs buckled. I fell down to my knees. Something was definitely wrong.

Isiah picked me up and carried me outside. It was starting to rain. It was getting harder to breathe and even harder to stay awake. I saw Carmen's face and smiled weakly.

"What happened?" Carmen asked Isiah as he opened up the backseat of his BMW and gently put me down.

"Something's wrong with the babies."

"What did you do to her?"

"I didn't do anything to her."

"Queen, are you okay?" Carmen asked me, ignoring Isiah's comments.

"It hurts so bad," I cried.

"Don't worry, baby. I got ya." Carmen got in the back-

Cynthia White

seat with me and wrapped his arms around me.

Isiah looked at him like he wanted to hurt him. I was glad he didn't. He went up front and got in the driver's side. He started up the car and took off. *"Forever My Lady"* by Jodeci was playing on the radio. I just closed my eyes and listened to the words.

So you're having my baby
And it means so much to me
There's nothing more precious
Than to raise a family
If there's any doubt in your mind
You can count on me
I'll never let you down
Lady believe in me...

I looked up at Isiah. He had tears in his eyes. If he wasn't going to be strong, I didn't know who was. I was starting to get to the point to where I wanted to give up. I felt hopeless. I knew that if I lost these babies, I would go right back to being the Queen I used to be. It seemed like every time I tried to do right, life came along and kicked my ass right back into reality. Maybe I wasn't meant to live a normal life. I was never one for the whole husband and kids thing. Maybe being alone was how I functioned best.

At the emergency room I was rushed ahead of all the other people who were waiting to be seen. That's when I really knew that something was wrong. I tried not to panic, but it was hard. I had started to bleed in the car. I was so close to passing out that I was starting to see things. My mother was there with me. She was haunting me. I was convinced that somehow she was behind this. She was going to

make sure that I was never happy.

Isiah and Carmen were right there by my side. Both men were prepared to be there for me during one of the most confusing, frightening times of my life. I didn't want them to leave, but at the same time I didn't want either one of them to stay.

*****

"Hello Queen," my mother said to me.

"What the hell do you want?"

"Is that any way to speak to your own mother?"

"I don't have a mother. I never did."

"You are so stubborn, just like your father."

"You shut the fuck up talkin' about my father," I snapped.

"You've got his temper, too."

"What do you want from me?"

"I want you to admit that you feel guilty for what you've done."

She didn't even have to say it. I knew what she was referring to. "I don't."

"You can lie to me, but you can't lie to yourself. You may not have liked the person that I was, but I was still your mother."

"If that's what you have to tell yourself."

"What do you have to tell yourself?"

"Not a damn thing. I don't lie to myself. I know I'm not perfect. I don't pretend to be this upstanding wife and mother when I'm really just a trifling, coked-out whore."

"The only difference I see is that your drug of choice is marijuana instead of coke."

"Fuck you! You don't know me. You never did and you never will. You treated me like I was nothing my entire life,

Cynthia White

and now I'm supposed to feel guilty for ending yo' pitiful-ass life. You didn't deserve my father. You were the worst thing that ever happened to him. Keep on blaming everyone else, but the truth is, you had it all and you fucked it up. It didn't matter if I killed you or if daddy would have done it. You had to be dealt with and that's what we call reality. You should try it sometime."

"You will reap what you've sown."

"Yeah, yeah, yeah. Get the fuck out of my face so I can get some rest."

*****

I woke up feeling different. I knew it was a dream, but it felt so damn real. The anger was overwhelming. I hated that woman so much, my own mother. She wanted me to suffer. I guess she loathed me just as much as I loathed her.

"What's wrong?" I asked Isiah when I saw the somber look on his face.

"You lost one of the babies."

"Which one?" I wanted to know.

"The boy."

I knew it was wrong, but I wished it would have been the girl. I knew that my mother was trying to tell me that my daughter would bring me just as much pain as I brought her. Maybe she would take my life just as I had taken her grandmother's.

"Is the girl alright? Is she healthy?"

"The doctor said she's fine. She's strong, just like her mother."

If he only knew. These days I wasn't feeling very strong, or very confident for that matter. I was starting to second-guess myself and every decision I made. That was dangerous when you lived in the environment I lived in.

"Where's Carmen?"

"He's in the waiting room."

"I'd like to talk to him, alone."

"Alone?" He laughed in a sarcastic manner and sat down in the chair beside my bed.

"Isiah, I know you don't understand the bond that Carmen and I share but—"

"Bond, what about our bond? What about our child growing inside you? It is my child, isn't it?"

"Must we go through this again?"

"Yes, we must. How do expect me to feel, huh? How am I not supposed to be jealous?"

"I don't know. Can't you just trust me?"

"No, I don't trust you, Queen."

That hurt so bad. I knew I had done a lot to him but to realize that he didn't trust me was awful. "Do you still love me, Isiah?"

"Yes, of course I do."

"At least I still have that."

"Baby, I wanna trust you. I really do, but I just don't know how anymore."

"I understand. I've tried to be as honest as possible without hurting your feelings, but I guess I went about it all wrong. I care about Carmen. We go back a long time. He knew my father in ways you could never understand. My father trusted him with my life. Yes, we shared one night together, but you and I have shared hundreds."

"Don't you see that makes it worse? We've had so many nights together you can't even count them all. You had one night with him. You'll never forget that one night."

"And I'll never forget any of the nights I shared with you."

Cynthia White

"Do you love him?"

"I don't know how to answer that."

"You just did."

He walked out of the room. I knew what he wanted from me. He wanted me to lie and pretend like everything was alright when it wasn't. I loved him, but for me to pretend that Carmen meant nothing to me would have been insulting to all three of us.

"How ya feelin'?" Carmen asked as he put on a brave face for my benefit.

"I'll be fine."

"Eventually you'll be fine, but how are you now?"

"I'm not so good," I admitted with tears beginning to form in my eyes.

"I'm sorry about the baby."

"Thank you."

"The doctor's confident that yo' little girl will pull through."

"Can I tell you a secret?"

"What?"

"I kind of wish she would have gone with her brotha."

"Why?"

"I don't know if I can protect her. Isiah and I are driftin' further and further apart, and I just don't know if I can handle it all. The pressure is just too much. Do you think I'm a terrible person?"

"No, I think you're a little more honest than most people, but not terrible."

"I just wanna be happy. Is that too much to ask for?"

Carmen got up from the chair and climbed into the bed with me. He put his arms around me and held me tight.

Isiah never returned. My head told me we were over. My

heart tried to hold on. I was released from the hospital the following day. Carmen had a limo waiting to take me home. I didn't want to go. I knew Isiah was there, and I wasn't ready to face him. I didn't want him to tell me it was over. I didn't want to watch him walk out of my life.

I decided to check into a hotel for a couple of days. I just needed a little time to myself to get my mind right. I had to figure out what I was going to do. I never in a million years would I have thought that I would end up raising a child on my own, but I had to be ready for that. Carmen was a much more complicated issue. If Isiah left me, I would want to lean on him so badly. I would want nothing more than to go to Hawaii with him and let him pamper me, but I knew it was wrong. His family needed him. Serita and his son depended on him. Even if he didn't love her, she didn't deserve to just be dumped like that. Nobody deserved that.

I did a lot of thinking while I stayed at the hotel. I tried to picture my life without Isiah, but I couldn't. I lay in bed and tried to sleep. No matter what I did, I couldn't see my future clearly.

"Hello." I answered my cell phone close to midnight.

"Can we talk?" Isiah asked in a sad tone.

"Is there really any point?"

"You actin' like it's already over."

"Why wouldn't I? You left me in that hospital alone."

"You wanted Carmen, not me."

"I wanted to talk to him, not marry him."

"Queen, you send me all these mixed messages then get mad when I can't read yo' mind. You change from day to day. I can't keep up."

"Don't you think things are hard for me, too?"

"I don't know what to think anymore. One minute you

love me and the next you're all up in some other nigga's face."

"I wasn't all up in his face."

"The hell you weren't."

"You know what? Don't come with me to Hawaii. I don't even want you there."

"That's fine with me." He hung up like some out-of-control diva who wasn't getting her way.

*****

The day was almost upon me. In twenty-four hours I was leaving with or without Isiah. Everything was packed except for the furniture. I had already ordered new stuff off the internet and had it sent to my new home. The only things I wanted to take with me were my clothes, shoes and handbags. I looked around at my room. So many memories surfaced. I smiled when Carmen walked through the door.

"Is he goin'?" Carmen asked, getting right to the point.

"I don't think so."

"Do you want me to come?"

"Do you wanna come?"

"You already know the answer to that."

"I just don't want you to go then end up regretting it."

"I wanna be with you, Queen. Nothing else matters."

"You say that now but—"

"Shhhh." He placed his finger over my lips to stop me from speaking.

He kissed me and there we were again. There was something so relaxing about Carmen that was exciting at the same time. He was older and wiser. He made me feel special, something every girl wants to be.

"Queen, I love you. I'm not doin' this to hurt anybody. I wanna be wherever you are."

"Even if that means leavin' everybody and everything you know?"

"Even if."

"Can I tell you a secret?"

"You can tell me anything."

"I love you, too."

This time, it was me who kissed him. I wanted to feel his enthusiasm again. He loved me with no strings attached and best of all, no ultimatums. With Isiah, I always had to try to be more together than I really was. Carmen knew I was confused and emotional and loved me in spite of it. I never thought it was possible, but I was in love with two men. My heart was pointing me in one direction and my head in another.

I stayed the night with Carmen. That was to be my last night in town, and I had no idea what the morning would bring. Carmen made love to me with everything he had. I appreciated that. It was the last thing I needed, but the first thing I wanted. Sharing those intimate hours with him further confused and upset me. Isiah still hadn't called. At least if he never showed up, I could leave with Carmen and not feel too guilty about it.

*****

The next day brought with it the moment of truth. Isiah showed up, making it that much harder to make a decision. I wanted to please them both. I didn't want to lose either of them. Up until the last few seconds, I didn't even know what I was about to do. My mind kept changing without my consent. I took a deep breath and began to speak my mind.

"I love you both, but I think I need to be alone for a while."

"Queen, if you think I'm just gonna let you move away

Cynthia White

with my child—"

"Isiah, please don't finish that sentence," I interrupted him. "Besides, you have another child, or have you forgotten? Nikki will need your help."

"Queen, you know how I feel about her. I don't love her. What are you thinkin'?"

"Maybe I'm not thinkin'. For once in my life I'm not gonna analyze the situation to death. Yes, I love you and yes, I'm carryin' yo' child, but that doesn't mean that you get to tell me how to live my life."

"That's not what I'm tryin' to do."

"Maybe not intentionally."

"Not at all."

"You sho about that?"

He didn't respond.

"And Carmen, I can't be the one to take you away from yo' son."

"I told you—"

"I know what you told me, but you know as well as I do that it would never work out. Serita loves that lil boy."

"So do I."

"I know, and that's why you need to be here for him."

"What about you?"

"I'll be fine. It's time for me to stand on my own two feet. I've always had a man in my life. First it was daddy and Uncle Moe, then Gauge. Then there was Isiah, then Marc, then Isiah again and finally you. I need to figure out who I am before I can give myself to another person. I need to find out what makes me happy. That's the only way I'll ever be a good mother."

I could tell by the looks on their faces that they were not happy. I didn't feel good about the decision I had made, but

I did feel it was necessary.

The driver opened the door to the limo and I got inside. As I got ready to leave, my mind was flooded with memories of my old life. I remembered the first time I met Isiah. We were at the mall. He was with Nate and I was with Jennifer. It seemed like a lifetime ago. I thought about the first time we made love. I thought about the day I murdered Gauge and how he helped me get rid of the body. I had made so many mistakes with him. I had hurt him so many times.

Then there was Carmen, the man who had been protecting me ever since I was twelve years old. I could no longer deny my feelings for him, and that scared me. I loved them both. I didn't know who to choose, so I chose to walk away.

I looked out the window at Carmen. He couldn't see the tears in my eyes. I thought about the first night we were together. He was everything I needed him to be. His strength amazed me. His passion captivated me. I wanted him every night that followed.

My dreams relived every passionate moment. I wondered how long it would take him to forget about me. I closed my eyes and blew him a kiss that he never got to see.

*****

Hawaii was just as beautiful as I remembered it. I must have stared up at the sky for half an hour. There was something so spiritual about the way the puffy white clouds faded completely into the blue. I felt this wave of relief wash over me. I was safe. My baby was safe.

I walked around my new home trying to get a feel for the place. There was so much space. My new furniture had already arrived. It was gorgeous. I sat down on my king-sized bed. The mattress was so soft. I lay back and closed my eyes. I didn't want to sleep, just rest. I wanted to be able to read a book from cover to cover without being interrupted by some sort of emergency. Or just take a long bubble bath without worrying that someone was going to burst through the bathroom door and try to kill me.

"I'm sorry I had to take you away from your daddy," I told my baby as I rubbed my belly. "He loves you so much. We both do." I smiled.

My smile quickly faded when I realized I was all alone. I was going to have to give birth all by myself. I knew it was going to be hard, but I could do it. After all I'd been through these past few years, I believed I could do anything. I was, after all, Hershey Aaron's daughter. Daddy had taught me so much, but most importantly, he had taught me how to survive.

After about an hour of trying to relax, I got up and went downstairs. I looked at all my luggage and sighed. I knew I had to unpack sometime, but I wasn't ready to tackle that just yet. I went into the kitchen to get my baby and myself a snack. I opened the cabinets. They were filled with all my favorite goodies. I made a mental note to call Monique and thank her. She really went above and beyond. I opened a package of chocolate chip cookies then poured myself a tall glass of ice cold milk. I took my snack out back and sat in a lounge chair facing the pool. I couldn't help but wonder what Isiah and Carmen were doing. I was glad my phone wasn't hooked up yet. I didn't want to be tempted to call. It was too soon.

I slept so well that night. I didn't wake up once. The next morning, I felt like a new woman. I even unpacked a few of my bags. I took a long, hot shower and enjoyed every second of it. I put on a pair of khaki shorts, a white wife beater and a pair of white flip-flops. It felt good to dress simply. I grabbed my Gucci tote bag and sunglasses and headed for the beach.

I sat down on my Betty Boop beach towel and took off my flip-flops. I loved the way the warm sand felt between my toes. I looked out at the ocean and imagined myself playing in it with my daughter. I wondered who she would look like, me or Isiah.

I lay back and pulled my shirt up over my belly. I looked up at the sun shining brightly, and suddenly I didn't feel alone anymore.

"Hi, daddy." I smiled.

Cynthia White